MW00916291

THE YARN WOMAN

By Brooks Mencher

Visit the Yarn Woman companion at
www.yarnwoman.com

Introduction

I was covering a street shooting for the Daily Bulletin when I met her. It was pure luck, but isn't half of life just luck?

She lives above a retired Art Deco theater in San Francisco's Sunset District with an old long-haired cat, her harpsichord and enough yarn to fill a railroad car.

The police call her the Yarn Woman; her specialty is the forensic study of textiles. But they ask for her help with some trepidation because they know that whatever crime she's unraveling for them comes with a lot of knots and baggage. And ghosts. There are always the ghosts.

"The Yarn Woman" covers my first three collaborations with Ms. M. They are presented here in chronological order, even as my work with her continues.

– Nat P.M. Fisher

GHOSTS
OF THE
ALBERT
TOWNSEND

The Beginning

Though it was still autumn, there was a hint of rain and a suggestion of winter when I first saw her. She was visible, but the light was dim and her form indistinct. For some reason she waved when she saw me — that much I could see in the late evening fog.

I smiled and waved back because I didn't know what else to do; I had no idea who she was. Her gown was blue or gray or white, I wasn't sure because it seemed to fade and I couldn't tell if she was in the fog or if she was the fog.

Yet despite the dark and the mist and the distance between us, I could tell her eyes were intensely green.

Then the strangest thing happened: A white and gray Silver Cloud floated across the street, as only a Rolls can float, moving against the traffic and through it, parting a vaporous sea of screeching tires like a mechanical Moses amid blaring horns and pumping fists, and it pulled slowly up to the curb, facing the wrong direction. A short, thick older man calmly got out and walked around the car. He was silhouetted by the headlamps and I could make out his enormous nose and protruding teeth. He graciously opened the rear door for her. They left, the Rolls nearly silent as it passed into San Francisco's neverland.

I waved again, trying to make sense of the other-worldliness of what had just occurred. I was left only with the image of those eyes, which I would never forget.

I didn't see her again until we were introduced by my boyhood friend, San Francisco Police Detective William Chu, two long years later during the first week of October. Yet this was the same woman; there was no doubt.

Detective Chu is no citizen of that misty other-world inhabited by mysterious green eyes and silent gray cars. He lives in the iron-shod underside of San Francisco, a gritty land peopled by tainted saints and homeless psychos, and the circumstances surrounding my introduction to this woman after so long were therefore harsh: She'd been called in as a consultant in a case that involved the grisly killing of an adult male and the beating and animal mauling of a six-year-old child. The detective's most important clue was an old shawl that had been wrapped around the girl, according to Chu, by "persons unknown." This fell perfectly into this Yarn Woman's area of forensic textile expertise: If Chu could find the owner or uncover the provenance of the wrap, he might eventually find the perpetrators of the crimes.

Chu relies on her because she has a knack of seeing what others don't, and in more ways than one. She'd worked with the SFPD, and with Chu specifically, on a number of earlier cases that I knew nothing about, and she had become a sort of myth among the cops – more like a resolute Diana than a seductive Venus, yet unreachable to mortals nonetheless.

The police call her their Yarn Woman; they have a name for everyone, though most are derogatory or at least laced with locker-room humor. But hers was bestowed as a *nom de guerre*; those few who knew her and worked with her had accepted her into their own ranks – as much as that's possible among the blue-clad.

When we were introduced, I was following up on an unrelated story, a shooting, and happened to be at the hospital where the six-year-old mauling victim had been taken, half-conscious and soaked in her own blood. And Detective Chu, urged, I can only guess, by the capricious Fates, decided I should meet this extraordinary green-eyed consultant whom he'd managed to keep secret for so long.

Unwilling to agitate the Fates, whose distant mumbling I thought I could hear, I agreed to an introduction.

Juliet Brown

I was pacing around the lobby of San Francisco General Hospital's emergency room early on Tuesday. There had been a drive-by shooting at 2 that morning and I'd been sent to the hospital to get what information I could on two of the three victims and feed it to the metro rewrite man at the Bulletin, where I'd worked for the past twelve years. The third victim died at the scene, and night metro steered clear of assigning manpower to a dead man whose name and vital information wouldn't be released by the police until next of kin were notified – and if it happened to be a juvenile, there'd be no information until the funeral. Another reporter had been assigned to get a statement from the SFPD, and rewrite would meld the two reports seamlessly together, supposedly, and produce a good twenty inches of engrossing copy. Any other day the whole shebang would be worth five inches and one phone call, but there'd been a dearth of news since a fatal dog attack the week before, plus the surfacing of an old schooner north of the peninsula about the same time, and the Bulletin had a lot of ads to wrap news around.

I'd been there for a few hours when suddenly the driver of a red Subaru Forester swung into the ambulance entrance and slammed on the brakes. The thing came in so fast I automatically leaped a few feet back, thinking the car might crash through the glass. I could barely see the driver. She had a child on her lap and they were wrapped, chest to chest, in a gray wool blanket. The steering wheel looked like it was rubbing against the child's back. Her head was a bloody, soaking mess and her face was pressed against the woman's upper left shoulder. She appeared to be unconscious. I don't know how the woman managed to stay on the road. And I don't know how she could see through enormously obvious tears that had mixed, on the palette of her face, with the girl's blood to form a pink cast that echoed the Subaru's salt-faded paint job.

She screeched in, rocked to a stop, locked the doors, cracked open the driver's window and laid on the horn. Three aqua-clad hospital aides rushed out to the car, but didn't know what to do. From my vantage point at the window, the situation was obviously stressing their young professional arrogance and at the same time demanded a level of leadership that was clearly lacking. One of them was shouting to the driver that she couldn't use the ambulance entrance and that there were certain procedures to follow, not the least of which was the ever-present question of insurance, and the idiot was madly motioning her to clear the drive. The horn drowned his voice, but both could be heard inside the ER nonetheless. The mother, bloodied, tear-wet and frantic, screamed for the workers to get either an emergency-room physician or a paramedic and a rolling gurney immediately. I left the room and stood unobtrusively outside near the ER door about fifteen feet from the car, and I could pretty much make out what she was saying, down to the expletives. Never did she stop hammering the horn and finally, after making her demands during brief interludes between the bleatings, she held it down without interruption.

The stubborn, locked-in woman was soon visited by three over-employed security goons who quickly made room for a physician in surgeon's pants and smock. He had a sloth hat tied on his head as if he'd just hustled out from performing a triple bypass. Only then did the woman relent, letting up on the horn and unlocking her door. The child was placed gingerly on a gurney by the physician and two assistants and rolled into the receiving area. She was soon out of sight behind swinging doors in the company of the mother. The security men wandered around looking tough but stupid, and, with chests puffed, one re-entered the building and another phoned for a tow truck.

When they left, I went over to the car, saw that the keys were still in the ignition, and moved it to an open parking area several blocks away. I returned to the waiting room with the keys. A tow would have cost her hundreds.

The adventure of the mother in the Subaru was far more compelling than another mere street shooting, and I was struck by the woman's sheer audacity. Either she was brilliant or her motherly fear had pushed her into temporary genius, for however bizarre her actions appeared, the end result was that her child ended up in the emergency room under the attention of a highly trained trauma physician within three or four minutes – nothing short of a miracle in the greater San Francisco Bay Area. Any other route would have taken six to nine hours no matter the condition of the child (triage is not a word used easily in these parts).

Cops trickled in as the morning progressed. I counted six. Half could have been related to the drive-by shooting, my original assignment, but the others had to be dealing with the woman and her child. Finally, Detective William Chu wandered in, looking up and down the hallway and through the waiting room. He looked dapper in his gray-brown suit and Bailey's fedora. A security man posted at the ER doors practically bowed. Chu didn't wait for an escort, but pushed open the double doors to the back and disappeared. Twenty minutes later he re-emerged, holding a small notebook and a reddish brown, blood-soaked sweater or shawl, which he'd bundled into a clear-blue plastic evidence sack.

I asked him about the girl and handed him the Subaru keys so he could give them to the woman.

He took the keys, smiled and said, "Hey, how about that Townsend?" as if he were talking about a baseball player. But he was referring to an old nineteenth-century schooner that had washed into the Bay after last week's severe storms, and was the topic of the week. I was one of the very few who hadn't seen it yet, and I wasn't lucky enough to get the reporting assignment. I'm a crime reporter: What did an old schooner have to do with crime, anyway? "Guess they found the old nautical records in the city archives. My mother wants photos, right?" he said.

I could get him the photos; that's what he was asking. The Bulletin sold photos on request, but Chu wasn't about to buy any. That would mean money. We'd worked on the "guanxi" system, a not-so-complicated Chinese system of reciprocal exchange, since we were in grade school. I knew what I had to do. I smiled back and asked again about the child.

"Not good," he said. "But not terrible. The injuries aren't as severe as they look. I mean, they're bad enough, but nothing is deep enough to be life-threatening. The thing is, the child is hypothermic. Bloodiest little kid I ever saw, too. Well, maybe not the bloodiest, but ..."

I asked him about the clothing in the bag. He stood there for a moment, weighing his options once again before deciding to include me in this one. This was a face-saving device — I understood he couldn't appear to be too helpful. Someone might see. But his choice, a few seconds in the making, proved monumental to me.

"You want to meet someone? I want you to meet someone," he said, carrying on both sides of the conversation. I'd known Chu since we were kids in North Beach-slash-Chinatown, and he had always talked like that. He is and always had been very important. But when you're used to it, it's just a character trait, kind of like an embarrassing cousin who's still a cousin nonetheless.

"Sure." Yes, yes, yes.

"The Yarn Woman. We have a private consultant," he said, as if it were a big deal for the department. "Textile forensics. Don't give me that, just because you can't spell it. You might like her ... you might not. Probably not. What do you think?"

Had I made some kind of face? "Not," I lied. I had no idea who he was referring to, but you can never let yourself sound too eager in front of cops and industry flaks.

"That's what I think. But you should meet her. Trust me."

I indicated that I trusted him.

And, I was "in." He'd talk about the case with me.

"The child was beaten, Teddy … thoroughly thrashed," he said. Teddy's not my name. My byline is Nat P.M. Fisher. The guys at work make a real thing of the P.M., and metro put me on the night shift almost 10 years ago partly because of it. I was told it was good for "buzz." Chu has called me Teddy since about ninth grade because he was and still is under the impression that because of my block head, husky build, wire reading glasses and a mustache, I look like President Roosevelt. He's managed to get most of the department to refer to me as Teddy, or on occasion, when the spirit moves, Mr. President.

He continued: "She's soaking wet, like she went overboard out on the Bay. Definitely saltwater. Hypothermic. Mauled. Of all this, that's the weird part. Then someone covered the bloody little thing with the sweater afterward, or maybe she was already wearing it. Not sure. She has bite marks, Teddy," he said, "but just the marks … no significant penetration. The blood comes from the beating, like someone bludgeoned the poor girl and threw her into some sharp rocks. The first five minutes of this assault is a category all its own, like someone tried to beat her, drown her, grind her on stones and then feed her to dogs. Of course, we know that can't happen ..."

Of course, we both knew it could happen. This was the real world, and that sort of thing happens all the time, especially in the Bay Area, where the macabre is an everyday occurrence and deviance expresses itself at the next level.

"Wrong order," he said quickly, "I'm sorry. Drowned first, then dog, then beating, then rocks. Like that."

I didn't know that it really mattered. Then a thought entered my mind. There'd been an animal mauling a week ago near Alta Park. A man, a transient, had died from it. It was a terrible, gruesome throat-rending killing and had spawned an enormous amount of interest and fear. I decided it wasn't time to go there with Chu though, not yet anyway.

"The mother?" I asked.

"Yes. The mother. Very shaken. Juliet P. Brown. P is for Patricia but she uses only the initial. She probably had nothing to do with it. In fact, she says the girl came back home … ran off for the morning, you know ... came back wearing a sweater that doesn't belong to her." He lifted the bag a few inches. He told me he was taking the clothing to a forensic textile expert for evaluation – a person he called the Yarn Woman, and he would phone ahead to let her know he'd be hauling me along. I was still surprised by the offer. He scratched the address down on a hospital flyer, handed it to me and turned to leave with the sweater under his arm. "Because I like you," he said, answering a question that I never voiced.

"Tomorrow morning at 6:30," he said. "She starts early. I don't think she attends to us mortals after about noon. I mean, really, you can't even reach her. She's very private. You might say she's eccentric – hey, don't say I said that. No, I mean it. You have to be very careful around her. Don't smile like that. And not a word. She's been involved in a couple of dozen cases at the department. She's worked with the feds, too. They call her the Yarn Woman. Have you heard of her?"

"Who are *they*?" I asked.

"We, Teddy, we. Cops."

Old San Francisco

It was 6:30 in the morning, an hour and a half after Mrs. Brown pulled into the ambulance drive. Chu had returned to Central Station on Vallejo Street in the Financial District. I gathered the available information on the drive-by shooting victims and phoned it in. It no longer interested me. The Yarn Woman and Juliet Brown and the beaten child took up most of my available brain. Though I'd been up all night, I wasn't tired yet – that's the problem with working nights – and right now I had a beautiful autumn morning to deal with and there was a ship I'd heard about but had never seen as it bobbed in the Bay. I was probably the only person in the city who hadn't checked it out, so I decided to go down to the Yacht Basin to take a look. There was no telling how long it would remain visible before sliding back into the silt.

It surfaced about a week ago. There'd been a fierce storm a few hundred miles offshore, and the churning waves hauled piles of driftwood and mounds of kelp onto the west and northwest beaches of the peninsula. The silt and sand on the seabed contorted like an awakened Leviathan, its water-muffled groans and gasps unheard by human ears. The minus tides combined silently with the writhing seabed to disgorge the vessel that local historians soon identified as the Albert Townsend, a steam-powered doghole schooner that had carried milled redwood from the small harbors, or "dogholes," of Humboldt and Mendocino, south to the Barbary Coast – the restless *enfant terrible*, San Francisco.

The Townsend sat heavily on a new submarine sandbank about two hundred yards off the Yacht Harbor just east of China Beach and the Golden Gate Bridge. Four or five feet of the rotting, creaking hull were visible when the tide was out, and it looked like the shell of a giant turtle. I walked along the slips at the basin, trying to ignore the wealth exhibited in some of the fancier boats that were moored there. As I stared out over the gray-green bay, muted further by a thick autumn fog, I wondered what was holding up the Earth if this ancient turtle was poking around in front of me instead of tending to business.

The first few days after the Albert Townsend had risen, cold marine mornings blanketed it in mist, and when evening ambled over the docks looking for run-down, oar-powered fishing skiffs of the same vestigial era – but finding only sleek white yachts and glowing fiberglass boats – it happily swathed the rotting hull of the resurrected schooner in the warm, loving orange light of a setting sun. After sunset, darkness slowly filled the Bay, and the Townsend melted into the night. Then, the lights of the city began to flicker on and you had to wonder if a dozen pairs of misty eyes were squinting through the muddy cracks in the hull – the ghosts of wakened deckhands and loaders and pilots who went down with their ship – aghast, as they must have been, at an incomprehensible city of lights a century and a half in their future. You could practically hear them mumbling.

San Francisco's a city of ghosts anyway, even without the Townsend. They're everywhere: on the streets, in the buildings, hovering like mist over the Bay. Everywhere you walk, the Gold Rush and the rise of industry on the West Coast float up from the graves of miners, merchants and moguls ... and rascals, raconteurs and rogues. In today's shop windows or hotel lobbies, yesterday's women with their china-doll faces stare out from old tintypes and albumen prints and say, "This is our city. It's ours."

And the men who influenced the architecture and attitudes of the City by the Bay a hundred and fifty years ago? The city can't or won't forget their faces or their names. From the de Youngs and Hearsts to the more bizarre Emperor Nortons, their spirits are very much alive and their names very much attached to every street, building, museum and park in this maritime metropolis.

San Francisco's ghosts are shaken and very happily wakened with every turning of the tide. They open a sleepy but curious eye whenever they feel a little thump from snapping fault lines that criss-cross the region like cracks in misfired porcelain. So complete is the presence of the city's past that if you walk down Bridge Street on a foggy night, you might suddenly find yourself in 1850 … or 1872 … it depends on the prevailing mood of the ghosts – both landlocked spirits and the old sailors the sea casts up. Like it cast up the Albert Townsend. I decided that the old schooner actually belongs here and so do its sailors. It should never be allowed to crawl back into the dark sea.

I walked back to the car. Now, the damn ghost ship and its ghost crew were bouncing around in my mind along with Juliet Brown, her daughter, the Yarn Woman, and another quart of oil that the car needed. That's what happens when you get too tired. I started drawing impossible relationships among them all. Not a pretty sight. I mean, what can the Albert Townsend and the crew that went down with it have in common with six-year-old Alexandra Brown?

The Yarn Woman

The street number Detective Chu gave me was out in the Sunset District in a mixed residential-commercial area of pastel-tinted stucco buildings amid very wide, flat streets at perfect right angles. I figured I would arrive at something like a makeshift tailor shop above a Chinese laundry. Maybe next door I'd find a Chinese takeout and doughnut shop like Lucky Golden Donuts or something similar. I tried to read the address on the paper as I drove west in the darkness of dawn, but Chu's writing was so abusive I had to stop, pull over, and slowly decipher it, make certain guesses and then drive on.

The address turned out to be in an alley – a little, lost Shangri La in a landscape of very pricey slag cement and concrete aggregate. The alley ran north and south and gave every indication of having been a real street until maybe sixty years ago. The asphalt was crumbled in places, revealing gray cobblestones alongside poorly mortared patches of rounded red brick – a testament to the age of the road. In the earliest days it had probably been one of the main routes leading to the Golden Gate on the north and the Presidio on the northwest, where household and industrial trash were dumped into the sea, a nasty local habit that actually expanded the peninsula.

It's hard to say why this street became a hidden back way. Time just rolled on without it, I guess, and when that happens, a place gets a dreamlike feel, like you've stepped back in time or slipped through a wormhole. I decided it was my week for wormholes, what with the old schooner. In that alley, I looked up and saw storefronts from the 1930s and 1950s where you'd expect to see slat-board backs of sagging commercial and multi-family buildings, trash bins and a supply of general urban refuse. But here, there was a lettered, lacquered facade for a tailor's shop, complete with a needle-and-thread sign overhanging a narrow sidewalk. And there, a second business was shuttered as if closed for half a century; a third was an odd mercantile in whose windows were paper box kites in red and blue and a five-man troupe of 7-inch marionettes in faded primary-colored enamels. There was a small cafe beyond that; it was crowded but the patrons all looked normal, as if they were really from the current century. Across the wide alley was the brick facing of a large, long warehouse with a stepped loading dock and a block-and-tackle apparatus that lifted unknown goods thirty feet up to peculiar doors above. A brick-and-mortar relief beneath the point of the shallow gable showed a sheaf of wheat with the year 1888 inset within a circle.

From what I could see, all progress had stopped by about 1960. I looked higher and saw the sky with puffs of fog coming from the west and nibbling at the building tops.

According to Chu's address, she, this Yarn Woman, lived at the Avaluxe Theater, which was poised solidly between the mercantile and a small confectionary and fountain that advertised Belgian chocolate, coffee soda and white, marshmallowy divinity.

The theater was two stories but had the height of three, maybe four, because the first floor had a 20-foot ceiling, and so did part of the second. It was narrow, as were most of the buildings in this section of town (except for the warehouse). By today's standards, the Avaluxe would be termed a mini-theater: It could seat a hundred comfortably on the main floor and another twenty-five on each side of the split balcony — a mere fraction of modern capacities. Yet in its day, it was one of San Francisco's premier (and premiere, as well) destinations.

The marquee jutted out a modest five or six feet from the facade and, in the morning dark, flickered in an ivory-peach light that bled through wayward, translucent red letters that had probably spelled "orchid" sometime in the past.

On the street level were two bronze-trimmed glass doors, and in each pane of early-century glass were cut-in images of stags leaping through abstracted leaves and flowers.

Because of its high interior ceiling and the modesty of nearby buildings, the Avaluxe loomed over the alley and seemed to dwell in agonizing nostalgia, staring toward a sea that was just out of sight and longing for a golden age just out of reach. But while the building itself may have seemed melancholy, its occupant was not. Somewhere inside was a woman as anachronistic and mysterious, in her own way, as the Avaluxe. And if she wasn't out of place in time, I was to learn, she was certainly as odd as if she were.

I peeked through the doors, careful not to touch the recently polished glass. It seemed more clear and resinous than modern glass, though I don't know why. It had slight waves in it from the early process of rolling, and a few noticeable air bubbles. A short, oddly built man caught a glimpse of me staring through it into the cramped lobby as he watered a plant on the north end. He wasn't more than five-foot-five. His nose and thick eyebrows protruded vigorously from his face. He had large gapped teeth that were overwhelmingly visible as he smiled at me through the glass. His block frame was supported by abnormally thick-looking bones, apparent especially in his Popeye-like wrists, which stuck out from the sleeves of his black jacket, and his black-socked ankles, which protruded from his trouser cuffs. He appeared to be in his seventies, and he gave every indication by the way he moved of being as strong, fit and vigorous as a man in his forties.

I had seen him before. I had to have seen him before, but didn't know where. It bothered me more than it should have, and ignited memories just out of my reach.

After he saw me, after he smiled, his nose fighting his teeth for the available space beneath his brown, nearly black eyes, he very precisely placed his gardening equipment on a tray and moved smoothly to a ticket kiosk in the center of the lobby, entering it from the back through a narrow door that reminded me of a train door in an old movie. He pulled at a lever that was not visible from the street, unbolting the front doors with a loud smack. The morning fog tried to follow me in, but the doors closed silently and quickly behind me. The Avaluxe was now receiving its guests for the morning.

I entered a lobby that was about forty feet wide and about twice that deep. The freestanding kiosk, of dark mahogany trimmed in black enamel with thin, repetitive chrome edge designs, was about seven feet tall and maybe five feet by five feet. Inside, there was a narrow mahogany shelf with several neatly incised roll-ticket holes and a heavy black dial-type phone whose ear and mouthpiece must have weighed more than a small dog. There was a small laptop computer and some complex electronic gadgetry, which were obviously misplaced. Below the shelf was the handle the doorman had yanked to throw back the bolts.

Twin majestic staircases, one on either side of the kiosk, wound to the upper level seating. The staircases with their wood balusters and carved oak newels, while adding an intense, overdone charm to the room, claimed much of the available space. A single elaborate chandelier, in which colored glass fruits accompanied long, waterfall crystals, was suspended above the north staircase, but it wasn't lit.

The lobby was crushingly close as a result of the twin staircases and the kiosk, and the woodwork kept the place dark. The furnishings were a collection of French antiques with a few odd-lot pieces of imitation Italian Rococo left over from the days of live theater. The wool carpet was a multi-colored flower pattern over a clay-green background. The place was cold but not damp, and old but not musty. In fact, the room felt very much alive, in spite of itself.

"Mr. Fisher, I understand?" said the Avaluxe care taker. I caught a trace of a Russian accent and wondered if it was mixed, just a little, with French. "Am I mistaken? Certainly not. She will remember you, rest assured." Remember me? He looked at a small gold watch that was dwarfed by the thickness of a hairy right wrist. His fingers were furred as well, and thick and knuckled like you'd expect from a life of hard manual labor or industrial manufacturing ... or someone who goes around happily punching brick walls. "I am Mr. Kasparov, thank you," he said. "I was expecting you a quarter-hour ago, Mr. Fisher. Time is liquid, hm? Please take a seat here." He walked me to a Victorian divan to my left. "Mr. Chu was detained, I am sure," he said, motioning me to sit and wait. "The Miss will be with you soon, yes. She's dyeing."

"What do you mean, dying?"

"Dyeing, Mr. Fisher, not dying. You spell it with an 'e.' You should know that. She is making color, Mr. Fisher. And may I offer you, for example, a hot tea while you wait for The Miss?"

Mr. Kasparov smiled broadly, vanished and returned a few minutes later carrying an avocado-cream ceramic tea set on a blackened silver platter. He placed it carefully on a delicate round table and left.

I waited, refusing to look at my watch. I decided that Mr. Kasparov was eccentric. Yet there was something magnetic about him. I couldn't help but like him and I felt comfortable with him, despite his formality, almost immediately.

About ten minutes later, roughly estimated, Detective Chu walked in with the disgusting garment bundled in plastic under his arm. He acknowledged his childhood friend, me, as officiously as he could to still save face in front of anyone who might be watching. In response, I gave him an old-buddy hug, purposefully squeezing him into his own parcel. Fifteen minutes after Chu's arrival, the

Yarn Woman — by now as much a fantasy to me as the ghostly deckhands of the Townsend — descended the northern staircase, the far one, from her apartment above and made her way across the room toward us.

She didn't look at either of us at first. In mid-descent, though, she turned her face toward us. I couldn't unlock myself from the gaze of those green eyes. I knew immediately and exactly who she was: the green eyes that evening in the fog two years ago were hers. And this doorman and caretaker who plagued my memory was her driver. Recognition and relief shot through me. Relief? Absolutely: I'd seen her again, finally.

Objectively, aside from the ... eyes... there was little particularly or immediately outstanding about this Yarn Woman's appearance, and it's only on reflection you realize how striking she actually is — it was like a dream you have to go back to and reconstruct bit by bit and you keep saying to yourself, "Oh, yeah, yeah. And then this, too." For some reason, at times you don't see the extraordinary at first; in fact, after I'd arrived at her very surreal residence on her chimerical alleyway (I wondered if I would ever find the place again), her fundamental commonness was unnerving. It lent an air of reality to a setting that might otherwise have been passed off as a momentary excursion through time and general sanity.

She wore no makeup and would have been no better for it. Her face was delightful, her build, though masked by layered clothing, appealing. Maybe she wore lipstick, but I don't know for sure. At first glance, her hair seemed an unremarkable brown, but when it caught the light it tended toward chestnut. It was almost long, very thick, probably straight or maybe waved as if exposed to humidity, and she wore it rolled or twisted and bunned in the back close to the top. Locks fell to the side and back because she hadn't caught it up completely before pinning it — it was home to a collection of knitting needles and yellow-enameled cedar pencils, the old kind, which held it up.

Her eyes were unquestionably otherworldly. They flashed out from a lightly freckled, slightly tanned or tawny face beneath the shadow of her dark hair. Her eyebrows were dark and elegant, and it was impossible to tell if they'd been shaped or were naturally arched and modestly thick. At first, you'd clearly see that her eyes were green. In the subdued light of the theater lobby, they glowed almost like a cat's and you had to blink to make the impression go away. But then, depending on the light – or later, I would learn, on her mood or concentration – they could be various shades of blue or aquamarine, even nearly hazel.

"Detective Chu," she said, holding out her hand. "Hi." She was wearing linen – loose sage pants and looser wheat-yellow buttoned blouse over an avocado-cream camisole with a burnt-orange Russian shawl over her shoulders. It was nearly autumn, after all, I figured. She looked like a falling leaf in human form. "And this is Mr. Fisher." I nodded, stood awkwardly and shook her hand. She's maybe five-foot-three at most, and I tried not to lean over to greet her. She had a tempered steel grip and was clearly athletic. "Hi. I'm Ruth," she said lightly. "I remember you." I noticed she had small hands and small feet, the latter in brilliant blue satin shoes. Though there was no way on earth that I could ever forget her, why would she possibly remember me?

"Nat Fisher," I said, the memory of that cold night in the city hovering over me like a spirit. I wanted to complete my introduction by saying I was a staffer at the San Francisco Daily Bulletin, that I usually cover crime and commercial fishing, and that I remembered her, too, and for two years had regretted not running like an idiot after the Rolls that had so thoroughly whisked her away. But I didn't elaborate. Unlike almost everyone I'd ever met, male or female, she didn't ask my vocation during our entire meeting, but after a few minutes I realized she had evaluated me quite thoroughly and had no need of such superfluous information.

"I understand you wanted to see me about a garment," she said to Chu.

She took a seat across from us and reached past the detective and spread a thick felt cloth over the table. Then she dragged over a powerful halogen table lamp. It was the only thing in the lobby manufactured in this century, except for the electronic gear misplaced in the ticket kiosk. She flipped it on and immediately a large black-and-white, long-haired cat leaped onto the table and sat there staring at me. It was uncomfortable. He … I assume it was a he … stared past me or through me with eyes that were, for a cat, very old and absent, almost glazed. She picked him up and put him in an empty fourth chair at the table, but he jumped down and departed.

"That's Methuselah," she explained. "He doesn't always come downstairs. He likes the roof. But you passed the cat test, Mr. Fisher" she said matter-of-factly, "which means we can get going. I'm really glad I didn't have to kick you out. It's such an awkward position, when the cat says 'no.' You can't explain anything to him, I mean, he's pretty set in his opinions. I pay him for his services at the end of the week." Her tone was so businesslike that it dawned on me that the woman was serious – and therefore eccentric – and I found that odd because I usually reserved that judgment for older people, certainly not one of her age … though I wasn't sure of her years by any means.

Chu, taking the cue, put the plastic evidence sack on the felt pad on the small table beneath the light. He snapped on a pair of skin-toned latex gloves and handed a second pair to her. I was still pondering the significance of the "cat test" as he opened the sack and removed a crumpled woolen garment. The yarn had mud ground into it, and dry weeds had invaded the weave in several areas. There were blood stains on most of it, and it was dry in a few spots but remained wet with blood, and, I assumed, water, in others. The blood-soaked spots leached onto the tablecloth. It didn't seem to bother her.

"The child was wearing this," Chu said, pushing it gently toward her and moving the cloth beneath along with it, "when she arrived at the hospital yesterday. She'd been badly hurt. Very seriously hurt. The mother, a Mrs. Juliet Brown, 34, divorced, no police record, restraining order against her ex, doesn't know where the child got the sweater, and the child won't tell her what happened. The child spoke to no one. The female officer assigned to the case couldn't get a thing out of her. Not a verb, not a subjunctive clause. After the assault, the child had obviously gotten into water and had become hypothermic, despite the sweater."

"The child, the child, the child," she said, disturbed at Chu's objectification of the daughter of Juliet Brown. "Okay, okay. Just a minute. First of all, tell me what you expect from me."

Chu, acknowledging the reprimand, said quietly, "I want to know where it comes from. A store? A particular maker? If it's homemade, what ethnicity? Who made it? What the hell is it? It doesn't look like a normal sweater. I am working in a very confined area of the city, about five blocks, so we may be able to link it to a specific person or family. Maybe a household. I looked at it and said it looks goofy enough to stand out in a crowd, Miss M. And, I thought, that's where you come in. Tell me about it. No, no ..." he held up his hand to stop her ... "I already thought about that: There were no deposits of used clothing on the street, we've already checked that. It's possible, of course, that the garment was a single discard, something the girl found in the gutter. But I rather doubt it. From what I can tell, which isn't much, the soiling isn't long-term. All that junk? That's all new. The weeds and dirt. I'll turn it over to forensics for full analysis after you take a look. We'll check for hair follicles, mismatched blood, that sort of thing. For now? I want to know where it came from."

"I see."

"The child couldn't possibly have put it over her own shoulders, she was hurt that bad."

"You said 'the child' again."

"Excuse me, then. The victim."

"So, go on. Tell me what you can about the assault. Why don't you tell me everything you know about the situation first."

Chu thought quickly. I knew him well enough to tell he was weighing his options. Finally, he decided to let her in on the full investigation to date, early though it was. "The girl is six years and two months old," he began. "She's very intelligent, apparently gifted. Her mother says she's musical and has a knack for mathematics. She slipped out of the house before dawn yesterday, probably around 5, possibly as early as 4, and was missing for at least two hours, until about 7. Mrs. Brown observed the child … I mean, Alexandra, Alexandra Brown … hobbling home on the sidewalk, coming from the north on Pierce toward Alta Park, that little park, covered in blood and wrapped in this faded, red shawl-sweater thing that didn't belong to her. She had no shoes and only one white ankle sock, soiled with sand and dirt, wet with blood and seawater. Definitely saltwater. Her long hair was soaked but no longer dripping, but she was unable to pull the hair away from her face because of the damage to her left shoulder, arms and hands, and the hair had matted into the facial blood as well. She was barely able to walk. There were bruises consistent with a severe battering, and numerous wounds consistent with the savage bite marks of a large dog. Her clothing tested positive for canine saliva; we know that much already."

"My God. Was she hurt terribly by the dog?"

Chu paused for a moment. She picked up on Chu's brief silence, and probed further. "So you're saying the dog didn't hurt her? What are you saying?"

He sighed. "There were bruises consistent with the tooth pattern of a large – very large – dog. Yet there were no skin punctures from the beast. And the bruising was not consistent with an animal grabbing and shaking a child, like it would a rag doll. That's why we could let her go home. That was kind of miraculous really, when you consider it, that there were no puncture wounds. They would have had to begin the post-exposure prophylaxis injections, otherwise. They may end up doing that anyway, I don't know."

A fatality from a week earlier came immediately to my mind. A transient had been killed within a block or two of Alta Park by a large dog. Police at the time decided it had been a massive pit bull on the loose and they'd scoured the area in search of the thing. The dog wasn't found and the story, from my end, was quickly eclipsed by all the other stories of the week, especially speculation about the Albert Townsend. The death was just a day or two after the old schooner surfaced. Taking advantage of the slightest break in the discussion, I mentioned the earlier death.

Chu seemed unhappy at my revelation but was basically forced to comment on it. "Yes, they could be related, but at this point, until forensics gets some results, we can't be sure."

"You weren't going to tell me about this earlier death?" she asked Chu. I couldn't tell if I was reading disappointment, surprise or anger in her question. Probably a mix.

"Well, yes, yes I was. I just hadn't gotten there yet," Chu said defensively. He smiled unconvincingly, but avoided casting a glance in my direction.

"And soaked from water, you say . . ." she continued.

"Saltwater. Ocean water, yes. The mother was naturally upset at the hospital, and was considered combative by the staff," Chu continued, as if reading from a book of police notes.

"Of course."

"Huh?"

"I said, of course. Combative. You guys are so predictable. Maybe she should have been arrested for caring about her daughter."

Chu ignored the commentary. He saw it as part of the package. "She parked in the ambulance drive, locked the car and jammed the horn until personnel behaved in the manner she desired. She had managed to drive with the child on her lap, both of them wrapped in a quilt she normally kept in the back seat. She obviously knew what to do about hypothermia; she had opened her own sweater, under the blanket, for direct contact with the child. And she knew how the hell to get into the emergency room at the head of the line. End of story. The hospital notified the police, and, of course, social services."

She looked up, the obvious question on her face.

"She was not molested, Miss M. I observed, upon my arrival, that emotionally, the child was fairly happy despite the injuries."

"I see. How exact is two hours?"

"I'm sorry?"

"Two hours exactly? The time she was gone. Or less? More? Three, if she left by 4?"

"We can't tell exactly because we are uncertain of the time she left the house. But we are estimating her absence at 90 to 120 minutes."

"And, this was the only time . . ."

"Only time?"

"Has it happened before? I mean, leaving the house so secretly."

"Possibly."

She waited.

"Well, apparently, yes. But only recently."

"How recently, Mr. Chu." She was growing impatient with having to pull the information from Detective

William Chu. From my perspective, it was a contest of wills: She wanted to know what the hell had happened, and Chu preferred to limit the information, apparently wanting her opinion on a very narrow aspect of the case, namely the sweater. He was proceeding on a need-to-know basis. But he sensed her attitude, and, surprising to me, finally adopted a more cooperative, even submissive air. I'd never seen him do this for anyone in my long association with the man.

"Just a few weeks, as I understand it."

Satisfied with Chu's newfound congeniality, the Yarn Woman took the sweater and carefully laid it on the table. I realized it wasn't a sweater at all. It had no sleeves. It was like a shawl, I suppose, shaped like a long, horizontal triangle … long like a scarf. The ends of it, which tapered into cords with tassels, hung over the round table. I morosely expected it to drip blood, but it didn't. When worn, it would have covered a woman's shoulders and back, but it was much too wide for a shawl. It looked awkward.

"Relax, it isn't awkward at all, Mr. Fisher," she said as if reading my thoughts. Then she inhaled deeply and seemed newly intrigued, as if she were looking at something extremely old, valuable or rare. She still hadn't touched the thing. She asked Chu to stand up. Uncomfortably, he did. She eyed the garment, then the detective, and went back and forth between the two several times. Finally, she thanked him and asked him to sit back down. "And the injuries, more specifically?" she asked casually, pushing the garment here and there to even it out.

"Her right shoulder was dislocated. It was lacerated, and with deep-purple bruises. She had puncture wounds – not from the teeth – and abrasions and considerable bruising. She had a mild concussion. Her right eye was blackened, with a nasty gash on her forehead near the temple. Bloody nose, torn lip needing five stitches.

Twenty-five stitches altogether, plus the knees. Her knees were cut and bruised and her feet were a bloody mess. Her head was deeply bruised here and here," he said, pointing to the area above his ears, "certainly from the dog, and she was either hit or bitten hard enough to bruise under her hair." Chu pointed to the back of his head.

"Around the crown, but not on top?" she asked.

"Exactly. The nurse practitioner in the ER indicated the injuries could be an attack or a fall or both. A dog attack. She was given a tetanus injection, but not specifically because of the head injuries."

Satisfied, she turned her attention back to the shawl.

"Mrs. Brown has no idea at all about where this sontag came from?" she asked.

"That's correct. Sontag? Sontag?"

"I thought you wanted my opinion on the garment, not its etymology. Is this a great day or what? This is great." The Yarn Woman almost seemed to glow. Chu had inadvertently broadened the inquiry. I got the feeling he'd made this mistake before. I could sense he was worried about time – and now he'd have to endure, from what I could predict, a bit of a history lecture. Chu looked at me, careful to show no expression on his face, but I knew what he was thinking. In that sense, he could not have sighed any louder in resignation.

The Soprano, Miss Sontag

"Mr. Kasparov," she said, lifting her voice slightly, "could you bring some more tea?" At this point, I realized she had a very lovely voice. I don't know how I missed it before. I wondered if she sang and if so, what. Did she read aloud? Recite poetry? The short, thick man, who had returned silently to his post near the kiosk, materialized almost magically and disappeared as quickly through a door to my left that led to a small commercial kitchen. He was back in moments, as if the tea were simply waiting for him to carry out.

"It was probably named after the great lyric soprano, you know," Ruth said. "Though not conclusive, the preponderance of evidence, so to speak, is clearly weighted in favor of linking this wrap, common in the second half of the nineteenth century, to the renowned Henriette Sontag, active in the first half." She smiled triumphantly. "I'm just saying."

Chu stared blankly.

"I mean, it's one of the prevalent theories on the naming of the garment. There was a whole team of etymologists working on this between 1910 and 1913, but, as they say, though they found still-warm bullets, they never discovered the smoking gun. Wait here," she said suddenly, and hurried to the staircase, taking the steps two at a time and returning moments later with an old journal in her hands and the cat following her down the steps, bounding along behind her. As she got closer, I could read "The Musical Quarterly" on the cover of the magazine. When she saw that I was trying to read it, she held it up to my face. It was Vol. 28, No. 1, dating from January, 1942. Then she sat down and began to read us selected excerpts from the pages devoted to the history of one Henriette Sontag, the bewitching lyric soprano, contemporary and muse to Mendelssohn and Beethoven, even Goethe, and namesake, apparently, of the peculiar garment on the table in front of me.

" 'Every man, married or single, fell in love with Sontag at first sight,' " she read. " 'Thousands proposed matrimony to her.' " The cat, Methuselah, hung on every word. "She reminds me of Mrs. Reynolds, who taught me much about music as well as textiles, especially knitting. But, but, let's stay on message here. I'll continue," and she lifted the magazine up again and I prepared to be lulled again by that lovely voice. " 'Hundreds (more or less) doubtless committed suicide when in 1830 she announced her secret marriage to Count (Carlo) Rossi, a young Italian diplomat, and renounced her stage career.' " She looked at us. "Love robbed the world. It happens." She began again. Chu, having come to terms with the situation, settled back into his chair. His eyes glazed over, but he blinked occasionally.

When she finished the reading, some six or eight pages and twenty or thirty minutes later, she folded the periodical and carefully placed it on the floor. "Well?" she asked us expectantly. "Is that something or what?"

"Very interesting," Chu said.

"I see," she said, sighing. She looked at me and added, "Consider it a study of how journalism in the mid-twentieth century sought to pay homage to a diva of nineteenth. Very unusual, I'm sure, and a professional challenge." Dejected, she put the journal and cat on the empty chair beside me. The cat stared at Chu, reprimand in its eyes. "The sontag was probably named after her. Where the hell else would you get a name like that, anyway?"

Science at its purest, I thought. She looked at me and smiled. It was a strange, almost crooked smile, and stronger on the left side of her face. It was charming. But the look in her eyes left no doubt that she had heard my thought as if I'd said it out loud. It wasn't a comfortable position to be in, and somewhat embarrassing.

"Perhaps we might first explore how the sontag is worn," she said, redirecting our attention. "In that way, we'll all be on the same page.

"Stand up, Detective, and I'll show you how it works." Hesitantly, Chu stood. She immediately draped the mangy thing over his back before he could dodge out of the way. This was about all Chu could stand. He flushed red, but with a deep breath he got himself under control.

"The evidence!" he said, his voice cracking. He could barely eject the words. "It hasn't even been to forensics yet! Really, Miss M ..."

"I have no decorum," she said to me, apologetically. "I never did get the rules down. Can you imagine what it's like to take all the evidence and stick it on someone's back? I feel terrible." She shrugged. I honestly couldn't tell if the woman was mischievous, incongruous or simply strange. Then she said, "What'd you hire me for anyway, Detective, if not to supply you with the needed forensics information? Your boys can take care of the blood and DNA later with no problem."

I suppose she had a point, though I was uncertain if Chu would readily admit it. Hearing no response within a reasonable period of time, her attention returned to Chu. She crossed the fabric in front of him from the left shoulder to his right hip and right shoulder to left hip. It was really quite amazing: The wearer of a sontag would have unlimited mobility of their arms, yet their back, front and shoulders would be warmly wrapped. It was clear that the female's household roles of the nineteenth century would be most easily accomplished in such a garment, whether she was splitting wood or cooking or plucking a chicken. She tied it in the back very conveniently. "It's also called a bosom buddy, Detective, unless a person like yourself is wearing it. Or Mr. Fisher, for example. The earliest pattern I've been able to dig up dates from 1859, but there's a better one in Godey's from January of 1860. Do you want to see it?" She was heading upstairs again.

"No, no," said Chu quickly. "That won't be necessary." His voice had returned. I, however, silently marveled at what must have been an incredible textile library upstairs at the Avaluxe Theater.

After a moment, she carefully removed the sontag by first placing the cloth from the table over the garment, then gingerly rolling them together off the detective. She carefully lowered them to the table and unrolled them.

Hovering over the sontag as it lay again across the table, she pulled a self-illuminating digital pocket microscope from a small bag she'd carried downstairs when she descended from her apartment. "It's a Brinell with a Leica lens," she said. I nodded as if I understood. I wondered how much a contraption like that would cost. Probably more than a car. She gloved up and held the scope and an end of the garment beneath the bright light. The device had a reticle inside that measured in microns. She was silent during her inspection. She hardly moved the sontag as she analyzed various parts of it.

As the minutes passed, the tenor of the room began to change. There was no clock anywhere to be seen, and I refused to look at my cheap Armitron for fear of insulting this Yarn Woman who might interpret the move as impatience. I hoped I had turned off the alarm, an embarrassing tune that never failed to chime at the wrong time. Nevertheless, I think fifteen or twenty minutes passed as she examined the old thing minutely. The seeming lightheartedness of her demeanor continued to evaporate with every minute that passed, until at last we were left, Chu and I, in the presence of a very serious textile conservator. Finally, she put the scope aside and snapped off the latex gloves. Her hair was disheveled, but it seemed only to augment the magnetism she exuded. Couldn't she do anything wrong?

"Detective," she said, "there are a flurry of points to

be made. I hardly know where to start."

"That doesn't sound good."

"Maybe it's not. Do you want to take notes? You don't have to; I'll type up the report tonight and have Mr. Kasparov fax it to your office. You'll have everything before you get in tomorrow morning. Unless you want it, like, this afternoon."

"Tomorrow morning is fine."

"Okay then. Curious ... you get a lot of police reports, right?"

"Yes, generally speaking."

"From other cities, other states?"

"On occasion, when there's an interstate element, or fugitive status ..."

"Have there been any museum thefts recently, local or otherwise?"

"Museum?" he said, thinking. "Not that I can recall."

"Okay. If you think of any, let me know. Now, let's talk about your garment. This is a sontag, a style of wrap that was popular during the Civil War and shortly after. It was, as you have seen, very utilitarian.

"This specimen was knit with handspun churro. That became clear under magnification. Churro is a kind of sheep brought to the New World from Spain in the sixteenth century. I don't know if you're that interested in the history, but a few hundred years later, the U.S. government decided the Navajo could have the sheep and they could make blankets and rugs and be productive members of society. That was the thought, primitive as it may sound to you today. Churro arrived in California during the Gold Rush, about 1850. Shortly after that, the U.S. decided the Navajo didn't really deserve the sheep after all and tried to dilute the breed and find substitutes. They killed so many to preserve the rangeland that the breed is now considered rare and endangered.

"Churro wool is very coarse, Detective. It's used for rugs, and it's not meant to be worn next to your body. The filaments are 38 microns at minimum and the crimp is one or two, maybe zero, per inch. That means thick and difficult to spin, knit or felt. I mean, it's used for rugs for God's sake, not garments."

"I'm not quite ..." Chu began, but she raised her hand to shut him up. He did.

"That's an important element in my final diagnosis, the churro.

"But to go on. This would not fit a tall woman. It's too short for even an average woman. The size and the apparent thinning and stretching of the fibers across the chest area indicate to me that the wearer was about four-foot-eight or -nine, built like a dumpling, and buxom.

"More, there is staining in the upper portion and particulate matter that lead me to believe it was used at least in part to cook in. There are indications of natural animal fats and oils. Yet there's no such contamination in the lower portion, or at least minimal, which suggests she wore an apron around her hips.

"Did you smell it, Detective?"

Chu pondered the question and then said that he had not.

"Well, smell it now. It's not going to jump you."

Chu leaned over and sniffed.

"And?" she said.

"Smells like pine tar. Like pine tar soap or something."

"It's wood smoke, Mr. Chu. She cooked over a wood stove."

Chu frowned. "I hardly believe that, Miss M."

"Well, believe what you want. There's soot in the weave. You can see a lot under high magnification, and I observed soot that had worked its way well into the fibers, not just topically. You may get soot from a fireplace, but foodstuffs come from cooking."

Chu thought quietly for a few minutes, sipping his tea and staring off into the void. Then he said, slowly,

"What I have, then, is a short, buxom woman who, in my mind, is a housewife (because of the cooking) rather than a career woman, who heats her home with a wood fire rather than using gas or electric. That does help."

"You have more than that, I'm afraid."

"What do you mean?"

"Well, she's poor, you know, because of her choice of yarn. She is an accomplished knitter, lifelong I would say, because of the stitch perfection in the work. So, you may add her economic status and age to your description of the woman. But that's not quite what I mean."

"Please go on, then," said Chu, remembering now why he had contacted her in the first place.

"She probably died a hundred and fifty years ago."

Chu was silent.

"This woman," Ruth said. "I said, she probably died a century and a half ago."

Chu was still silent. He used to do this when the math teacher threw a crooked equation at him. He'd just stand there, calculating. Then he'd answer, and most of the time he was right. "That's not good," he said.

"You're telling me."

"And you're saying …?"

"Your sontag dates from about 1870, perhaps as early as 1865. As you know, I am one of the individuals that museums contact to authenticate their acquisitions. I am coming from a place of knowledge in this matter. I suggested that your perpetrator has worn this particular garment for perhaps the last two to three years, based on soiling, and I don't mean the most recent incident with Mrs. Brown. I am taking into account the general wear and the stretching of the fibers, which I mentioned. It was, however, in a controlled microclimate display case prior to two or three years ago. This piece belongs in a museum, and I suspect it had been in a museum. It's in remarkable condition, just remarkable. I've never actually seen a perfectly vintage sontag. Never this old."

"Well, okay," he said slowly. "What has led you to this understanding, shall we say?"

"A combination of things. The churro, of course. The excellence of the work is indicative; the edging style is historically accurate. The dye and mordant, yes, cochineal with a chromium-iron mordant is my educated guess, as well as the effects of such on the fiber. The manner of soiling is important, and its depth in the fiber mass. The condition of the dye in relation to the fiber surface – though it would be nice to see that under higher magnification from a stereoscopic microscope. There's very modest felting that has involved fiber breakage.

"Frankly, the wetting of the fabric has slowed the crystallization or aging process, which is a benefit, but we should get this back in a microclimate case as soon as feasible.

"The edges, of course, have already reached a state of embrittlement – once it entered the natural environment (as opposed to one of controlled temp, moisture, air flow and pH in its display case). They are the first portion to be attacked by the aging process during the drying process. The edge fibers, under magnification, show signs of cracking from folding or bending."

She smiled and waited.

"I'll run a check on museum thefts ... over what period of time did you say?"

"Three years, maximum, two years minimum, based on physical aging."

"Fine. Done." He sighed. "I don't have a suspect anymore."

She put her hand on his shoulder. "Get over it." Her comment wasn't exactly comforting. "If I were you, I'd start looking into that earlier killing, the dog-mauling one."

"There's always that," he said.

"Detective Chu," she said, "are you going to arrest Mrs. Brown?"

Chu, caught off guard, obligatorily rolled his shoulders.

"Then you have other suspects?"

"No," he said. "But I'm not sure what Social Services will do. They don't exactly communicate well with law enforcement. Personally, I'm not interested in Mrs. Brown as a suspect, but, personally, Social Services is operated by morons who respond quite readily to public opinion. They have an agenda of their own, and they keep it close to their collective chest, so to speak. I can't tell if public opinion will have a role in this," he said, looking slyly over at me.

"I see," she said. "Then I'd like to visit her as soon as possible."

There was quite a pause. Finally, he said, "Okay. That would be fine. Time may be important here."

"I'll need an introduction. A woman who uses the ER the way she did won't just allow a visit from out of the blue. We could arrive together and you could introduce me."

Chu, normally a very sober man, seemed even more so. Like me, maybe he was holding onto his sanity. "I could contact Mrs. Brown tomorrow for further inquiry; you could accompany me," he said. "I would bring the sweater, of course."

"Sontag."

"Whatever."

"I have a microclimate case upstairs that we can use until protective arrangements are made for it."

"If you think it's necessary."

"Yes."

"Fine. You'll have the sontag in its safe environment. Then, after I introduce you to Mrs. Brown – you might find her abrasive but I am sure you can handle it – I would have some sort of emergency and leave you two to talk." He looked at his shoulder. There were blood smudges on his wool-silk suit. He didn't say anything.

"But," he said, directive in his voice, "you have to tell me everything Mrs. Brown says, after the introduction. Even things that don't seem pertinent. You know, we, the department, will be knee deep in this by tomorrow. Everyone's got their eyes on the mauling fatality, and hearts are going to break when the papers print that kid's photo. She's a cute one and the press will be on it like flies. This isn't the time to discommunicate."

I knew he could be right about the girl's photo, especially if she was cute. I didn't know if she was because I hadn't seen her face the morning she arrived at the hospital, and I didn't take the comment about the press as an insult.

"Discommunicate," she said with a smile, "surely not. I'll just have a little visit, and maybe bring Mr. Fisher along to take notes for you." Which made me feel great.

"Tomorrow."

"You know, like mid-morning or something."

"What's mid-morning? Ten?" he asked.

"Ten-thirty would be fine. I don't have her address. We could meet you there."

Chu scribbled out the address and ripped the page from his notes, handing it to her. Both were standing now, the chat obviously over. I stood to leave as well.

"I can't read this, Detective Chu."

He took it back and snuffed, then put it on the table. "I've got until tomorrow to come up with a new inquiry direction. The press is going to be on this like..." He looked at me and shut up. Then he smiled. "Do the right thing, Teddy," he said.

"Always do."

"Thank you Miss M," he said, turning to the Yarn Woman, and left. The heavy glass door on the right swung slowly closed after him. I was still standing in front of my chair.

We stood alone in the lobby. "What are you doing tomorrow morning, Montag?" she asked.

“Um, Fisher,” I said awkwardly. Montag? “Nothing pressing.” My so-called schedule was adaptable to the needs of the moment. “Trying to make your detective look like he knows what he’s doing.”

“I see.”

“It’s the least I can do.”

“I’m sure. Well, can you read this?” Unfazed by her own mistake about my name, she handed me Chu’s note.

I told her the number on Pierce Street. It was just south of Alta Park, which was a little grassy space where people often walked their dogs.

“I think it’s very useful to be multilingual,” she said, taking back the note. “Mr. Kasparov can speak six languages. But I don’t read scribbles, myself. Here,” she said, picking up the magazine tribute to Henriette Sontag, “don’t forget the journal. But I want it back.”

Hauper

We arrived at Mrs. Brown's residence at the prescribed 10:30. She lived alone with her daughter in a common three-story apartment building that looked like it had about twenty-five units. It was run down but not a wreck, but even so, the one-bed apartment wasn't cheap. Unless, of course, she'd lived there for the last fifteen or twenty years and lived under the protective wing of rent control, which I doubted.

Mrs. Brown was not looking her best, and for good reason. Disheveled, she bore a distraught look and deep shadows had taken residence beneath her eyes. We sat in a very small living room, wedging ourselves into two chairs and a micro-sofa. Chu didn't sit, but made his introductions and made his exit, using an unnamed emergency at the office as his excuse.

It was cool inside, but despite the chill, Mrs. Brown was in a sweat: Her blouse was soaked under the arms and her mousy hair, between medium and short and cut in no particular style and not particularly clean, was pasted to her face here and there with perspiration. The visible lack of care seemed to me typical of an overworked single parent with little time and less energy. She was about five-foot-eight and probably in her mid-thirties, with a pleasant, pallid face that seemed marred by a little more than her fair share of life's general sadness.

There was an open purse beside her chair. It was ivory-white leather with a brass snap closure, and the lower corners were very worn. She didn't seem to be the type who had more than one or two. She wore unpressed wool slacks that had pilled.

"I understand you wanted to see me about my daughter," she said flatly.

Ruth nodded.

"And you are?"

"I'm Ruth M. Detective Chu thought we could talk just a little. Just fill in some blanks."

"I mean, are you with the police, or are you from Child Protection?" She was referring to Child Protective Services, a branch of the city Social Services Department that takes children from their homes – purportedly for their own safety.

"I'm a consultant, Mrs. Brown. Forensic textiles is my area."

"No shit. I'm Juliet Brown. I'm 37, divorced, have no police record, one child, full custody, a restraining order against the ex that's good for a hundred yards or twelve months, whichever comes first," she said, reaching for the strap of the purse and twisting it. "She's six now. She reads novels, takes my romances, and is up through algebra. Okay?"

"Is she here?"

"She's watching TV or playing a game on it, I don't know."

We could hear the TV in the background. The child must have had good ears, because only seconds passed before she appeared at the doorway. She wasn't a pretty child, and neither was she enormously cute in my opinion. But her looks were somehow endearing and Chu, I decided, had been right about her probable influence on the press. More striking than her appearance was her presence – she was a 150-watt bulb in a 60-watt world. She was wearing a short-sleeved button-up shirt with a pattern of different-sized squares in bright colors. Most of her small body was wrapped in gauze and parts were coated in a fiberglass and plaster casting compound. She slowly sat down there, propping her back against the jamb, and listened. Clearly, she was in pain.

Ruth explained that Detective Chu had asked her about the sontag, which she said was the shawl that the girl had been wrapped in. She asked Mrs. Brown if she knew anything about where she thought it might be from, if she'd seen it before, and so on. "It's obviously sized for a mature woman, and you don't have any idea where she got it?" she asked. "Have you ever seen anyone in this area wearing anything like it?"

"I have no idea at all," said Mrs. Brown. "The Russian women wear shawls, but they're not like what she came back in."

"No. Very different. Do you have any neighbors who might be described as short, say four-eight or four-nine, buxom, plump."

Mrs. Brown was very near tears. "Everyone," she said.

"Mrs. Mullins," mumbled the girl under her breath. The mother didn't hear. Ruth heard but didn't show it.

"Well, your daughter acquired it within an hour of your home, possibly half that time," Ruth said. "So you might have seen her, is all."

"Fine," said Mrs. Brown.

"That limits it somewhat, geographically, is what I mean."

"I gather." There was a long pause. "I expect to be investigated for supposedly endangering my child," she said finally. "The police were all over it. I really don't know why I'm talking to you. I need a lawyer."

"Well," said Ruth, turning her attention to the girl, "Detective Chu said you're musical. Do you have an instrument or is it voice?"

"I play the violin," said the girl from her doorjamb.

"Yes. A little half-size violin," said Mrs. Brown. "She's had lessons for a little more than two years. She has another recital next week. Obviously, she won't be able to play."

"Yes I will," said the girl.

"What are you playing at the moment," Ruth asked.

"Currently? Vivaldi," said the child. "And I can almost hold the bow because I just tried." She looked at her mother, her face a blend of childish anger and adult pity.

Ruth, who'd been carrying a basket that she usually used for whatever knitting project she was working on, had stuffed some sheet music into it before the meeting, and she started digging it out. The girl limped over from the doorway and began picking up the papers from Ruth's lap.

"Do you play violin?" she asked.

"No. Well, a little. Mr. Kasparov plays; he's my friend. I have a harpsichord."

"I know," said the girl, pointing to the title of one of the Schumann pieces. "Is it small? Is it golden? I've seen pictures."

"Yes and yes," said Ruth. "Oh. How should I call you?"

"It's Alexandra," interrupted Mrs. Brown, which brought the child, who had seated herself with difficulty beside Ruth on the micro-sofa to more easily peruse the papers, to her feet. She hobbled out of the room carrying some of the music with her.

"It's Alexandra. But she won't answer to it," said Mrs. Brown. "She's gifted, I've been told. But, Ms. M, gifted is never easy. It's just work most of the time. Her father tried to make her." She shrugged.

"Make her?"

"Answer to Alexandra."

"I see. What does she prefer?"

"Hauper."

"Hopper? Like a rabbit?"

"Hopper, like the artist. But she prefers to spell it H-a-u-p-e-r to avoid confusion with the rabbit thing. She calls herself Hauper, and refuses to answer to anything else."

"Hauper. Hauper Brown?"

"No."

"Just Hauper, then. One name."

"Duh." Pause. "Do you have children?"

"And she's six?"

"Six years, two months, one week, one day." She looked at her watch, then looked up. "The damned police wanted to know everything. I mean everything. You're not even a person."

"Well," Ruth said, unfazed, "I'd like to invite you and Hauper for tea, nevertheless. Can that work? No more questions for now. Maybe she could bring her violin. I'll bet she'll be playing it within a week. I do have a couple of questions for her about her adventure, but I don't need to deal with that immediately … it can wait."

"Don't we all. God. I don't believe in punishment; that was her father's, um, peculiar gift. She'll tell me things when she's ready. That's the way she is." Mrs. Brown got up and went into the kitchen. I could hear the hiss of a soda can opening, and she returned with a Pepsi and four glasses in her hand. I think the glasses were clean, but they were fogged from abrasion, the way old tumblers can get when they somehow survive years without breaking. She poured out the can without asking if anyone was interested, and placed them on a battered coffee table that was situated between us.

Hauper meandered out, took her glass, and disappeared once again.

"Maybe she'll mention something to you," Mrs. Brown said wistfully. "Yeah, we can come to tea, and then I could find an errand, leave you alone for a while, like fifteen minutes or so, and then come back. I could go shopping, get a fur coat or something for myself. Go to a body shop and price a paint job I could never get. Is there a spa nearby?" She looked sadly up from her soda and sighed. "She won't talk to me. She wouldn't talk to the cop woman. She's going to mute me into prison, Ms. M. God. That's exactly what's going to happen. Then what? Wham, her father. She wouldn't talk at the hospital and hasn't opened her mouth since. But, then, no one's had a harpsichord, now, have they? That could work. A piano wouldn't do it, guaranteed. But really, I don't know if she ever discusses anything with anyone. She's solitary, a solitary little girl. She got my mother's brain; it sure didn't come from her father."

Clearly, Mrs. Brown wasn't just going to send her daughter off with a stranger. A quick thinker (re: the ambulance driveway at the hospital), she'd devised a fifteen-minute slot where she was out of the way but well within reach. She'd worked out a scenario that gave the girl at least some room to express her thoughts.

"In fact," said Ruth, "if you have the time now, we can all go over together. My friend, Mr. Kasparov, was going to pick me up shortly anyway."

Mrs. Brown may not have been elated at the development, but it added a distractive level that she appreciated. There was no argument, and Hauper, who'd been listening from another room, was ready to go. I could hear the sound of a zipper, probably from a bag or purse.

Mr. Kasparov soon arrived. Mrs. Brown was no more dumbfounded than I would have been at the sight of the man driving up in a 1957 Silver Cloud I, duotone in white and gray. It floated up Pierce to Mrs. Brown's apartment, and we could see it from the window. The look in the girl's eyes, when they landed on the Rolls, is etched in my memory.

Mrs. Brown wasn't sure what to say, but Hauper was down the stairs, albeit clumsily, before Ruth could gather up her sheet music. Mr. Kasparov double-parked the white and gray automobile (does anyone call a Silver Cloud a "car?") and Hauper got in as if she'd always belonged in a Rolls, snuggled down into the leather and waited for the rest of us. At the last minute, Mrs. Brown decided to take her Subaru, not wanting to trouble Mr. Kasparov with the return trip. But she allowed Hauper to ride in the Rolls ... as if she had a choice.

Mr. Kasparov started the engine. The six cylinders fired in silence; the duel carburetors breathed in a whisper.

With one exhale they were three blocks down the street. In fifteen minutes they were halfway to the Avaluxe Theater.

The Avaluxe

The upper floor of the Avaluxe Theater is home to three apartments and eight studio dressing rooms, original to the 1925 building. Most of the rooms have curtains or delicate rice-paper blinds on the windows that face the alleys, back and front. Their doors – tall, heavy oak monstrosities with bronze fittings forged by Titans – open into a single hallway whose oak-floored corridor is twelve feet wide, and at the foot of each doorway is a walnut and ebony inlay of one of the signs of the zodiac in Art Deco abstraction, with the twelfth sign situated in front of the hall door that leads to the staircase and the lobby below. I don't know if the other units are occupied.

They arrived at 11:30. Ruth and Hauper ventured up the north grand stairway in search of the golden harpsichord. The door to No. 8 slowly opened inward, floating on its hinges like a boat on water. They were greeted by a very old, longhaired jellicle cat that walked out and promptly sat down at the girl's feet.

Hers is a loft with a fifteen- or twenty-foot ceiling. This is the only room of its kind in the Avaluxe; it's adjacent to the silver-screen auditorium. The rest of the roofline isn't as high, and the other residences are hardly as magnificent.

Her main room is about forty feet by forty feet. One wall has the entrance with the door from the celestial hallway; across from it are cathedral windows beginning a foot above the floor and continuing to within a foot of the ceiling. The view outside is one of brick walls, rain-pooled rooftops and perpetually gray sky.

The wall on the right is a triptych bookshelf extending from floor to ceiling and from corner to corner with a ladder on a running rail. It's full to overflowing.

The final wall on the left as you enter the apartment is

a waterfall of hanging skeins of yarn alternating with branches of lavender. The bundles, which are meant to keep moths at bay, scent the room.

Beneath the woolen waterfall and stacked against the wall are boxes of roving and sack upon sack of raw fleeces still in the shape of the sheep who'd been relieved of their precious wool. There were a half-dozen spinning wheels in the room in no coherent order. The rest of the floor is covered with the largest, most extensive stash of yarn outside of a Chinese loading dock. There are paper bags and plastic sacks overflowing with balls, skeins and cones, spilling like avalanches on the precipitous edges of the wool mountains. They have been piled into plots or sections like city blocks in miniature. You have to crabwalk sideways between little communities made of the wool of sheep and goats, rabbits, buffalo, yaks and camels and alpacas and God knows what else.

Near the wall of skeins is a twelve-foot round table about knee high, surrounded by chairs and one small red sofa or loveseat. This is her work table. The room has few other furnishings – a desk and small round table with a marble top near the windows and a few other pieces. There's an outdated stereo with a turntable near the door and an admirable series of amps and preamps fit for a person whose interest in sound is more profound than average.

In the middle of the room, a circular area has been shoveled free of yarn (there is a red snow shovel propped against one of the piles to keep the square clear), and within this barren spot are two or three spindle-backed chairs, another spinning wheel, and a small, delicate, gold-leafed harpsichord that's clearly not of this century. It's hidden by the surrounding yarn.

Hauper was appropriately dwarfed by the sheer volume of the flat. Miss M, who hadn't taken off her long coat during the entire visit with Mrs. Brown, tossed both their coats on a yarn-encrusted, spindled chair near the round table. She was wearing bright yellow, loose fitting silk trousers of the type you might see on a swashbuckling Arabian sailor a century ago. She had a blue silk top and a scarf over her shoulders and back, and wrapped once around each arm near the biceps. The mere sight of her dress cheered the girl.

The cat, Methuselah, eventually re-entered the apartment and Ruth responded appropriately to His Majesty by walking over and closing the door.

What sort of name is that for a cat, anyway? "Methuselah is a character in a children's story I'm fond of," she told Hauper. " '... a fearsome leopard, black as night, prowling through his forest ...' It's an odd story, but, then, so is all of folklore. A story can be odd and real at the same time, huh?"

Hauper immediately took to the room. The mounds of yarn balls and shanks of hand-spun stirred up her adrenalin, and she began her visit by limping briskly around the perimeter of the room five or six times, and then navigating the very narrow paths between the mountains of wool. She hurt, but it didn't stop her. She recognized the labyrinth for was it was and took this pathway and that, left, right, zipping forward and circling around, until at last she ended up falling over into a blue hill of alpaca.

It was a little later, as she ventured again through the narrow avenues of Yarnville, that she discovered the Yarn Woman's harpsichord and was so enraptured by the sight of the intricately detailed, gold-leafed specimen that she stood stock-still and breathless despite her recent yarn pentathlon, and then she sat down with a flop, unable to take her eyes off the instrument.

Ruth brought two cups of tea and sat down beside her. They fell into a discussion about the history of harpsichords, more or less, especially the history of this one. She had a natural affinity with the child, just as she did with cats – or with humans if they had enough intelligence to be around her … and if she felt so inclined. After a few hours, the two were seated quietly at the low, round table in the corner of the room, eating crackers and discussing Methuselah, the cat.

They talked about music. They discussed the planets and gravity and the Great Barrier Reef. Velveeta cheese was mentioned more than once. Mayonnaise was frowned on, even scoffed at. They had coffee. But nothing more significant than steaming Sumatra or an oat cracker passed their lips. The Yarn Woman didn't ask Hauper about her ordeal. The time was spent forging the first bonds of friendship. Only after an hour did the child say anything relating to her present condition, and it was no more than a passing reference to a man on a corner near the park and how he had leered at her and had begun to move in her direction.

Ruth tried not to display too much interest for fear of shutting Hauper up again. "Jerk," she said softly and left it at that.

"Willem Bracken didn't like it. Didn't like that man," said Hauper.

"I bet." Who the hell was Willem Bracken? The name sounded so familiar, like a character in an old book. At this point, though, Ruth wasn't about to pry.

Hauper looked around the room, her face echoing a gamut of emotions and finally settling on comfort. "I'm not going to think about it. I hope you don't mind."

When they returned downstairs several hours later, Mr. Kasparov informed them both that Mrs. Brown had peered in the doorway upstairs, decided the situation was satisfactory and left only fifteen minutes ago. Mrs. Brown had suggested Mr. Kasparov drive Hauper home in the company of Ms. M, and after about a half-hour they departed in the Rolls.

The Arrest

There were three police units at Mrs. Brown's apartment building on Pierce when Mr. Kasparov, at this point about a block south, calmly took evasive action and signaled a right turn onto Sacramento, exposing only the driver's side to the police activity at the apartment. Hauper was talking animatedly in the back seat and didn't notice where they were. Mr. Kasparov's action was so smooth that even a Rolls Royce could go unnoticed in the general law-enforcement hubbub. Ruth was sitting behind Mr. Kasparov, so when he turned she gained a full view of the activity. Mrs. Brown was being solemnly led to a police cruiser, her hands cuffed behind her. She looked up absently and her face registered shock when she recognized the Yarn Woman looking at her from the back seat of the gray and white Rolls. Mrs. Brown quickly shook her head as if begging, "Please, don't stop." Moments later, the big cop who had her by the arm, leading her to the cruiser, pushed her head down and guided her into the caged-off back seat.

"Mr. Kasparov, would you please take us back to the Avaluxe, then," said Ruth calmly. "Thank you. Mrs. Brown had earlier suggested that Hauper stay the night with me, and maybe we can dig up an old movie for the screening room. I think that would be a good idea, all things considered."

"Ah. Does young Hauper like automobile movies?" asked Mr. Kasparov. The casual tone of his question was poor cover for his eagerness.

Mrs. Brown's arrest occurred shortly after her arrival home from her brief visit to the Avaluxe. The police, responding to an interrogation request by Child Protective Services, were awaiting her arrival. It was probably the easiest arrest they'd ever made, but the absence of six-year-old Alexandra added the necessary ingredient to turn the case into a media frenzy within hours. The girl wasn't with Mrs. Brown; she wasn't already at home. Therefore, she had disappeared.

Her frightening absence added new life to the situation — not just the public memory of her extraordinary wounds but the mauling death just a few blocks from the apartment the week before, and while the media and their adoring public love a tale of woe and suspense, those directly involved in such a tragedy see it in a wholly different light. Recognizing the sensationalistic situation for what it was, Mrs. Brown refused to give up her daughter's whereabouts to the police, and this practically convicted her of any atrocity one could imagine. She was, in the minds of the public, guilty in the disappearance of young Alexandra Brown.

The media had moved into high gear by the following morning, in time for earliest feature-news shows. One of the networks had gotten some pretty good cell-phone footage of Mrs. Brown's arrest from one of her curious neighbors and pretty soon they all had it. Though Mrs. Brown appeared to be genuinely confused in the forty-five-second clip, once the segment aired, smoldering suspicions ignited. Now "guilty" in Alexandra's disappearance, she was also linked to the mauling death of the transient the week before. The neighbor (we should all be so lucky as to have such concern exhibited on our behalf) had caught two of the arresting officers wondering aloud how this single working mother could have managed a murder and a disappearance so expertly, because "she's pretty, but she doesn't look so smart."

Pretty, however, is a temporal thing. Mrs. Brown is not unpleasant looking, but the arrest video showed her at her worst, hair hanging, old clothing, generally disheveled with dark circles under her criminal eyes. She was guilty, guilty, guilty. You could see it for yourself.

The level of sensationalism grew as the soap opera

unfolded, and after a cable news network gained possession of three hospital photos of the poor girl's injuries, it could easily have been measured in kilotons. Money for the photographs was secretly exchanged, I learned, and though a few thousand dollars may not seem like much money to many, it was a heap of cash for the low-level non-union caregiver who worked the hospital's night shift. I talked with her; she sent most of the money back to the Philippines, where work and income and a sit-down dinner were mostly just other people's dreams.

Under the circumstances, that $3,000 for the photos should, really, have been in the neighborhood of $20,000, legality aside. With the photos flashing across TV screens, child-abuse pundits magically appeared on both the cable and network news shows, suggesting that the only remaining mysteries were where Mrs. Brown had dumped her daughter's chopped-up, dog-gnawed body parts, how she had managed to murder the transient the week before without being detected, and where she kept the half-wild beast-dog that she had used to take his life. How, they asked, had young Alexandra stumbled onto the vicious canine killer? Was it in the cold, dark basement? How had she miraculously escaped? Where on Earth was she?

Speculation spread like the mold in the basement of Mrs. Brown's 1950s apartment building, but there was no evidence of a dog down there. Responding to public fascination, the police turned out in force, examining every inch of the building and neighborhood. At least thirty cops combed the area for nearly two days, though it must have been difficult for them to work amid all the TV cameras and mikes.

Public pressure finally forced police to respond to the accusations of kidnap and murder against Mrs. Brown. They tried to keep a perception of public safety foremost. Detective Chu's department superiors as well as the District Attorney (who was looking down the throat of a municipal election just over a year off) demanded, first, results, and second, a reasonable explanation of what had occurred. Chu was finally forced into a statement that Mrs. Brown was a "person of interest" in the fatality and a "suspect" in the disappearance. What else could he say? In front of the cameras, he remained adamant in pointing out that the woman had been arrested only, and had not been charged with any crime whatsoever. In bowing to his superiors and the D.A., Chu kept control of the investigation. He managed to round the mandatory bases of 24-hour news coverage while expertly dodging the flying hardballs, relying heavily on well-rehearsed explanations that the killing and disappearance may or may not be related, and that Mrs. Brown's arrest was solely for the purpose of interview, and he no-commented his way through the most torturous interviews and "pressers." Then, after the abuse, he smiled like he always did. It was very disarming. Chu is an extremely handsome man (he practically glowed beneath the camera lights), and he often found this quality useful in dealing with the media and could play it to his advantage when necessary. Inevitably, however, the networks would pull away from Chu, broadcast one of the photos of Alexandra (they had obtained one from about year ago showing her as a very happy child, and often contrasted that with one of the stolen photos from the hospital) and immediately engage one of the commentators who would then comment on the bitter innuendos and rumors that Chu refused to respond to.

The worst of the commentators turned out to be the neighbors. They voiced enraged shock that such a heinous, vicious criminal as Mrs. Brown could live so close to their cozy homes – though it appeared to me, as I watched the clips in endless replay on CNN, MSNBC and the major networks, that they'd been given their lines by a docu-drama director, plus thirty minutes to practice the tears and hugs and sanctified head-shaking, before the director let loose the cameras. Yet when I started asking around, not one of them even knew who his neighbors were. Nevertheless, amid the tragedy there was a certain joy in the air at their realization of newfound community and new cause *de vive*. This new life might also, unfortunately, be known as the death knell of reason.

Hauper, of course, remained with her friend, the Yarn Woman. Ruth decided, as they sailed around the corner as the arrest played out, that it was appropriate not to deliver Hauper to the authorities, come what may. And what came is that barely twelve hours later, millions of people around the nation, even the globe, knew for sure that all that was left was to find the poor child's body, the grim remains of a six-year-old, auburn-haired violin prodigy, wherever the pieces had been dumped, hidden, burned or buried.

Having the "dismembered, murdered" girl in her care wasn't particularly worrisome to Ruth. And Mrs. Brown, for her part, maintained complete silence about her daughter's location to both the police and her court-appointed lawyer, whose eyes betrayed belabored exasperation with the woman. Ruth didn't feign ignorance about where Hauper was, either; she just made it clear she wasn't going to tell anyone, which infuriated the police and fueled the filicidal rumor mill. She was quite a bit like her daughter.

"Why would I want Hauper to be turned over to foster care or a juvenile holding tank?" Ruth said later. "Child Protective Services? Get it straight." With someone like Ruth M in your bullpen (and I'd barely just met her) I realized that Mrs. Brown had every reason to keep her mouth shut and feel confident — at least, as confident as the circumstances allowed — in the welfare of her only child. There must have been some unseen and unheard communication between the two women, I thought, but that, for sure, was not within the range of my rather limited male understanding.

Hauper was still talking in the back seat of the Rolls,

mostly to herself and quite happily, as they drove silently on. The automobile arrived back at the Avaluxe at 6 that evening, after they'd stopped for popcorn kernels and a half-gallon block of Neapolitan ice cream. Everyone stayed in the car while Ruth ran into the market. She tried not to look into the security camera in the corner behind the counter, and checked to see if the Rolls was within its limited range. It was not; Mr. Kasparov was not new to this sort of thing, apparently. The TV news coverage was just revving up, setting the stage for the morning's frenzy. I arrived at about 7 after Mr. Kasparov had called me, requesting my company, and by 8, Ruth, Mr. Kasparov, Hauper, and I were safely ensconced in the Art Deco glamour of the 1930s. We had a great evening — we spun forward to 1958, however, to watch Robert Mitchum in "Thunder Road," a pristine 35mm black and white film courtesy of Mr. Kasparov the Collector, and made popcorn in a pre-war glass and steel popping contraption. I preferred the vintage cartoons he had somehow gathered into his celluloid repertoire. Mr. Kasparov was a strange man; there was a lot to him that was obscure and that I would probably never fathom. I liked him; I don't know why. What I did know at that point was that despite the automobile and a collector's penchant for obtaining automobile movies, he was quiet, generally happy and poor as a church mouse. He kept up with the car because he was an accomplished mechanic who used genuine parts bought cheaply on the Russian black market; some, I understand, are ordered on eBay from Kiev in the "Buy Now!" category, others are apparently shipped in to Oakland by tanker. I didn't know how he got the thing in the first place and realized I probably would never know.

Hauper slept in Ruth's apartment very comfortably that night, oblivious to the arrest of her mother and the insanity of the slavering media, and she had the purring company of the old cat who slept beside her. If only it could last.

A Walk in the Fog

Of course, neither the hand-wringing neighbors on Pierce nor the overbearing press that blocked up the streets within a mile of ground zero understood that the resurrection of the schooner, the Albert Townsend, which bobbed in the Bay a mile directly north, was intimately linked with the macabre attacks on the transient and Alexandra Brown. In fact, the events were so closely related that by the time the sea pulled the schooner back into its cold, dark grave a few days later – by the time Mrs. Juliet Brown once again saw the light of day instead of the cement walls of her prison cell – all the Yarn Woman could say to her was, "Mrs. Brown, do you believe in ghosts?"

Only in San Francisco.

By the morning after the arrest, the old schooner had already begun its slow slide back into the silt of the seabed. No one watched – San Francisco was preoccupied with murder and dismemberment. Another day passed as the networks ground out their tragic stories. Less than three feet of the hull remained above water. Soon, her ghosts would return below decks, never to look landward again. Maybe this time they would be gone forever. Did they know there were only a dozen hours of sunlight left for them? Life is so fleeting. By late morning, as if to prepare the Albert Townsend for the coming darkness, the sky grew gray and a cold breeze moved in from the Pacific. A hundred miles inland, the harsh summer sun burned down at more than a hundred degrees and the clash of the hot and cold fronts created a bloated, intoxicated fog that crawled up from the sea and limped through the streets and alleys, looking for old ghosts and grog, looking for somewhere to settle, looking for home. From the beaches on the north end of the peninsula, you could see only faded shades of white-indigo and white-gray where once there'd been a separate sea and a sky; now they were one. The old hull was hidden by the thickening fog and its prying, curious fingers. You couldn't see the ghosts, either. Not at first.

Ruth and Hauper rose late after their second night together. Everything seemed fine. Hauper's spirits were good, though she missed her mother. They decided to spend the day with Felix Mendelssohn, Igor Stravinsky, and Methuselah, the best friends a person could have at times. Mr. Kasparov had been kind enough to deliver sandwiches at about noon and soon the day had melted into the afternoon. At the Bulletin, I continued to be assaulted by commentators on my desktop television and wondered when the insanity would end. But the inhabitants of the Avaluxe remained safe from the broadcasts and broadcasters, insulated as they were by the absence of twenty-first century technology.

Yet even the best of circumstances can grow tedious to a six-year-old. Eventually, Ruth relented to Hauper's restlessness and they decided to take a walk in the late afternoon, venturing out into San Francisco's thick, cold summer fog and trusting in the anonymity it might provide. Though she recognized the risk involved, Ruth has never been one who responds to intimidation. I don't think she even sees it.

When the marine fog sets in, you can't see a thing around you and the usual mad thrumming of the city is smothered. It's cold and you think of sitting by a wood fire. You wear a thick sweater, even a coat. The odors are stifled, the whole world is muffled. If you happen to be hiding a child who half the world thinks has been killed, the fog is a curtain between you and the prying eyes of San Francisco and the world. Standing at the window overlooking the western extremity of the city, Ruth and Hauper could practically hear the ghosts beckoning them to go out for a walk. Ghosts like the company. They like the fog, too, because it's safe.

Staring into the endless, unfocussed gray, it's easy to imagine the nineteenth century schooners that sailed into port from the north, carrying the redwood foundations of San Francisco, which at the time was the tenth largest city in the nation. And when the wind comes up, even just a little, you can readily see why some of those ships lost their bearings, foundered, and slipped beneath the waves. Buried in silt and sand and the endless refuse deposited by a burgeoning Victorian metropolis, the old ships were lost to the light of day. But that doesn't mean they were gone forever. They just slept. Nineteenth century San Francisco and its sunken schooners have never really been lost. The Old City and sea just hide from the light, waiting for the morning fog or the evening dark. They wait for night, and they sleep.

The Yarn Woman and Hauper could no longer resist a walk in the fog. But then, Hauper couldn't resist much of anything while she was at the magical Avaluxe, from its movie screen to its small puppet theater and even its little kitchen downstairs that had, in ages past, played host to the palates of the glitterati. They spent an hour dressing appropriately for their covert sojourn into the foggy city, wearing long skirts and soft shoes, sweaters and knitted leggings. They were warm. Each had a handbag. Hauper wanted badly to begin their walk at Alta Park, near her apartment. Fine. Why not increase the risk? Surely, no one would see them; in the fog, no one would recognize them. But were they like spies or like ghosts?

It was evening before they left; Mr. Kasparov drove them from the Avaluxe through the city, north and then east and north again, forcing the Silver Cloud to crawl across the foggy land at a blind crustacean's pace. He slowed to a stop near the park, and Ruth and Hauper disembarked. Mr. Kasparov was unhappy. He saw no purpose to their exposure. They hadn't thought it through. Anything could happen. Ruth would be jailed, Hauper would begin a life bouncing from foster home to foster home. Mr. Kasparov was *extremely* unhappy.

"Trust us," Ruth said to Mr. Kasparov.

"You, I trust," he answered. "It is the other 8.2 million people in the broader metropolitan area that give me pause."

They compromised: Hauper and Ruth would walk north on Pierce to the water, and Mr. Kasparov would meet them in a few hours. Or something like that. He sighed. It was the best he could do.

Soon, the pair had made their way to the intersection of Pierce and Pacific. By now it was about 9 p.m. and the daylight was well gone. Strangely, though, the streetlights were off. They probably hadn't gotten the power back in this part of the city after the big storm eight or nine days ago. Or maybe streetlamps didn't exist on this particular stretch; Ruth couldn't remember and Hauper was rarely out at night and had no way of knowing. And the lights from the houses? There weren't any: It was a power outage for sure. Finally, as they grew accustomed to the dark, they detected candles here and there in some of the windows, but the fog was thick and it was as if the little firelights floated somewhere in the ether, just out of reach.

For all the exciting, adventurous lack of bearings, there was no doubt in Hauper's mind where they were when they arrived at a pair of crooked little plum trees set back off the street. Candlelight could be seen distantly through the branches. As they walked back between the plum trees, the fluttering lights of a small cottage grew visible through the mist. Ruth followed the girl to the misty house.

The wooden stairs creaked as they walked up to the porch. The plank decking was blue or blue-gray, and a small oil or kerosene lantern, a cheap one with a carnival-glass reservoir and a long thin flue, was in the window. Spider webs in the lower corners had gathered a few insects, which were visible once their vision became attuned to the sparse illumination.

There wasn't an electric light for blocks around, and the cottage, removed from the street, seemed to be nestled into a dim, gray world of its own. Ruth glanced at the old, weather-gnawed door and then looked down at Hauper, who looked up. Hauper knew just where she was; Ruth understood that, weighed the probabilities and then smiled. They knocked. They waited. They both knocked again and finally heard shuffling inside. The door opened slowly and before them stood a short round woman with a candle glowing in a cheap tin-handled holder, and in the same hand were long, thin knitting needles bent with years of use, and a mass of off-white yarn trailing on the floor behind her.

"Young Hauper!" she said happily, and invited them in.

Lucy Mullins

Her name was Lucy Mullins. She'd been passing the foggy evening knitting by kerosene lantern and candlelight, no mean feat for older eyes. "I put several of them side by side, for the light," she said. "Candles, you see." She owned the house and had lived there with her husband for longer than she cared to remember, yet she seemed oblivious to its decrepit condition. It was one of those San Francisco shacks that had stayed in the same family for decades, somehow safe from modernization or yuppie gentrification but without enough funding for a new paint job.

Mrs. Mullins had brilliant blue eyes that flashed from a very round, red-cheeked face. Her short, thick gray hair was standing stiffly on her head, thrusting to her left, and it came down well onto her forehead. She appeared to be in her fifties or sixties, and was definitely Irish and perfectly San Francisco.

Her husband was away, she said. "He's up the coast, you know. He works on the ships, sometimes at the docks. But tonight … ah, tonight's Ladies Night, we call it, and I don't miss him so much when there are other people around. They are on the way, and since you both are here already, you are invited," she said with a laugh, holding up what must have been a note confirming the imminent gathering of a number of her friends. She seemed very pleased to see Hauper. They were perfectly at ease in each other's company, and Ruth realized their friendship had been longer than just a few weeks and was much deeper than mere acquaintanceship.

Ruth looked from the note that Mrs. Mullins had so triumphantly held up to the interior of the house and decided immediately that the old cottage was very deceptive. When they first entered, it seemed to her that the house was cold, damp and drafty like so many of the city's older structures. It probably had no foundation. But by the time they were through the door, Ruth found it actually quite warm and inviting.

The room also seemed to play with her. As they'd entered, Ruth had the impression that the small foyer was a musty, wizened shell in a shack that hadn't been cleaned for decades. The old wood floor was dusted with fine grit, and it grated like sandpaper under her shoes. But the roughness lasted only for a step, for as she entered further everything was swept cleanly. The redwood wainscot panels inside were polished, and there were actually two or three small, framed etchings on the foyer wall to their left, just before the arched passageway into the small living area, which appeared comfortable though not plush. Like many of the older homes and apartments on the peninsula, there was a little coal-burning fireplace toward the back of the great room, inset into the wall, and the coals were banked and hot. The floor had a warm oak glow. The walls were filled with framed maritime drawings and prints, all of them of obvious sentimental value to Mrs. Mullins, and most of them quite old — well over a century, Ruth guessed. Several quaint oil lamps on this particular evening added to the golden hue of the room, and there were unlit candles here and there in glass holders. There was even a small brass ship's lantern on this perfectly Victorian stage, and one candle near the fireplace had a silver holder with a circular, ridged reflector.

Mrs. Mullins had much to say about Hauper — how she enjoyed the girl's visits and that she was both "a dear girl" and "very talented." Hauper smiled, blushing: She'd been coming here for quite some time, sneaking out early in the morning and returning home before her mother rose. Friendship, to Hauper, knew no age barrier, and she'd grown to love the old woman and her house and her dog.

"She has a fine time playing with my Willem Bracken," Mrs. Mullins told Ruth with a puckered smile.

Ruth's ears rang at the sound of the name.

Hauper took her usual place on a small loveseat with carved legs and arms. "She reminds me of my youngest," said Mrs. Mullins. "Patrick." She went on to talk at great length about Pat, who was always getting into some sort of trouble, but he had the "sweetest disposition! And that hair … the orangest batch of fuzz you ever saw!" Of course he'd grown up and left home like the other two boys. "He took to the sea," she said, "like his father.

"Now, Ethan, my husband, he's gone for weeks at a time. Sometimes for months."

"Mr. Mullins is at sea, then?" asked Ruth.

"Lord, I've been waiting for that man since the day we married," said Mrs. Mullins with a smile. But then her smile weakened. "The weeks get long, though, Dear. Very long. It's not the time so much as what's in the heart. With the boys gone, now it is just me and that man's dog that stay here, waiting." She fixed her skirt and pulled down her shawl. It was then that Ruth noticed how the woman was dressed.

Mrs. Mullins's shawl was a rusty autumn red combined with a bright burnt orange. The contrast was increased by an occasional descent into a ruddy brown, surely accomplished by hand dyeing. It covered Mrs. Mullins' back and shoulders and then each side wrapped over her shoulders and across her chest, down under her arms, and tied in back at the waist like an apron. She wore a sontag. The finishing touch was an elaborate, crocheted gold-brown edging that ended in a pair of tying tassels. The knitting was tight, with no cabling and no decorative stitches other than the edging.

Ruth waited a few minutes. "He's worked at sea his whole life?"

"Knows no other," said Mrs. Mullins. "We married at sixteen and we've been lucky. I can't say I've been unhappy. Three good boys. Two of them is married. It's just the waiting. Sometimes I feel awful tired of it. It weighs on me, Dear. I feel it in my eyes, you know."

By now they'd seated themselves in chairs near the coal fire. "Your sontag is lovely," said the Ruth. "May I look at it a little closer? Under the light?"

"I suppose," said Mrs. Mullins, blushing. She moved over to one of the oil lamps, and Ruth studied the look and feel of the wool, the patternless knitting and the garish crochet work. "It's just an old thing I wear on a foggy day, Mrs. Hauper. I'm always at least ten years out of fashion, don't you know?"

At the older woman's waist, under the garment but still visible, was a wide leather belt. There was no buckle and in its place was an even wider area stuffed like a flat pillow and punctured with small holes throughout.

"That's my pin holder, Dear," said Mrs. Mullins, following Ruth's gaze. "It takes the strain off my down wrist. You would be surprised what a wonder it is for socks."

"I don't doubt it," Ruth said, "once you get the hang of it." Ruth knew there was something wrong, something out of place with the whole thing ... the porch, the foyer, the coal-warmed room, with Mrs. Mullins herself. Ruth took a deep breath. After all, she thought, it would have to be the 1870s, maybe the 80s for a sontag to be out of fashion for ten years. And the leather knitting sheath?

"I'm sure," said Ruth again after a while. "It's lovely. Absolutely. I'm sure your husband is warm and well in all the clothing you've knit for him, using that. He's a very lucky man. Did he have the sheath made especially for you?"

"You can tell! Lord, girl. Yes, down at the docks. He put in that little pattern you see along the edge. He used a nail head, and he filed that cross into it, of all things! Yes, filed in that little cross there, and tapped that right into the leather with his hammer. You wouldn't know it wasn't done by the tack man himself. Ethan found the man and worked out a trade and gave him a little bone piece with a picture of a schooner on it. Ethan has a talent for chipping into bone … you know, to while away the time when he's on ship, like my knitting. Here, let me show you a few pieces."

She went over to a low hutch beside the entry. Seven pieces of butter-white ivory of various sizes were carefully placed on top, arranged in order by size. The work was delicate and accurate, reminiscent of a Dore engraving. "I have this one saved out for my young Hauper. It's a picture of Willem Bracken, then, isn't it?" She held it up for Hauper, in the seat, to see. "I think today would be a good day, don't you?" she said to Ruth.

Ruth smiled and nodded. The piece, so polished that it glowed, showed a dog of great size beside a sailing skiff.

"Do you ever go down to the docks, Mrs. Mullins? To watch the sea? Or out to the ocean, to the west?"

"Oh, no," said Mrs. Mullins quickly. "I dare say, I just stay here at the house. I can't bring myself to step outside for the longest time. I do just fine alone, I suppose. But I miss watching the shadows as they play on the sea, the silhouettes of the ships on the water, coming in, going out through the Gate. I think about Ethan out there, you know."

"You watch the boats go under the bridge?"

"What, dear?" asked Lucy. "What bridge?"

Ruth paused, quickly analyzing the older woman's response. There was no Golden Gate Bridge; it wasn't finished until 1937. Finally, Ruth smiled. "I think it's a beautiful night for a walk, Mrs. Mullins. Perhaps we can take your dog down to the water?"

"Indeed, a walk will do him good," said Mrs. Mullins. "I do not know about myself, then, Mrs. Hauper. I don't much like walking tonight. It nervouses me. But my Willem Bracken dearly loves the walk to the sea. I do so much want to take a walk to the water, Dear, but I don't know ... I can't seem to drag myself that far from home, you know. Honestly, Mrs. Hauper, I don't know why it's been so long ... I suppose I feel like I can't go so far these days. I get so tired." She seemed genuinely confused about the very possibility of leaving her home, however small and cramped it might have been.

"How did you name him?"

"Oh, Willem Bracken? From the old children's tale, don't you know? You know the one? Willem Bracken."

"Patrick used to play with Willem Bracken outside, I gather?" Ruth asked.

"Oh, he loved that dog. Pat's gone to sea now. He was such a strong boy. Now, your Hauper loves to play with that dog, and that is for sure. But he is not as young as he used to be. Getting a little gray in the muzzle, I would say! She comes over every once in a while and just goes straight to the back. Is that not so, Hauper?"

The girl smiled and looked toward the back of the house.

"You can go get him, Love," said Mrs. Mullins.

Hauper was up and out without another word. She came back with a dog so large that Ruth's mouth dropped involuntarily. He was the size of a pony, and he claimed a corner of the room away from the fire where he curled up with Hauper.

"I guess you know about that old dog, then," said Mrs. Mullins.

"I'm not sure," said Ruth, blinking.

"Well, I will tell you. He has not got much sense in his head sometimes, and at the same time he has all the sense in the world. One day, then, that Patrick of mine fell into the Gate off his little rowboat, being out on the water without Ethan, as he shouldn't be. That water, you see, can turn on a person. A strong swimmer would be hard put and might be drawn under. But Willem Bracken, he is there with the boy and leaps from the boat and grabs him and pulls him along as he swims ashore. But that Willem

Bracken is so big he doesn't know his strength, you see, and bless me if he didn't maul up Pat's head pretty good. His head! Good Lord, pulling him along behind as he fights the current all the way to shore. It's a strange sight, seeing that dog of Ethan's haul your youngest along by the crown of his head, I will tell you. Oh, it wasn't horrible, just a mess. The boy is still missing a little patch of that red hair of his to this day. But that's what he does, Willem Bracken, don't you know."

"And Hauper?"

"Oh, that would be the same. They are friends now, you know. I'm sure he would haul her through water if she fell in or up a mountain if she fell down! And make a proper mess of her, and hurt her some, too, I'm sorry to say." Mrs. Mullins voice dropped and Ruth could see her blushing even in the dim light. "I would not be surprised if she got herself into a little trouble day before," she carefully admitted, "for I see now she has a small flock of bruises upon her."

"You made the sontag?"

"Oh, surely. I mean … do you mean this one," she said looking down at herself."

"No, Hauper's"

"Oh, the one I give to Hauper?" Her eyes feigned ignorance.

"I'm afraid it has blood stains. Was it your own pattern?"

"I picked that up from a friend, Dear. Someday I'll write it down, I suppose. I've been working on one for Mark's wife. He is my oldest. She's small, you know. I mean, you know, in the chest."

"Willem Bracken just does that?"

"Does what, Dear?"

"Willem Bracken. He just carried Pat by the head? Or Hauper?"

"Oh, Ethan taught him that, you see. Like a bird dog, but," she laughed quietly to herself, "but, bigger."

Mrs. Mullins lost herself in thought for a few minutes, then picked up on her tale of Willem Bracken. "What, with Ethan being away so much, he wanted a dog looking after us all the while he was gone. Only God knows where he found an animal that size. He spent day after day throwing things for him to haul back, and used bigger and bigger things – fifty pound of driftwood – until Ethan was sure Willem Bracken could haul all the children in off the tide if he had to. But that dog, he never did take mind of the part of doing it gently, like a retriever. Or maybe he did the best he could, with all that power, you see. As I say, he doesn't know his strength. But that's what my Ethan did, and he named that dog for the children's story and the dog does the same thing in the story, as you may know."

Ruth smiled. But she couldn't find the right words to respond immediately.

Tea was served. At least an hour passed in comfortable conversation. Then the guests arrived. A knock on the door surprised Ruth, but Mrs. Mullins answered it quickly, for the older woman was spryer than she first appeared. And having guests, in this case Hauper and Ruth, quickened her spirits.

"Mrs. Hutchinson!" she said. "What a surprise! How very nice to see you. Please come in." She happily motioned the woman through the arched passage. To Ruth, she added, "Mrs. Hauper, this would be Mrs. Hutchinson. Her husband founded the city's humane animal group, you know. But," she winked, "we know it was our Coralie who was the force behind him. We know that, for sure! Got us our Willem, she did, from somewhere. A land of giants, I am sure."

Mrs. Hutchinson smiled and greeted Ruth warmly. "I'm very surprised to see you, Mrs. Hauper. You have no idea. How very kind of you to visit. I suppose you might be surprised to see me as well?"

Ruth smiled, but remained silent.

Mrs. Hutchinson turned her attention back to Mrs. Mullins. "Lucy, dear," she said "I have wonderful news for you. I have learned that your Ethan is homeward bound and that his ship is due this very night! Yes, tonight."

Mrs. Mullins nearly fainted at the news, and both Ruth and Mrs. Hutchinson grabbed her before she could fall. "That's why I sent that note, Dear," said the visitor, "but I wanted to tell you the news about Ethan in person. And the rest of the ladies are on their way. How long has it been since we visited?"

Mrs. Mullins, having regained her breath (but unable to stop the trembling), said, "Why, it's been weeks, Coralie, weeks." Mrs. Hutchinson smiled, but Ruth saw something strange in her smile: It hadn't been weeks, that was clear enough. How long had it been?

"Weeks it is, if you say," said Mrs. Hutchinson. "But we've all come around tonight to walk north and watch old Ethan's ship arrive."

No sooner were the words out of her mouth than there was another rap at the door followed by a flurry of knocking. A gleeful Mrs. Hutchinson threw open the door and a chorus of voices shouted in greeting. Ruth saw no fewer than seven women standing at the door, and two more were arriving in a small coach pulled by a brown mare. It appeared that someone had actually rented one of the surreys from Fishermen's Wharf to come calling on their old friend, she thought, still holding onto the current century as best she could. These women were an odd fellowship, but friendship is a remarkable thing.

After the last of the women climbed down, the trap departed, heading north into the fog, which, after a moment or two, obscured the horse and left only the clopping of its hooves.

Soon, they were all walking north, hidden by the fog. Like an acting troupe, they shouted lines, sang spurts of songs, commented on one another's clothing or hair or voice. Hauper and the dog, Willem Bracken, weren't the quietest in the group, but neither were they the most boisterous. So festive was the mood that Mrs. Mullins vanquished her fear about leaving the house and found herself singing with the rest.

A very good viewpoint, from which they could watch any vessel enter the Golden Gate, was straight north. "I'm certain the fog will thin by the time we finish our walk, and as it is dark, we shall see the lights of the ships," said Mrs. Hutchinson. "And even if the fog remains, we should be able to hear the deck hands, for they'll pass close to shore, I'm sure."

There were no visible street or house lights when they set out. There were no cars. Visibility would have been better in a dream. They practically walked on clouds as the city blocks fell behind them. After they passed Jefferson Street, Ruth knew that only Beach remained. But, strangely, they passed Beach and came to another intersection. A small sign read "Tonquin." That was confusing. And the next street after that was named "Lewis," which was even more confusing: Ruth was sure there were no such roads.

It had been about a mile to the shore, and though the distance was hardly noticeable, time passed in a peculiar fashion. It was night when they began, yet it was now daylight. They had arrived at the beach and no one was tired. The fog had thinned and then vanished, and the night's cold was no longer cold. The daylight was blue and sharp and there was a soft breeze off the water. Ruth looked around and what she saw amazed her. Many people were milling around the shore, and, coupled with the brightness of the day, reminded her of a Cezanne painting, complete with women in full white dresses – though there were only a few white dresses because most of the women wore darker colors. Long skirts covered every ankle. Men very busily and purposefully strode through this summer picnic scene, and Ruth didn't see a bare head among them. All wore caps and hats. There were a number of children playing in the waves in front of her along the small beach. Hauper and the immense dog were just leaving a small group of children, stomping back through the sand to where Ruth stood. It seemed like only moments ago that it was dark, foggy and empty except for the party of women walking to the waterfront.

Momentarily lost in the crowded scene beside the sea, Ruth began looking around for the other women in her party. She found them not far to the west and well out of reach of the lapping water at the head of the bay, and she and Hauper made their way in that direction. Just beyond them, on the sand, Ruth saw a tall man dressed simply, in the fashion of the sea – canvas trousers of indeterminate color, a wool sweater, a second wool sweater that was cabled above the welt, a knitted cap pushed back on his head revealing a broad forehead and a ring of bright orange hair. His beard was short and a mix of white and orange – the hair and beard being the only thing of color about him other than his light blue eyes. His smile, however, was as electric as his beard.

"Ethan!" shouted Mrs. Mullins, spotting him for the first time. Her skirt ruffled as she ran from the group into his arms, splashing into the tide which had crept in at the last moment as if to add a spray of diamonds to their embrace. "I've been waiting so long!"

"Lucy! I'm here! Ah, it seemed I would never get back!" They could see a rowboat that had been pulled up onto the sand and the hull of the mother vessel was visible a hundred yards offshore.

"I've just been waiting, Ethan," she said and hugged him with all her strength.

They held each other for a moment and, amid the growing crowd at the beach – it seemed by now that the number of beach walkers had swollen to well over a hundred – the small group headed by Mrs. Hutchinson worked their way east to a less crowded piece of sand.

"And there's that Willem Bracken," said Ethan, holding the dog's huge head in his hands as he knelt down. But he was looking at Hauper.

He rose and looked back at Lucy. "I couldn't get word to you, Lucy. Now, let me look at you! And how's that Willem Bracken, has he been a good dog for you?" He patted the beast's side. "He looked after you while I was away?"

"He's been a good dog, Ethan. He knows his business."

"I'm sorry to be away so long. But you were sleeping," he said, laughing. "Turned out I had to wait for that schooner to creak and crack and wake you up. Good lord, it's been a long time!"

"Oh, I heard that ship, and that's for sure. I heard it in my dream not two weeks ago. Oh, Ethan, I'm so happy you're back."

The clear autumn day was unparalleled. They sat in the sand, watching the water breathe. All of them could see the hull of the old schooner protruding from the sun-glowing sea like the back of a turtle. Yet it seemed perfectly appropriate – the kind of thing you don't particularly ponder.

Ethan, who stood well over six feet, looked down at his wife as they sat there. He placed one hand in his pocket; the other was wrapped around hers. "There was a wave out there the size I have never seen before so close to shore," he said, "and we dropped six fathom as it was coming on, and all we knew was that it covered us completely. Lord, we just lay there in that trough and waited for the water; it was coming, that we knew. Then it was over us. That was outside the Gate. It was awful dark, Lucy. Then that wall of the sea just fell down on us."

"I'm sorry, Ethan," she said. "Did it frighten you?"

"No. It didn't that. But it pulled us down. And then I had to wait for you. We drifted into the Gate, down at the bottom. I was here, you see, at the seashore, for an immense amount of time. Couldn't seem to get away, wanted to walk home but just ... couldn't get off the ship. Days and weeks, and longer. And I knew you were at home sleeping and I, good lord, just couldn't get to the air. You know, we promised not to leave each other. You remember. So we both waited, it seems. I waited and you waited." The man's smile was nearly as wide as his shoulders. "Ethan Mullins, the king of waiting! But all along, I knew you'd wait for me, too. And I was right, Lucy."

"I'd always wait, Ethan. We promised."

"Well, then one day, let me tell you. That old Townsend finally come up for air and I could get to the beach." He nodded in the direction of the skiff. "One day I was here on the beach, thinking you might be out and walking, and the air was clear and wet, and, for goodness sake, Lucy, I looked over and standing there was that dog, Willem Bracken, right there on the sand, and with him was a wee girl the like I never seen before!" He looked at Hauper. "She was you, Dear," he said to the girl. "You had dropped your wrap on the sand, and it looked to me like you was getting too close to the water, and then, and then you got into that water too far, Dear. A wave no bigger than a barrel pulled you on in, but that Willem Bracken got ahold of you! I made sure you put your shawl back on, as you should. But I was overjoyed, and between Willem Bracken and asking our young lady here about your welfare, Lucy, well ... and there she was wearing your wrap and shivering after the dog pulled her ashore ... Then I squinted my eyes and rubbed them and tried to see the girl, and I could, but it was like a dream and I kept drifting off. My eyes. That dog of yours danced around like he was crazy, and the child, well, she danced with him as best she could for she was quite chilled, that's all.

"And I guess you got the word from the girl to come out and see us, Lucy. Old friends came back to get you, and Coralie here was one among them. And the girl here."

They grew silent.

"I waited for you, Ethan. I feared to go outside that I might get lost in a dream. I feared getting lost in a dream that wasn't my own. Sometimes I tried to leave the house, but I just ended up back there. Never here, never here at the water. Then one morning the child wanted to walk that dog to the beach and it was a cold day, that, and we put the orange wrap on her. But Willem Bracken came back alone. Oh, I worried for an hour, but Willem, he wasn't worried, so I knew that all was well. I trust that dog, Ethan, more than a person. And didn't see her again until this very day." She smiled at Hauper. "And I hoped maybe, just maybe, you'd be getting around here yourself."

The day actually was like a dream to Ruth and Hauper, and very likely the rest of them. The Yarn Woman, in fact, had difficulty remembering parts of the day she spent on that beach. What she told me, she told me in snippets, her voice often trailing off and leaving those green eyes somehow wanting. She remembered the picnic-like atmosphere, from morning until afternoon, spent with Lucy, Ethan and the rest, though it was difficult for her to describe the transition between the picnic and the present. It seemed that the day's affairs were going along happily and then, so very normally, she and Hauper realized that their stomachs had gone unattended for what seemed like forever. Then the gray and white Rolls pulled up nearby, and Mr. Kasparov opened the doors for them, yammering about them being out all night. All night! When they looked out of the car windows, though, there was no one else around. It was like waking up — like going to bed at night, in the silence of the dark, and then realizing that your eyes were open, that you could see the magnificent light of day and that there was nothing in between the two states of waking, not even the opening of your eyes.

The Albert Townsend

Mr. Kasparov, who had set aside his anger and disappointment as he always did with The Miss, drove her and Hauper to Lucy Mullins' house as requested. But when they walked past the crippled plum trees, they could find no structure lurking behind. The plum trees were gnarled, their dark skins twisted and dry, their leaves brown and crisp. Ruth could make out the spot where the little house sat, and as she walked further into it she saw the old brick and a half-buried iron grate from the coal fireplace that only a few hours before had so warmed the house and those inside. She looked up to see Hauper. She smiled as they stood silently amid the overgrown weeds and the trash that the city seems to cough up wherever there's room.

They weren't surprised, but it made them sad if only because of the exhilaration they felt when Lucy and Ethan embraced; it was as real as the ivory "chip" still in Hauper's pocket. She pulled it out and held it up as if trying to conjure it all back to life. She went over to the spot in the yard where, so long ago, Willem Bracken was fond of sleeping. She put her hand to the ground and found it still warm, as if the beast had only just gotten up to go about his rounds.

They turned and walked up Pierce a few blocks. It really was morning, and it was Friday. They came to a place where a large commercial building had been torn down, leaving a gaping hole in the ground. A galvanized steel barrier fence had been pulled across it, but over time it had fallen over in places, creating a second hazard to anyone walking on the sidewalk. Ruth looked down into what used to be a wide, deep basement. It was a twenty foot drop, nearly vertical, at the bottom of which were large pieces of cement and other rubble.

Ruth called the police emergency number from one of Mr. Kasparov's cell phones. "I'm on Pierce, near Broadway," she said, raising her voice over the sound of the traffic. "There's a big hole here, where a building used to be. I'm here with Alexandra Brown. Yes, that Alexandra Brown. She's fine. Of course we'll wait. Yes. Thank you."

She folded the phone and dropped it in her bag; she didn't like phones and hardly ever used one.

She looked down into the hole again and, squinting, thought she could see one of the girl's missing shoes. There was no doubt they were down there, both of them. And a sock. She looked over at Hauper, who turned away.

"Fell?" she said to the girl.

Hauper nodded.

"Dog pull you back up?"

"By the shoulder. I told him not to."

"Well, maybe it was for the better."

"I wonder where he is."

"I don't know."

"Mrs. Mullins?"

"I don't know."

"Thank God you didn't spout a bunch of crap that wasn't true, Ms. M," said Hauper. "Adults always do that. Like, oh, Hauper, we'll see her again, when you really don't know. Don't ever treat me like that."

"I wouldn't dream of it," said Ruth. "You can cut the Ms. M stuff, too, by the way."

But it was enough for Ruth to understand how the girl had received most of the physical damage. After nearly drowning, she either decided to check out the crater on the way back to Lucy Mullins' house, or simply lost her balance at the edge where the fencing was open. She must have slipped. But would falling into the hazardous crater be enough to exonerate Mrs. Brown?

Later that day, police retrieved the shoes from the bottom of the pit and the sock from a root along the side. It was decided, in light of her re-appearance while her mother was imprisoned, that her injuries had been from the fall. She'd struggled back up out of the foundation area and somehow managed to crawl home. Obviously, she'd run off on her childish rounds again when Mrs. Brown was arrested, and here she was found after spending a day and night on the street.

Mrs. Brown was released two days after her arrest. The charges were dropped. Eventually, the old sontag was returned to her, and she gave it to the Ruth, blood stains and all. But Juliet Brown was a woman of mixed happiness after the arrest. How could it have turned out better? Her daughter was safe; and she'd always been safe. Yet Mrs. Brown also found that friends and neighbors had begun to avoid her. Even people who had never known her shunned her; when they saw her, they saw only the police mug shot, the one with the ratty, sweat-soaked hair and the bags under the eyes; the one printed in the nation's newspapers. The only thing she lacked was a cigarette hanging out of the side of her wicked mouth. She might always be seen as the monster she was portrayed as on those few long autumn days.

With Mrs. Brown free and the Townsend swallowed once again by the sea, I concentrated on tying up the loose ends. But first I decided to amuse myself by reading the edition of Musical Quarterly that the Yarn Woman had pushed my way. I had slipped it into a plastic zip bag to protect the edges — I always worry about damaging other people's books. About midway through the piece on Henriette Sontag, I found the name she had so cryptically called me. It seems that the diva had a devoted fan, a certain British diplomat who followed her across land and sea to attend her performances. No stranger to the press, he was dubbed Lord Montag because he followed Sontag. I wasn't sure why Miss M had called me that — it could have been a joke, a nudge, who knows. I think I prefer Teddy. But maybe it alluded to her openness toward working together in the future. I could be the follower. I didn't know how I felt about that, exactly.

My own research into the Albert Townsend the following week was successful. Old stories from the Sun and the Bulletin, on microfiche at the Sutro Library, showed that Ethan Mullins went down with the schooner on Feb. 14, 1872, having almost reached the Golden Gate despite a northwest winter storm. Sixteen men were lost, no survivors were listed. The vessel had sailed from Caspar Point with a full load of redwood. Mrs. Lucy Mullins died in San Francisco in 1874; three sons survived her. Patrick Mullins was barely 16 at the time, working at sea. There is even a small mention of the dog, Willem Bracken. A city map of that decade, also in the library's archives, revealed Tonquin and Lewis streets along the north edge of the peninsula; they no longer exist.

I re-investigated the fatal mauling of the transient. Ruth had asked me earlier if the man had shown up on the national list of sex offenders. He had not. But I called Detective Chu who told me, finally, that the man had a series of arrests and charges relating to children, none of which had ended in conviction. The information, however, was enough for me to understand how a dog that size had registered a significant threat to Hauper, resulting in a fatal attack. That, I decided, was a damned good dog. I did, however, have a hard time admitting to myself that it was a ghost.

I didn't find the old folk tale of Willem Bracken. Ruth, however, was familiar with it. "I have it somewhere upstairs," she said. "It's one of those strange tales that have been traced back to vague, but historic, events. In this case, maybe the seventeenth century. Those old stories are like ghosts. They wake up now and then, shouting at you.

"Do you believe in ghosts, Mr. Fisher?"

She waited. "I said, I wondered if you believe in ghosts."

She waited longer. "Do you believe in cats, then?"

THE
FISHERMAN'S
WIFE

Prologue

"Some say the selchies shed their skins if they want, and wander much as people do about the villages on the islands, or at times along the sand, or at other times on the rocks. By their eyes you can tell them, and by their song, for they sound like women crying. Then they walk back to the surf barefooted, and, once in their skins again, they return to the sea."

— *Cormac McGregor, Lochinver, Scotland, 1835*

A Body on the Beach

At 1:45 on a cool July afternoon, Friday walked into Betty's Crab Shack in Half Moon Bay because he knew Deputy Avila would be eating fries and drinking an iced tea with two lemon slices, one white packet of sugar and a pink one of fake sugar. There would be a straw in the glass and a second one with the wrapper still on the table beside it. Avila would see him enter, the screen door banging behind him, and say, "Happy Tuesday, Friday," which would make Friday smile; that's why he went there, to give the deputy some comic relief. He never bought anything, he just provided Dennis Avila the opportunity to say "Happy Tuesday, Friday," and then they'd both chuckle and that was about as good as it got. Avila would hand him the clean straw and Friday would carefully unwrap it and test a sip of the iced tea.

But this particular Tuesday, Friday wasn't happy; he was agitated and uncomfortable. That morning, he found a body on the beach near Pigeon Point, about thirty miles south of Half Moon Bay, where he always walked to watch the sea lions or to take a moment to study what he considered to be ancient script on the sea cliff walls, which he found marginally better than the New York Times and significantly better, in his opinion, than the San Francisco Bulletin, though in both cases, perhaps, less up-to-date. The "script" was actually half-fossilized shellfish in half-pressure-set sandstone which had been sheared off cleanly through erosion, leaving curlicues of white shell shavings that did, with little effort on the part of the unlearned beholder, resemble flowing Arabic writing.

After Friday's discovery of the human remains, he hitchhiked back north to Half Moon Bay, which might have taken about an hour but today took three because he was upset and nearly unintelligible after finding the body, and he was booted from two cars before getting his third and final ride from a drunk in an old BMW. But at last he found Deputy Avila at Betty's Crab Shack, right where he was supposed to be, and nervously informed the lawman of his discovery.

Avila took care of it; Friday was relieved but still not happy. His day was ruined, and probably the whole week, maybe the whole month. Friday didn't like death.

By Saturday, four days after the remains were found, they still hadn't been identified. But it wasn't simply human remains to either Avila or Friday. It was something more dreadful, something that didn't want to be forgotten. Friday, an Army veteran of Desert Storm, the first Persian Gulf War of 1990-91, had seen a lot of dead men. It was the faces he remembered, and, oddly, the positioning of the bodies as if frozen in the middle of a dance. Yet death wasn't the part that bothered him most about his discovery on the beach. As for Avila, the younger of the two, he'd seen only a few dead men in the line of duty, but, like Friday, it wasn't death that really mattered in this case. Seeing dead men didn't really get to him.

It's never easy to find a body, but for Friday, this particular discovery was incredibly difficult, and it was all he could do not to weep, to shake, to clench all his muscles into a single, tight, shelled mussel and scream somewhere inside, where it would have echoed for years. He wondered if mussels screamed. Probably they did.

On every one of those first nights, Friday had nightmares. Nightmare, singular, because the dream was always the same. He could only remember fragments, like pebbles of glass that even when melted together formed an incomplete picture with an interrupted, wavy image. What he remembered most about the dream was the emotional content – the enormous feeling of being trapped and the precipitous, shrill worry of running out of time. He woke up, sometimes so fast it was dizzying, always sweating, only to find himself curled up on broken-down cardboard boxes where he had gone to sleep, insulated from the sandy ground but chilled from his own sweat. He should have been a mussel. It was the dream that was the worst part of that death, for Friday.

Those four miserable days passed and they were once again at the cafe when Friday finally told Deputy Avila about his nights with the recurring nightmare. He remembered a woman in the dream. He remembered her face, perfectly. There were birthmarks on her neck and running from her forehead to her cheek. "Like a dog, Denny," Friday said gravely, his voice cracking like his sun-exposed skin. "I mean, like when they have to shave the dog to stitch him for some reason, and like, you see the darkened areas where the fur has, like, spots. I mean, say, if this dog had something like a sticker and they had to shave the hair off and get the thorn out of there, you know. The fur. Like that. You know?" They reminded Friday of the spotted dog he had as a child … his hair had to be shaved off and his side stitched after the animal survived a close encounter with a pickup bumper.

The woman was very pretty, and her skin was pale, almost pink, as if she suffered from vitiligo, with dark birthmarks remaining here and there like islands in a pallid sea. Her eyes, at first glance, were brown and deep, but as Friday stared into them he realized that the glistening eyes had no white showing at all. With eyes like that, she had to be either angel or devil, and he didn't know which.

"But she must possibly be the demon," he said slowly, "because in the dream, she's chained. Fenris was chained then, wasn't he, Denny? Fenrir, the Fenris Wolf. And Prometheus was chained. And Fenris brought the Twilight of the Gods after he bit Tyr's arm off and Prometheus had the liver disorder." Dennis Avila smiled in spite of himself. Friday had always been the smart one. But there wasn't much left of him after the war.

"I see her face at night," Friday said softly, stirring his coffee with the small stainless steel spoon. He reached for another packet of white processed sugar, which he chose over the brown packet of natural, crystal cane sugar. He pulled the top off a miniature chemical creamer, chosen over natural half-and-half, and poured it in. Avila picked up a clump of french fries, placed them carefully on an available saucer and pushed them over to Friday along with the ketchup. He'd never bought Friday a meal – Friday would have nothing to do with Avila's charity. He'd take money or food from someone else – maybe anyone else – but not San Mateo County Sheriff's Deputy Dennis Avila. But he didn't mind sharing the chips or maybe a cup of coffee as long as it didn't have a fancy Italian name like crappu-whatever. He enjoyed sharing, which is different from charity. You share thoughts, or love, maybe literature, but you don't share coinage. Coinage belonged to Caesar.

Nevertheless, during the last few days, an unnerving obsession with the discovery settled on Deputy Avila as well. He hardly ate. He hadn't slept more than an hour or two at night and those few hours were filled with a continuous nightmare ... like Friday, he felt trepidation so strongly it was palpable, as if some sort of deadline was quickly approaching – time was running out. That's how it felt: Time was running out. His nightly nausea was accompanied by sharp body pains and sweating, and over and over he counted the days since the discovery of the body. One, two, now four. Shit, four, and no identification.

"I see some guy with a rifle," said Friday, "I mean, in the dream, man. And he's on this troller, this boat, and the booms, like, they're up, high, and he's like shooting over the side. And she's like on the rocks, man, on the beach. The woman with the patchy skin is on the beach there, watching him shoot and he's, like, only thirty yards offshore, and he's, like, 'I'm a really good shot,' you know? The boat's really close. You know where the seal cave is? There. And she can't move. She gets covered with sand and there's even sand in the boat and she can't get loose from there. God, it's like she's going to drown when the tide comes in. I don't know how she's in the boat and on the beach at the same time, so don't ask. She's tied, like Fenris, you know? Can't get the binding off. It's dark and all the seals are getting spooked, the seals on the beach. Can't see the boat anymore. I can hear the gunshots. Man, it's an M15 for sure. You think I don't know the sound of an M15? I can hear him drop the clip and the bullets, like they're all over the deck, Denny! I know she's on the boat and on the beach. I mean …"

That's crazy, but Avila didn't say it out loud. How could he, when he was having the same nightmare?

"What's Mom say," Friday finally asked. He peered at Avila over his coffee cup. He hated how it had little brown drips going down where his lip touched the cup. It's because the wall of the mug was so thick. Embarrassed, he wiped it off with his thumb.

"About the body?"

"What'd she say, anyway?"

"She came down to the station after I mentioned the sweater we found on it. Funny how the sweater's still there, and he's mostly intact. Not the face, of course, but the rest, being covered …"

"You still have that sweater?" asked Friday, placing the cup on its saucer.

"What?" Avila knew that Friday had changed the subject; it only sounded the same.

"I mean, that one Mom made?"

"Well, sure." She made it when they were in high school more than twenty years ago. It fit neither of them anymore, especially Avila. Friday, who was little more than skeletal, could wear it, but it was tight, short, and the sleeves were short.

"That's good. Can I borrow it for a week? I can tell the wind's coming in. What'd she say?"

"About the sweater?"

"Yeah. Not ours, his. The dead man's."

"Well, she looked it over and said someone could probably identify it – or identify him because of it. She said it was a traditional pattern or something. She gave me a phone number. I haven't called."

"Man, how come?"

"Huh? Oh, I'll get around to it."

"It's been like four days, man. That's practically a week." Friday dumped in a fourth sugar and then a fifth. "Four days. Day Four. One, two, three, four. One more and it's five. Five is like, unlucky. Unless you're Chinese, then it's four. It's very bad. You ought to do it. I mean, sometime soon. You know, soon? Denny, you know?" Good advice; Friday was, after all, the elder brother by two years.

Avila smiled. "They'll laugh at me."

"They don't need to know, dude. Whisper. You mean the other deputies, right? Anyway, they'd laugh at the dreams maybe, but they wouldn't laugh about calling someone on the phone. Would they? Call an expert?"

"Maybe."

"What, did she give you the name of another astrologer like last time?" Friday shook his head softly. "We don't do astrologers these days; doesn't she know that? Reagan did astrologers, you know? Ronald Reagan and his wife, Nancy. Reagan. Very much so. Or in Syria back like 2,000 years. They did astrologers and myrrh, dude. Ask anyone."

"No, it's just that it's an outside consultant. That's all. I have to go through the channels. I have to get the okay and the money, and the budget is in such pitiful shape these days."

"Here," said Friday, leaning sharply to his left and jamming a thick, sun-reddened hand into his jeans pocket. He opened his fist on the table top, depositing a handful of nickels and dimes and five quarters. "I used up the phone card. But you call that number. I'm running out of time, man. And there's more where that came from, if you need it. I'm good for it."

Friday stood up, pushing his chair with the backs of his knees. He wrapped the fries in a piece of tinfoil the waitress left earlier out of habit. "Love you," he said and turned for the door.

"Love you, too."

An Appointment

Uri Mr. Kasparov reached for the phone to his right. It was 5 a.m. and he was seated in the Deco kiosk of the Avaluxe Theater checking his email on a netbook that he'd set up slightly to his left. He was already an hour into his day. Both communication contraptions were nestled on a narrow, dark mahogany ticket-taker's shelf alongside a stack of paperbacks and a week-old edition of the Kiev Segodnya that he picked up from an old Soviet-era informer who lived quietly on Clement Street. There was a long scissors on the other side of the black rotary phone and a few empty 35mm film canisters and a bulk loader. His hand hovered over the receiver a few seconds and he twisted his thick wrist to look at his watch. He smiled, his huge gapped teeth working their way into the air of the kiosk.

"Mm?" he said. Anyone who called at this hour really didn't want to speak with anybody, but probably wanted to leave a message. That's what Mr. Kasparov liked about email. "Have you considered email?" he asked, his tone formal yet friendly. He smiled as he spoke, as if his unseen friendliness had some degree of effect. He listened to the voice on the other end.

"The Miss is currently occupied." he said, "May I take a message? Oh, I see. She does not like to be interrupted, I am afraid. No. I couldn't think of it. I see that it is ... 5:03 a.m." He fiddled with the receiver cord, running it between his thick, knuckled fingers. "Ah. How interesting. Well, I will construct an approach, then, if I may call you back shortly. Yes? Now, if you would please give me the situation in brief for my presentation."

He waited on the phone, listening carefully, minutely, to the radio-like voice on the other end of the line. After a few minutes he closed the conversation, hung up and picked up his newspaper. Avoidance was the wrong approach, he decided, and picked up the receiver again, risking a call up to apartment No. 8. It was now close to 6. His face contorted with each ring, as if it were forcing an electric current into his eye. She picked up on the eighth ring, which was not a good sign.

"No, no," he said. "Yes. Of interest! Of great interest! Yes. Yes. If I may . . ."

With that, Mr. Kasparov began an itemized presentation about the body that had been found on a beach about sixty miles south of San Francisco and how a consultation with her might lead to its identification. At first, the Yarn Woman was reticent to work with a law enforcement agency she wasn't familiar with, but Mr. Kasparov, for reasons he wasn't sure about, convinced her of the need to participate, and she resigned herself to listen to him. An hour or so later, she asked him to call the San Mateo County Sheriff's Department to set up a meeting. "And call Mr. Fisher," she added, "See if he's interested."

"He is," Mr. Kasparov said. He turned to dial.

I had worked with the enigmatic forensic textile consultant whom the police refer to as "the Yarn Woman" on one previous case. She, however, had worked with the San Francisco Police Department on more than twenty cases, some as serious as multiple murder, as well as more than half a dozen with federal agencies including the FBI, ATF and TSA. Yet I had never heard of her until our paths crossed a few months ago regarding a missing child and deadly dog mauling. And I had not seen her since – she is reclusive. She's eccentric. I think she spends her days knitting or lecturing on fiber history. She has a harpsichord; I do not know if she plays professionally but I have no doubt she is excellent. Her eyes are unforgettably green and she, herself, is unforgettable if, I must add, as etheric as mist. The phone call from Mr. Kasparov Uri Mr. Kasparov, a political refugee from

Ukraine during the Brezhnev era who had, for reasons unknown to me, become the Yarn Woman's driver and, for want of words, self-assigned bodyguard, offered a welcome glimmer of hope that I would see her again just as I had begun to feel great despair over the matter.

I was careful not to seem over-eager. I told Mr. Kasparov I would have to re-arrange my schedule but that I would be available.

* * *

The drive down the coast to Half Moon Bay took less than two hours. Mr. Kasparov pulled off 92 to eastbound Alpine, humming an old Roger Miller tune as he sat alone in the front seat. Ruth and I were in the expansive back seat with the stereo turned just high enough for Bach's Four Lute Suites to drown out Mr. Kasparov's warbling "King of the Road." We were about an hour ahead of the commute traffic from the city to the small, used-to-be fishing town. I usually work nights at San Francisco's largest daily newspaper, the Bulletin, but my metro editor was interested in the story and I'd have to juggle my hours later in the week to come up square.

Mr. Kasparov parked the Rolls among the C350s, the 328s, some 911s and other tell-tale signs of Half Moon Bay's emergence from commercial fishing village obscurity to high-end playground for new, moneyed residents and the traveling rich. But still, the 1957 White Cloud I drew a few stares. It was the kind of car most people only see in photographs or possibly at the Concours d'Elegance at Pebble Beach once a year. Mr. Kasparov wore gloves when he drove it. I had always found it strange that Mr. Kasparov, an unmoneyed refugee from Soviet-era Ukraine, had such a vehicle. He certainly had nothing else. His regular employment was as caretaker of the old, retired Avaluxe Theater, which he took very seriously. And, he drove for "The Miss."

Ruth studied the hand-painted sign over Betty's Crab Shack. The scent of fried, battered fish ambled drunkenly out through the screen door, which she pulled open, ushering Mr. Kasparov and me in first, and then let it slam behind her. In her opinion, the satisfying smack of wood against wood was far better than a door-top bell or the dreaded laser-beam trip at your feet that signaled, over and over, your arrival.

A dozen people were seated at the cafe tables and their attention was briefly diverted to the clacking door before they settled back into their burgers, chowder and chips. A vagrant who'd been walking toward the exit stomped out as if he'd been insulted by the noise. He was thin and tall but masked his height by crouching over like Kokopelli without a flute. He cast a brilliant blue eye at Ruth as he crushed past her into the great yellow-blue glow of Half Moon Bay's summer afternoon, and mumbled something intelligible.

She didn't turn around to watch him. There was no need. She felt the sand from his clothing scratch has he brushed by, and though his shirt was stained, he didn't smell. His skin was red from the sun, the deep red of the homeless, and his hands were cracked and puffed. Yet his nails, chipped, were relatively clean. His hair was uncombed and something between blonde and red-gray, and strafed his neck and collar as it tried, with difficulty, to escape from beneath a grease-blackened red baseball cap that advertised Puralator oil filters.

He took a long look at her after he pushed past her; I moved slightly to the side to clear the way. It wasn't a wolfish look – it was more of a scientific evaluation through piercing eyes that peered like blue buttons from a sun-swollen face. He threw the door wide and let it bang a second time, smiling as he took the five wood stairs down to the parking lot.

Ruth spotted the uniformed San Mateo County deputy waving from the back of the cafe, and she walked in his direction. He was about five-eight, easily two hundred pounds, and wide like a linebacker. His patrol hat was perched on the back of the chrome and yellow-marbled Naugahyde chair next to him. She could see the impression of the band in his glistening black hair, short-cropped though it was on the sides and back.

"I'm Deputy Avila," he said, holding his hand out, the alto tone of his voice in contrast to his size. "You must be ... I understand they call you 'the Yarn Woman.' I mean, you are the Yarn Woman, right?"

"Flattery will get you nowhere," she said, but that smile... She nodded and shook his hand.

"You couldn't have timed it better," he said. It was 2 p.m., within a minute of their appointment. He noticed she wore no watch and had no pendant timepiece visible over what he perceived to be two blouses layered over the top of a camisole. Instead, there was a simple brass band on one exposed wrist and nothing on the other. He ignored the bracelet and studied what he could see of her forearm. She appeared athletic but kept herself under long sleeves. She was shorter than him by at least four inches, exuded both physical and inner strength, and yet because of the style of dress he was unable to gauge her weight with any certainty. He didn't have to – he wasn't trying to describe a suspect.

She, in turn, noted the rough quality of his hands, which indicated a lot of common labor despite his job. There was no ring. She decided he worked on his house, if he had a house, or, she smiled, his mother's house. He took care of his mom. Duh. It would have been like having a second job. She probably hammered on him, however softly, about getting married. He was about forty and Mom was probably running out of hope.

"I'm Ruth M, Deputy Avila. Thank you for calling. This is Mr. Kasparov, who drove us. He's a very old friend. And this is Mr. Fisher. He's helping me but also works at the Bulletin."

My position as a journalist wasn't a deal-breaker, but it took a few minutes and a couple of promises before he felt comfortable in the presence of the press. I figured he needed all the help he could get on this one, anyway, and that might be in the way of publicity.

"I haven't ordered," he said, waiting for her to take a seat across from him. He nodded to Mr. Kasparov and me and motioned us to sit as well. We sat at a chrome-rimmed, red-Formica five-top that matched the yellow seats only in the chrome and marbled effect in the Naugahyde. She sat with the entry door to her left, with her back to wide windows that looked out onto the small harbor. The many-paned glass had been hand-set, secured at the edges by strips of wood and copious amounts of clear silicone caulking. A few fly fossils were embedded in the hardened silicone as if it were amber, but the windows were otherwise perfectly clean, and the small fishing boats, amid a mix of yachts and sailing vessels, were clearly and beautifully visible – to Deputy Avila and to Mr. Kasparov and me. The sun glanced off their Furumo sonars high in the erect trolling booms, and the plastic side windows of the cabins reflected the slow-breathing water of the harbor. Avila, however, had no worries about being distracted from the woman at hand – a compliment unvoiced – and her company would make for a rather pleasant day after all, he was sure, despite the task ahead of them.

He handed her a menu and suggested the fish and chips. "The red snapper is really rockfish," he said, making an effort at conversation. "The Atlantic has red snapper."

"Right. What kind?" she asked. Avila looked up at her over the top of his menu, his eyes questioning her. "I mean, there are 13 commercially viable species of scorpaenidae," she said happily, "and almost 60 Pacific species in five general classifications, each with a couple of sub-categories, so I was just wondering what kind of scorpionfish."

"Chilipepper," Avila said, feeling a degree of pride in his unhesitating response. He might even have been right. He'd heard the things discussed on the docks since he was a kid, but he could only remember chilipepper. Oh, there was bocaccio – he remembered bocaccio, too.

"Sounds good," she said, smiling. Her smile was more in her eyes, he thought. Who knows what she meant with the mouth part of the smile – it was hard to decipher because she seemed to smile only on the left side. He found himself intrigued, but pushed it aside.

We all ordered fish and chips and iced tea.

"Your brother didn't want to stay?" she asked the deputy after the waitress, our ticket in her black apron pocket, wiggled off to the kitchen. Ruth had easily recognized Avila and the homeless man as brothers, which from my point of view wasn't possible. They appeared to have entirely different genetics. I would have guessed that Avila was a "Port-u-guee," one of the ethnicities to settle in the coast in the 1800s, and the other man Irish. Where Dennis Avila was dark-featured, his brother was light-skinned with light hair that had been tangled and thinned by the sea wind. Dennis was husky and short; Friday was lithe and a good six inches taller. His outer appearance was that of a typical homeless Northern California male: sun-damaged skin, chaotic facial hair, and the usual clothing.

"No," said Avila, recovering from his surprise. "That's Friday. He's a couple of years older than me. He's had a little trouble since the Gulf War. He's not fond of talking, you know. He prefers to be on the beach. Our mother bought him a pretty nice Dundee hat – $200 and change – so he'd give up the Purolator, but he lost it. But anyway," he began cautiously, "you know, Mom wanted to come down and listen in. She said she wanted to meet you, Miss M ..." He lifted his chin slightly, looking at the screen-door entry, and said "Well, well; there she is now," nodding toward the door. "Imagine that." He smiled, embarrassed. He stood and waved at her, a broad smile crossing a face that had thus far shown nothing but straight-lipped business. Then, catching himself, he overruled the movement of his waving hand and wrenched his smile straight again. Finally, his eyes assumed their usual three-quarter-open, omniscient cop look.

Ruth turned to see Mrs. Avila just as the screen slammed behind her. She was in her mid-70s with a thick batch of white hair that had once been dark red or chestnut. Some of the red hue remained. She was short and wide like her younger son and she wore blue. Her shapeless dress was sky blue, patterned with nickel-sized tarnished gold ovals. The short sleeves revealed thick, strong arms that were no stranger to heavy work. Her modestly pointed patent leather indigo shoes had an older nurse-like quality – the heels were thick and about an inch and a half high. She had on thick supportive nylons, loud finger rings with bellowing stones, a thin watch that cut into her fat wrist and a cream cardigan, unbuttoned. Mrs. Avila was accomplished at applying makeup, but there was nothing anyone can do to make penciled eyebrows look real. She was *dressed,* and looked like she might be ready to settle into a series of Manhattans or an Old Fashioneds for the remainder of the afternoon.

Ruth spontaneously gave Mrs. Avila a warm hug at the table, which surprised the older woman. She commented on Mrs. Avila's lovely sweater and its workmanship, and though she could easily identify the pattern, the yarn and the source of each, she did not – there are some things you just don't do. It's enough to know what you know.

The hug left Mrs. Avila briefly off balance, a feeling she was hardly used to and didn't particularly like. But how many women had even met the Yarn Woman? Everyone knew her name, or had read her evaluations and commentaries on everything from stitch histories to natural mordants, but few had ever seen the recluse. She was much younger than Mrs. Avila had expected.

Deputy Avila had already ordered his mother a chef's salad, and after overly long introductions Mrs. Avila took a seat to Ruth's right, the big windows behind her and the cafe's seating area before her. She could watch the comings and goings in the cafe at will.

A Fisherman's Sweater

After lunch, Avila drove us all to the recently renovated, state-of-the-art county crime lab in Redwood City in a department cruiser. This would take the day, I realized; I'd half-hoped he would bring the garment in question to the cafe, knowing all along it wouldn't happen. There were forensics concerns, of course, as well as the disgusting thought of looking at a corpse's sweater over fish and chips.

Though the crime lab wasn't a beehive of activity, there were a number of workers around nevertheless, all wearing long white lab garments and plodding through their daily responsibilities. The rows of steel-topped counters were extraordinarily well lit by wall-length windows, emphasizing the need of natural lighting in forensics work. It had been billed as the first "green" forensics lab in the nation when it opened a few years ago.

At Avila's request, a lab pathologist cleared a portion on one end of a long steel examination counter, a sort of free-standing table that ran the length of the room, and retrieved a parcel from a climate-controlled metal cabinet. He handed Ruth some latex exam gloves and then placed the sweater on the steel. Avila motioned for Ruth to open it up. His mother, standing behind Ruth, frowned. The pathologist assumed a position away from the table, busying himself with other matters but occasionally glancing at the progress he assumed we were making.

"This was on the man my brother found five days ago on the beach a few miles south of the harbor," he said. "Five days. This is Day Five."

"That's a heck of a sweater," she mumbled, snapping the gloves on and staring intently at the clumped, wrapped article, entering a thoroughly pensive, observant state of mind. You could practically hear the lock snap as she closed the door behind her. It seemed to me that she was utterly gone, that only her body made any movement to remind us of her existence.

Ruth picked it up and briefly studied it through the wrapper, holding it up to the light and putting it back on the metal table. She made a mental note that it weighed just over twelve hundred grams including water weight, but dry it might have been around nine hundred. She wrote nothing down. Then she carefully removed the sweater and placed it on the sterile surface.

She looked up once at Mrs. Avila and smiled. Mrs. Avila, who'd grown momentarily accustomed to Ruth's withdrawal, was shocked a second time by the sudden display of life. Uncertain what to do, she smiled awkwardly back and together they hovered over the sweater.

Ruth examined it minutely. She had a triplet magnifier and with it she studied the yarn in several places — the cuffs, the belly, the ribbing at the bottom, the tip of the neck, and the sleeves, which appeared elongated due to the action of the seawater. She had gauges and rulers and used them to evaluate the process that created it, determining the needle size, and stitches and rows per inch. She seemed particularly interested in the cuffs, one of which was severely mauled, the strands torn and the weave unraveling. The measuring of the thing was probably the only aspect that Mrs. Avila, an accomplished knitter herself, clearly grasped, and in grasping it she felt a camaraderie with the peculiar woman beside her.

Ruth took no notes on the physical characteristics. There was no need. She could, at will, memorize a complex knitting pattern in moments, just as she could remember an entire crossword puzzle solution, much to the chagrin of Mr. Kasparov, who enjoyed solving them of a Saturday or Sunday morning without her mischievous assistance.

Then Ruth smelled the material, crushed it while holding it near her ear, and turned the body of the sweater inside out — which gained the older woman's heightened attention, as if she were waiting for bells to ring. I found myself watching Ruth's eyebrows, unsure whether I was simply distracted or purposefully trying to follow her line of thought. I wondered if she had them shaped, or if they were natural. But in their movement, I saw clearly that she, too, saw something clearly. I just didn't know what. She seemed pleasantly surprised. I had no idea why. She became agitated, I think. Her eyes, which had been their usual emerald, seemed to shift to a more aquamarine color.

Mrs. Avila had briefly seen the sweater early in her son's investigation, and whatever anomalies she observed compelled her to recommend her son find an expert. To Mrs. Avila, there was only one expert, and she fortunately lived in the same state, almost the same county. But it took her a while to find the name, which she'd scribbled in the border of a pattern she'd downloaded several years ago. Her own jotting, done hurriedly and so long ago, was nearly illegible. Ultimately, though, she managed to decipher it, producing enough of a phone number to make contact.

The sweater was now back on the table, half inside-out but neatly arranged. Ruth raised an eyebrow, then picked it up again and pulled the left arm through so the full sweater was inside out. Mrs. Avila, who was fairly dramatic, even entertaining, gasped. Unflinching, Ruth fingered the shoulder seam and then straightened the sweater, right side out now, on the smooth, cold steel. She picked up a cuff in each hand and held them above the table as if conducting a seance. Each breath was held a long time before slowly exhaling. She continued to hold the old thing, hands on top as if she were a psychometrist. Mrs. Avila followed her every move.

Laying down the sleeves, Ruth turned her attention to the right cuff, the one that was mangled and torn. She worked out an end and carefully poked it into the view area of a portable hand microscope she'd taken from her bag, a Brunel with a reticle that measured in microns: She mumbled that she was interested in the fiber's response to the obvious tension that resulted in the tear.

"Denny has forensic microscopes, Miss M," said Mrs. Avila, "if you wanted to use them. Don't you, Denny? They're very powerful."

Ruth woke from her concentration. She stood for a moment, as if disoriented, then said, "Oh?" She looked expectantly at the deputy, who introduced her to the lab's microscopes via the pathologist, who was their king. They gravitated from a rather mundane digital model with a flat screen to a Leica FS C – if you ever wanted to buy the latter you had to talk to a sales rep to get a quote. She never did … she held to the theory that if you have to ask, you can't afford it.

She stared through the binocular lenses, knowing full well she'd learn nothing she hadn't seen with her own portable. She did, however, fully explore the capabilities of the Leica with the rather enthusiastic assistance of the pathologist. The rest of us swallowed our boredom for the next forty-five minutes or so as the two talked about Leica technology. By the time their conversation had veered into the old Leica 35mm rangefinder cameras of the early twentieth century, and the many Russian copies produced before and after the War – the Zorkys, Kievs and Feds (Ruth owns a Fed camera made in the mid-1960s, a gift from Mr. Kasparov some years ago) – Deputy Avila gently returned them to the to the current century and case at hand with a series of coughs.

Pulling herself away from Leica history and the wonders of the FS C, Ruth took a few deep breaths and then separated the strands and split the plies that made up the end she'd worked out. By the time she finished, locks of her hair had fallen out of the perpetual twist she wore, which had been fastened in the back as she always did with knitting needles and, today, a chopstick. It was a nice chopstick – black-enameled. The two needles were sevens.

Ruth's face had a quizzical look, as if the stray strands in her gloved fingers perplexed her. Familiar with her face and eyes, I deduced that she'd found something of importance in the frayed yarn. I had no idea what, and I doubt that Mrs. Avila did, either.

From what little Deputy Avila could see, the sweater's overall condition was good except for the cuff and belly. He was aware of the dried seaweed, which he thought would be of little interest to the Yarn Woman. The right cuff must have gotten caught on sharp rocks, he decided, and possibly yanked with the dead weight of the man's body as it tossed in a deep-water current. The abdominal area was mauled and he could see that some of the strands of yarn were frayed or abraded there. Yet, had the cuff been complete and the gut unmarred (and had the thing not been found on a corpse), it would have had long life in it yet. More, it appeared to be practically new.

"So what do you think?" he finally asked.

She sighed. He was pushing her. "Tell me about the victim."

That was no problem — there wasn't much to tell. "Based on the size of the bones and the muscle and other tissues, the coroner believes the deceased to be an average male, five-ten or eleven, weight about two hundred, and with nearly black, undyed hair, age mid-30s. There was no visible loss of body mass from marine scavengers, and the legs, arms, and torso are intact. Skin, intact, but with damage from abrasion and other factors. He's certainly not facially identifiable, though he was submerged for a day at the most, maybe less, and it's the pathologist's opinion that my brother discovered the body the day it washed up. We've had him for five days now; the time of death would be maybe six days. And I've found no missing persons reports that apply to him.

"The man's death was probably by drowning, but there was also damage to the surface tissue in the abdominal region — the skin and muscle under the sweater, shirt, and undershirt — is damaged and there appear to be something like dog bites and bruising. I think you can see the bite damage on the sweater. I don't think the guy's local, but it's not like it used to be here ... I don't know everybody anymore. My mother," he nodded in Mrs. Avila's direction, "said the knitting could possibly be identified, like maybe a certain family pattern. I thought you could help with that, or with anything that came to mind regarding the fabric.

"So, that's the point: What can you tell me that would help me identify him and notify his next of kin? It's a suspicious death, but it's not a homicide, I think. I just want to know who he was."

Ruth thought for a moment. Mrs. Avila watched her expectantly. "The pattern," Ruth said, "won't help us as much as other peculiarities in this garment, Mr. Avila," she said. "You're looking for the name of a dead man, and I'm confident that with a little luck we'll be able to find that. But his name is only the beginning ... because I think you have to find this man's widow. If she's still alive, her life is in peril ..."

Full Disclosure, Almost

Deputy Avila stared silently at the Yarn Woman. The look on his face was severe. "Wife? Danger? What do you mean?" he asked, his voice level, almost robotic. The gears in his mind were moving slowly, but with power. To his credit, the man didn't discount her opinion as I would have expected, but seemed genuinely interested in this surprising diagnosis.

Ruth, assured now of an open, if unconvinced, audience, continued, "… and if it's been a week or so since he died, as you said, the chance of finding her alive grows slimmer and slimmer for each day that passes."

"I told you!" shouted his mother. "Didn't I say that, Dennis? I said there was a woman involved, a wife! And, Miss Ruth," she said excitedly, "I got the brush-off like you wouldn't believe!"

"You said it was his mother," Avila said, addressing his own mother.

"Mother, wife, whatever," she shot back. "The point of it is, 'female.' The point of it is, 'in danger.' Look at the similarities, Denny."

"You said the pattern was the clue," Avila snipped, "and that's not what I'm hearing here."

"I was on the right track, Dennis. Admit it. You're acting just like your father used to."

Avila ignored her and watched the Yarn Woman expectantly.

"Basically, this sweater is an old style called a gansey," Ruth said, "which originated on Guernsey, the Channel Island, about four hundred years ago. It could have been earlier — you know how it goes trying to date things when the written record is lacking. Knitting, you see, knitting isn't really that ancient. Not like weaving. According to the research, it's been around less than two millennia, but it wasn't known in Europe until the Middle Ages.

"Your sweater," she said, nodding at the garment she'd carefully folded and replaced on the metal table, "clearly reflects the original patterns and it could as easily have been made several hundred years ago as yesterday, except for one thing."

Mrs. Avila moved closer to the sweater as it lay on the cold steel, waiting.

"It appears to be very recently finished, of course ... but the strangest aspect is the Scandinavian influence on the traditional design." She looked up and said, "Not only is this made in a very old Swedish two-strand technique, but one of the strands is what's known as Z-ply, that is, it's spun and plied backward ... as if you had to tighten a bolt, for example, by turning it to the left rather than the right. (She looked closely at the deputy to make sure her analogy had sunk in. She was sure it had.) That is, it's opposite of the generally accepted – universally agreed-upon – standards. What's more, it's been done commercially and not by hand. That makes it extraordinarily rare – I have no doubt I can find the maker. I need time to research it, is all. This may mean little to you, Deputy Avila, but as far as this investigation of yours, it's everything. Well, almost everything."

Mrs. Avila touched the cuff of the arm, somewhat in awe.

"And," Ruth added, "there are ... religious ... elements that are clearly from the distant past, more closely related to the pagan Brits than the Christianized Norse."

But our interest grew. She had her audience well in hand. Yet she re-directed her discussion even as we waited.

"Here is what we know:

"She used five-ply yarn, which, in itself is unusual these days.

"It's hebridean wool. I know that because I'm familiar with various yarns produced by the many breeds of wool sheep. It's one of my specialties.

"I know of no hebridean flocks in the States. They're from Wales, for the most part. Or Cornwall. The breed, a 'black' sheep, is actually dark brown, and originated on the islands off the west coast of Scotland. Oddly, they gray slightly as they age, just like people. And it's old, dating to the Iron Age. The breed was almost extinct until recent efforts to revive it.

"The sweater is a bizarre combination of two traditional styles: It's the Scandinavian two-stranding of a Channel Island design, making it a thick, nearly waterproof garment. The two styles, though geographically disparate, date to the same time frame, three or four hundred years in our past.

"The addition of the Z strand kept the yarn, in this technique, from twisting up like a corkscrew.

"The sweater's fitted. Unusual."

Mrs. Avila nodded. Her son remained stolid.

"The deceased," she continued, "was a Hercules, a bodybuilder."

"How could you tell that?" asked Dennis Avila.

"As I said, the style is traditionally very boxy – it goes straight down. But this one's been fitted. It's tight below the welt, that is, at the abdomen, and then she started the cables above the welt. This would make broad shoulders, or a deep chest, appear even broader and deeper. It's all about style. Anybody would have looked good in that sweater, but the man you have in the morgue would have looked outstanding."

He nodded.

"And there are the hidden things in that sweater, mysterious things," she said, finally.

This, apparently, was what the older woman had questioned, had been waiting for. Mrs. Avila drew closer to the gansey on the exam table, then returned her studied gaze to Ruth. "What did you see?" she asked.

"There is a pattern below the welt, nearly invisible.

This is where, for centuries, a man's initials or surname might be knitted in, using purl stitches. Isn't that right, Mrs. Avila?"

"Very much so."

"The initials were used, sadly, to help identify a body that washed ashore after being lost at sea. Fishing has always been a dangerous vocation. According to current U.S. Labor statistics, it's the most dangerous job of all, with more than 121 deaths per 100,000 workers."

"… Just in passing …" the deputy said.

Ruth explained that the knitter, the man's wife, twisted the two strands to create the shape of a fish. I was unable to see it on the front side of the garment, but it was visible to me from the back, where, as Ruth noted, one could see it in the floats – the unused yarn that extends for a stitch or two on the back side. Normally, as I understood it, the two strands would be different colors and the knitter would twist one color to the front, which would have made the fish red, for example. The other color would be "floated" on the back side. But these two strands of yarn were the same color.

"So what's the point?" Avila asked.

"She hid it, like she hid a tan-colored strand in the shoulder seam." Again, Mrs. Avila nodded. She smiled. "I have to ponder that a bit, but what we have is enough to start your identification process, Deputy Avila."

By now it was nearly 4 in the afternoon. Avila looked at his watch, his first mistake in a long, long day. Avila didn't know about watches and the Yarn Woman. Her eyes grew narrow, her smile straightened and her lips grew thin: When a man looks at his watch, it means he's no longer in the moment. He's thinking of other things.

Ruth sighed, her eyes showing resignation rather than her usual disdain. She must have liked the man.

"Mr. Avila," she said, using the honorific rather than his title, deputy, showing at least a degree of disappointment, "your man was a fisherman by trade, and not simply because he was wearing a fisherman's sweater. The sweater was meant to work in, and the fish is indicative. He is not one of your recent 'immigrants' to the coast, but from an older fishing family. Surely the sweater, because it's so well executed, even unique, would be recognized by other fishermen who knew him. I would suggest showing it around at the fishermen's unions here and up the coast as far as you think the body could have drifted – maybe as far north as Crescent City? The currents flow southward so I don't think I'd waste my time with the southerly ports.

"Your man was young, under thirty, despite what the coroner says. He was built like Adonis; I can tell this from the increases after the welt area and the cabling in the chest and shoulders. I assume he belonged to a gym, that his diet was regulated and that he took muscle-building supplements. Have the coroner checked for steroid residue or maybe other supplements like commercially available andro or creatine. So, you can check the marina, the gyms and the vitamin and supplement outlets.

"You already know he had black hair. But he was a rogue – so please check the bars and taverns. He married into one of the old local families within the last year or so."

"Surely, you can't tell that from the sweater, that he was married, and a trouble-maker," Avila said, causing his mother to frown.

"I'll discuss my reasoning in the written report. But if he wasn't married (a very slim possibility), then he was at least in a relationship with the young woman, and her family would have been very upset about it, about him as a prospect. It's clear to me he was a violent type. Perhaps he has a police record? ... specifically relating to domestic violence, fighting in bars, that sort of thing. His wife was definitely afraid of him in the end, Deputy Avila. Very afraid. I feel that she was frightened enough to defend herself if she had to ... or kill him if she had no choice."

Then she stopped talking. It was abrupt. There was

no summary statement, just that smile.

"Check your watch again," she said." He looked down at his wrist. It was nearly 5. But still the Yarn Woman wasn't quite finished with Dennis Avila, and added, "If you still have a few minutes, I have some questions before we part."

"I've told you everything I know about the body, and I have no reason to withhold information at this point. Because of your help, I'll narrow my search down to the harbors and local taverns, the gyms and supplement or vitamin stores. If you could investigate the backwards yarn thing ..."

"Right. Then tell me about the dreams, Mr. Avila."

Both the deputy and his mother nearly choked. They looked at each other and a fog of uncomfortable silence descended.

"Oh, tell her, Denny," said Mrs. Avila, her voice short and exasperated yet somehow relieved, and her hand waving in mock resignation. "But how did you know about the dreams, Dear?"

"Both your sons haven't been sleeping. That's obvious; the rest is a guess." Ruth M, however, never guesses. I'd been around her long enough to know that.

After a while, Avila nodded as if to himself. "Okay, then." He was quiet for a moment. "As far as the dream," he said, "I think it's similar to the one my brother is having," he said.

"It's the same," said Mrs. Avila to Ruth. "Exactly the same."

"Well, the same, then," he said. "And it's the same dream over and over. The deceased, well, I see him with a rifle on a boat, his boat, some small dragger. Something like that ... I can't tell. Friday, my brother, says it's a trolling vessel, a salmon boat, rockfish boat. And onshore, there's a woman. She's very pretty, dark hair, very large black eyes. Dark brown eyes, I guess. Her skin has two tones, sort of pinkish white and then a brownish tan like large birthmarks. They're even on her face, but mostly on the chest and shoulders. The rest of the woman is covered but I can't tell what with. It's dark, or she's dark.

"She's on the rocks and she can't move, but she's singing. I can't remember the song, but in the dream, it's like a song you've known all your life, a ballad or something like that. The melody seems very old, like some kind of folk song. There's a small cave, a blowhole where the water runs through, and she's in that, and the sand starts coming in and she's trapped. The sand keeps coming in, but now she's in the boat. For some reason, she becomes trapped in the boat instead of the cave. It sounds stupid, I know. But it's the feeling ... it's a very strong feeling of being trapped and having time run out. It's horrible, the feeling. Not the rest of it. The rest is just regular dream stuff. It's incoherent and, frankly, stupid. But it starts every time I close my eyes."

"Friday has the same dream, Miss M," said Mrs. Avila. "He told me. He's sure it's a troller. Denny was never good with boats ... I think Friday knows where the little cave is, too, I mean, in real life. But he's the quiet one. Quieter since he was in the service." There was a long pause before she continued. "There's nothing we can do, you know. He gets his disability, the SSI, and something from the Army from the first Gulf War. They hold it at that little grocery store in town for him."

"I see."

Clearly, the meeting was over, but there was an unfinished feeling to it. For Deputy Avila, it got too personal for comfort. Ruth, however, broke the silence by saying, "It's been a pleasure, Deputy Avila, and I enjoyed meeting your mother." She turned to acknowledge Mrs. Avila. "May I call you?" she asked.

"Please, dear," said Mrs. Avila, who then scribbled down her phone number on a scrap of paper she found in her purse. "Perhaps ..."

"I would look forward to it, Mrs. Avila."

"Kate, please." Triumph glowed in the older woman's eyes.

Ruth then turned back to the deputy. "I'll find out where the yarn came from and get back to you. If I get lucky, it'll be in the full report, which I'll have for you tomorrow. I'll need your email address – is an MSWord attachment okay? I'll cover all the reasons for my conclusions."

"Please," he said. "But use the old program; they haven't updated our software for years."

"Do you mind if, say within the next few days, I come back down from the city to speak with your brother?"

"That's fine, if he wants to. He probably won't, but … I'll ask him, kind of prepare him. He's not nearly as rough as he appears. He does have a home. But he doesn't talk much to strangers."

"He lives with me, Dear," said Mrs. Avila. "It's just that he mostly prefers being outside. You know, since the fighting."

"Does she sing for your brother, Deputy? Mrs. Avila?"

"Pardon me?" said Dennis Avila.

"The woman in the dream. Does she sing for Friday?"

"In the dream? I don't know, now that I think of it," he said.

"Yes, she does," said Mrs. Avila. "And it haunts him, Dear."

Back to the City

We returned to San Francisco after the interview with Avila. On the smooth ride back, Ruth sat huddled in silence with a pair of headphones covering most of her head. I wondered how she kept her hair up all day, but then remembered seeing her re-pin it occasionally. I worked through my notes on a netbook, to which she was oblivious. Mr. Kasparov had something horrible playing softly on the stereo, but I had to admit that the sound itself was exceptional.

It was dark when we arrived in the city. I wanted to know what she was going to put into her report. She'd offered not a hint, and I decided it was just better to wait than to ask. What was she going to share with Mrs. Avila by phone? I wouldn't wait much longer than a day anyway, since she'd promised the report by tomorrow. I left them at the theater, chugging along across the Bay Bridge to my apartment in Oakland, where all the flotsam that has been priced out of San Francisco housing seems to end up. I knew it wouldn't be long before I'd be priced out of Oakland as well, but pushed the thought aside.

Ruth spent the remainder of the evening at her harpsichord, lost in thought. Her pensiveness was unrestful, though, and dreadful dark hollows grew beneath her eyes. She could feel them like clay weights, pulling at her. She couldn't help but look in the mirror, and though she could do nothing about the eyes, she re-pinned her hair. At least it was something. She showered and changed and tied a silk bandana across her forehead. She wandered out into the back alley to breathe the night air, and she watched the moonlight play on the sweet-pea petals for a few minutes. Now cold, she went back inside, slowly climbing the north staircase to her rooms.

She sat back down, shuffled her sheet music and then let it fall to the hardwood floor. She dimmed the lights and sat again at the delicate instrument in the middle of the yarn-strew hardwood sea. Her cat, an old black-and-white creature appropriately named Methuselah, sat behind the sheet support on the harpsichord and stared at her, wondering, maybe, if she'd at least pick up the music. He batted at her hands, but she didn't seem to want to play. What could he do? He yawned mightily.

Ruth rarely talks about the harpsichord or her music. What was there to say? Like her crates of yarn, pedal-powered spinning wheels – some of them quite old and from distant lands – and bins of needles, they are as much a part of her as her body, maybe more, and for that reason she kept private counsel about them. Nevertheless: I learned from Mr. Kasparov, my Yarn-Woman informant, that the harpsichord was 20th century French, a copy of a seventeenth century Blanchet masterpiece. The original, which had survived the French Revolution, was now in a Russian museum. So I understand. I don't know how it got to Russia, nor does Mr. Kasparov. He saw the Blanchet once some years ago, he said, and noted that Ruth's "copy" was smaller than the original.

"Hers was a gift," he had quietly informed me. "From a certain Mrs. Reynolds. I was a player in the negotiations. It was just a bit part," he said, smiling broadly, his teeth protruding. But there was a wistful look in Mr. Kasparov's eye the day he had so brazenly betrayed that mote of confidentiality about his "Miss M." Though the finer points remained a mystery, I was certain that his relationship with Mrs. Reynolds had been either intimate or at least respectfully close. I didn't pry, not because I didn't want to, but because one simply does not pry into the lives of Ruth M and her compatriots. It's very bad form; you have to be very delicate.

Prior to her possession of it, the gold-leafed harpsichord had been damaged over time. Ruth and Mrs. Reynolds had it restored at some expense. "Mr. Fisher," Mr. Kasparov said, huddling close to me in the lobby of the Avaluxe one day so as not to be overheard by the stars of the silver screen, whose black-and-white photos lined the walls, "she had to survive on what yarn she had for quite some time in order to afford the rehabilitation of the instrument. Mrs. Reynolds acquired it in imperfect condition, knowing what would be required, and she located a noted maker to undertake the restoration, and The Miss was quite agreeable." It was hard to tell, but I'm sure I saw a wry smile somewhere under his nose. It wouldn't have been difficult to make her yarn last until the end of time. Like foundation concrete trucked to a building site, you'd measure her yarn in cubic yards.

Ruth played the instrument for hours at a time, sometimes with the aid of a sheet of music but more often without. After we'd become acquainted, I noticed that after extended periods of music – mixed with spinning or knitting – that could last for days, she emerged from her meditations pale and weak, her normally tawny skin white and waxy, her thick hair damp and limp, curled, even matted, but still pegged up in the back with needles and sticks. She was always very hungry. There was usually only one way to revive her: Chinese hot and sour soup.

At 1 the morning after our return from Half Moon Bay, after a few hours at the keyboard, she rose from her harpsichord and made tea. Then she knitted for an hour or so, starting the ribbing for a pair of socks (using, I was told, a flexible cast-on of 72 stitches). Then, never looking at a clock (because she didn't have one and wouldn't own such a monstrosity), she set it down on her large round table and resorted to picking up her phone. She had no cell, though she occasionally borrowed one from Mr. Kasparov. All she had was a vintage 1940s dial phone in the apartment whose receiver, like its twin downstairs in the ticket kiosk, doubled as an Olympic free-weight. She spun the dial, appreciating the solid rotary feel and the sound as the inner spring pulled it back to 0.

"Are you up?" she asked me. Her absurd question

was typical of her dry, overly exhausted humor.

"Yes."

"Great. I'm working on the yarn."

"Don't your eyes ever get tired?"

"It's not late for bar flies. Or for you. Are you interested?"

I was.

"It's troubling," she said.

"What?"

"Time is our enemy, my friend. Time is big trouble in this one. It's been a week as of now."

"But what about the sweater, the yarn?"

"I'm ordering yarn. This is important." She perked up. "God, talk about great stuff. Five-ply from Wales. That's why I love this job. Can you believe it, I have to order yarn from halfway around the world in order to solve Deputy Avila's case? Can it get any better?" Clearly, she had solved many parts of an investigation that were still obscure and mysterious to my eyes. How did she know she'd be calling Wales? What had she seen in the pattern? It looked fairly normal to me. And it sure looked warm. I was sure it would have fit me ... though it might have been a little on the short side.

I extrapolated for a second but couldn't come up with a valid reason for having to order yarn to solve Avila's mystery. Was she padding her investigation fee in a manner than only a Yarn Woman could? I decided not. She didn't work that way. "I'll be there," I said and hung up. How could I resist watching her order five-ply yarn from halfway around the world? How exciting. Yet, if she said ordering more yarn was important, I decided, it was. She'd explain the finer points when she felt like it.

My old jacket was hanging limply over a chair. It was not a pleasant jacket. It was stained with blue ballpoint ink and smudged gray graphite. It needed cleaned. The cuffs had frayed. I threw it on, grabbed an extra pair of reading glasses, my netbook, mechanical pencil and a notebook, and shoved them all into a canvas shoulder bag with a Vietnamese noodle-house logo that had been mostly worn off. There was a small camera in my jacket pocket. That was about all my equipment, except for an old Zippo lighter that had belonged to my father and that I found useful on the street if I needed to light a source's cigarette.

Ordering Yarn from Wales

The subsurface locks of the Avaluxe's glass doors smacked open and then closed. She was out of the kiosk and up the stairs practically before I could get in. Her blue robe caught the air and there was a glimpse of loud pink and lime-green wool socks over muscled calves and bare knees. She didn't say a word or look at me. But I was greeted by her proxy, Methuselah the cat, who followed me in and led me up the stairs to No. 8. The big oak door – by that I mean the door is about ten feet tall, wider than normal and made of solid oak – was open about five or six inches. The cat momentarily came alive and burst through the door, leaped onto a low round table in the left corner of the room, and slid to a stop. He then went to sleep sitting up.

The Yarn Woman was now seated near the windows that looked down on the western side of the metropolis, and a gentle rain had begun. Her thin blue linen robe was loosely tied. Her hair was up, of course, her face calm, her emerald eyes soft but quite awake. Who on earth could look so nice at 2 in the morning? I took comfort in the slight shadows beneath her eyes.

The rain may have been nothing more than the surf spray carried inland on the wind, but it hissed lightly against the windows, creating a sound like that of the distant, brushed cymbals of a jazz drummer. There was an open laptop computer near the cat and I assumed she'd started her official report for the sheriff's department. The screen was sleeping, like the cat. Ruth, at the opposite corner of the room where the cathedral windows met her wall of books, was now seated at a small round, marble-topped table with the antique phone. She raised her hand in a wave as she dialed the last of a long series of numbers, something that anyone else might have done by simply popping the keys on their cell phones. The rotary had gone around enough times (I assume in an effort to reach

Wales) that she woke the cat again. He meandered across the floor, leaped onto her small phone table and sat squarely in front of her, parking himself on the piece of lined paper and an old, half-sized catalog she'd just set in front of her, and stared off blankly the way older cats do. He pawed at the pencil – it could have been a mouse disguised as a pencil; you never know.

My many questions, of course, would only be answered after she completed her phone call, not the least of which was how she knew which yarn company to call in the first place, and, secondly, what scrap of information she was seeking in Wales.

"Yes," she said, holding the phone in one hand and gently pushing the cat off the papers with the other. But he moved back. She waved me to a seat near the window, a small spindle chair with a webbed seat. "I'm calling from the States. From San Francisco. Yes, I can hear you very well, too. Quite amazing. Here? It's nighttime. … Yes we do have earthquakes now and then. That one was 1906. Pretty still since then. (Brief silence.) Except for 1989. Got a bad one then."

More silence.

"First, I need to know if I can order five-strand hebridean in a Z-ply. That's the deal-maker, I'm afraid."

She waited.

Methuselah waited.

I waited.

Ruth stood and punched the air. She mouthed these words: "Got it, first try!" She blew me a kiss and sat back down, settling her bottom comfortably into a thin pillow for what I predicted would be a long phone conversation. She picked up her pencil.

I was enormously optimistic, even happy, though I sure as hell didn't understand what any of it meant.

"In that case, I'd like to order some yarn. How do you ship? Okay, great. … No, that would be fine. I'm actually ordering for myself and an acquaintance who didn't have enough to finish a project. I think she's already ordered twice and now she wants to add a cap. ... It's a gansey. Could you tell me about grams and meters, please? For the hebridean."

(A longer pause as she listened.)

"Natural. I think her last order was just a couple of skeins, with an equal amount in Z-ply. I think she might have ordered Z-ply alone a few months earlier, I'm not sure. Does that sound familiar? Could you check your records? ... Well, that's the embarrassing part – I'm not sure of her name. We've only met a couple of times at the knit meeting and I'm bad at names. We knit together once a month at the library. You'd probably remember the orders ... they were from California, about two or three months ago and the other maybe six months before that. I'm just guessing. The postal code would probably start with 9-4-0 ... No, I don't keep very good records, either ..." She looked at me, held her hand over the mouthpiece, and said, "I think they found her!" and then turned back to her note paper and the cat.

"She ordered from San Francisco?! Oh, that's great." She looked up and winked. "Perfect. There was nothing else from California, right? Oh, from Yuba City?" She was silent for a minute as the person on the other end of the line discussed the Yuba City order. There was, of course, no Z-ply. "No, that's too far inland to be her, anyway. I guess I'm lucky there's only one possibility. ... Just general delivery? Interesting. ... Yes, I thought she'd only ordered a few S and a few Z. You suggested how many? She should have listened the first time. Could you tell me her first name? ... Not a she? Oh, it's on *his* credit card? Of course ... don't you love it?"

She covered the receiver with her hand and said to me, "Oh, this is beautiful. This day gets marked on the calendar. You have a calendar, right?"

The conversation continued. "No, she was working on the gansey and she was just a bit concerned that her first order was of a slightly different hue to what she started with.

"The age of the sheep? I didn't know that was possible," she lied. "Well, people get gray, the tensile strength of the hair changes, why not animals? Natural is natural, right? No, my guess is she had a few skeins from a friend or something, and then ordered enough, including the Z, to get going. Yes. Really? Sure, I'll wait."

She looked up and said to me, "She ordered Z-ply only, and that was about two months before this last order of S and Z. So that would have been to go with her original stash so she could double strand the whole thing. Our lady has quite a record ..."

She tapped the desktop with her pencil.

"Let me get a pencil," she said into the phone. "Two months ago is about right. No, it's very helpful, thank you. Yes, well, for me I'd like eight skeins of Z and the same of S. And she asked me to get one more of each for her. Me? I'm still looking through patterns, but something with a decent collar. Okay, better to have too much than ... just a minute, I have a cat here who's interested in what I'm ordering." She nudged Methuselah off the paper.

"The cat wants some yarn, too. I don't know; that's what he just said. He's looking through a pattern book right now and wants another six skeins, not Z though, just S. For a vest. Cabled on double moss ... No, it's an old pattern. Yeah, the cat's old, too. Really old. We always modify them ... You, too? What do you do about the open arm holes so they stay down on the shoulder? (A very long pause.) Good idea. The Avaluxe, San Francisco. Apartment 8. You're kidding. I'm notorious? *You* should have called *me!*

"So how much did I just order? Good lord. No, no. I can always sell the cat. He's very valuable. Just ask him." She put the phone to the cat's ear and nose, then listened again.

She stayed on the line mumbling mm-hmm's and I-see's, and whatever the person on the other end was saying, it was profound enough to draw Ruth's tired face into a wave of pensive expressions. She finally voiced some extended courtesies and thanks, gave up her credit card numbers, and hung up the heavy receiver, shaking her arm to bring back the blood flow. She floated across the night-black windows to a small, very used red sofa beside the wide, low circular table. She'd have to sleep sometime, and she was pushing herself into the cushions as if that time were now. Sensing that, the cat came over and sat down on her.

All this, of course, left me seated in a little chair by the window. I stood and drew the tall drapes closed and settled into one of the softer chairs by the table near her. Already, she was breathing softly. There was no sense leaving, and I was unsure how I would lock the main door behind me anyway. By morning, I thought, I'd have explanations to both the phone call and her theories about the fisherman's wife.

An Old-Time Religion

"The fisherman's name was Thomas Royce Case," Ruth said. We were drinking a select Earl Gray at her round table amid sheet music, half-started knitting projects, half-finished sweaters and a half-sleeping cat, and the sun was now well up. She'd wandered off to bed sometime during the night (her room is behind the huge triptych bookcase) and was lounging now in her linen bathrobe. I hadn't been quite as comfortable, but it didn't matter. "Tom Case. That's the dead man. He's from here. I've already been downstairs and talked to Mr. Kasparov, who is notifying Deputy Avila. But I couldn't get the address without raising suspicions. I'll find it on my own."

I nodded. "He's from San Francisco, Case?"

"That's what they said."

She made it look so easy, but I knew her discovery was a combination of intelligence and luck. Not only had she been able to tell what was used in this so-called gansey – this, despite the dunking in seawater – but she could identify the breed, weight, and brand of yarn, the backwards spin. The luck part was that of the 133 orders that this small sheep farm in Wales had received from the U.S. in the last quarter, only one was from coastal, northern California for that specific kind of yarn.

But I wanted to know more of the man's story, whatever it might be, and how she could make such bold statements as to his troublemaking past.

She needed little prompting to begin elaborating on her perceptions, from the creation of the sweater to the destruction of the lives that hovered, like moths, around it.

"The story of Tom Case's sweater began with the ribbing," she said, "and ended with the ribbing … or lack thereof. That is, the sweater is a love story that began with passion and ended in fear and fury, in betrayal and death."

The sweater was completed in three phases, she

explained, which she could tell from the graying of the hebridean sheep over time. Mrs. Case had begun with yarn she'd apparently either had on hand or had gotten from a knitting friend. She ordered the backwards yarn, then, to begin the sweater. It was slightly grayer, though not to my eye. Perhaps under a microscope? She ordered a second time because she didn't have enough.

The fish was knitted into the design early. It was hidden because, she said, Tom Case must have ridiculed his wife's beliefs, her superstitions. And the tan strand she mentioned in the shoulder seam? "The strand," she said, looking briefly out the windows into the bright morning, "... was also observed by Mrs. Avila. Kate. This is the imperfection that will keep the roving evil eye away. It's very common in Middle Eastern carpets, and in indigenous weaving throughout the world. In fact, it appears in the fiber work of nearly every culture in some form. We have to keep the evil eye away from our loved ones, especially at sea. Therefore, we introduce a flaw: The devil doesn't covet the imperfect.

"This type of magical imagery, the fish, has been in the human family at least since the Lascaux caves 17,000 years ago. The fish and the off-colored strand are examples, anthropologically, of sympathetic magic, what we might call superstition. Her religion is old, a folk religion, as I said, and it's very much a part of her. Why did she hide the fish and the strand? Because Tom Case didn't share her beliefs. I can only guess that he was hostile toward that. He probably ridiculed her. She was still crazy about him when she started the sweater, but she was afraid of him. That's why I say he was a rogue, might have a record of violence. So she hid the fish and the tan strand to bring him success at sea and protect him as well. She secretly accomplished her goal against his will.

"Everything seemed to be okay, though, for a while. All the time she was knitting the body of the sweater, things were fine between them. But then," she said thoughtfully, as if recalling her examination in the lab, "then, the sleeves. I got to the sleeves."

I was waiting for whatever she was leading up to. But she had to warm up the tea first.

"You've heard the saying that care must be taken for the fire that burns brightest?" she asked, adding a splash of milk. "Well, the sweater is a record; it's the evolution of a love affair from its passionate beginning to its fatal conclusion. When I got to the sleeves at the crime lab, the tragedy just unfolded." She paused, pushed a lock of hair back up into the stack and re-pinned it. She sipped her tea. Methuselah repositioned himself on her lap and seemed disgusted at the interruption.

"Months had passed as she knitted this sweater for the man she loved. She'd finished the body, stopped at the collar, picked up the right shoulder and completed half the arm. I can tell this from the various grays in the brown. And then the tragedy occurred. He did something to break her heart so completely it could never be mended. He might has well have killed her. Maybe she was beaten. It's possible he betrayed her ... maybe, there was another woman. Or man. Maybe he was angry, threatened her, threatened her child, I don't know. We may never know. But she either feared for her life or was engulfed in uncontrollable fury.

"Mrs. Case returned to her sweater. She ordered the rest of the yarn for the sleeves. She used his credit card again, meaning she didn't have one of her own."

Ruth then described two ways to knit a workingman's sleeve. You can keep the sleeves short so they don't interfere with the fisherman's daily labors, or knit a ribbed cuff so it pulls tight at the wrist and you can push up your sleeves and they stay there out of the way. Without ribbing, she said, the cuffs sag, and they can get caught in machinery or other equipment – ropes and hooks, pulleys, nets and belts and saws and that kind of thing. But Tom Case's sweater had long sleeves and no ribbing.

"The style of a non-ribbed cuff is uniquely Scandinavian," she said, "but even so, it's only used with such items as mittens, not with sweaters. Somehow, this Scandinavian connection keeps surfacing. But on top of that, she actually increased the stitches near the end to make them sag more. I counted four increased stitches over the last three inches. That's almost a half-inch."

"He caught the cuff in some of the boat's machinery?" I said, mostly to myself. "But if that's the case, then she killed him."

"The right cuff finally caught on something," Ruth said, "and there was enough torque involved to mangle and tear the yarn. That's a lot of power – yarn has a high tensile strength. In some manner, Tom Case was pulled violently to his death by something grasping or catching his cuff while at sea. Machinery? The booms and gears on his fishing vessel? I don't know.

"I'm convinced he did something terrible to Mrs. Case before he died. I don't think she had a choice. I want to know who this woman is, why it seems that everything about her is two hundred years old when clearly she's young. And where is she? Is she okay, or is she a captive somewhere, waiting for the sand and tide to drown her? I believe in dreams, Nat, especially when the dream is the same – and shared by two brothers. Why do the Avila brothers feel so much fear in their dreams, like her time is running out? Because it is. It's running out."

One Clear Fact

It took Deputy Avila quite some time to confirm Tom Case's identity because there were no fingerprints, nothing a friend or relative could look at, and DNA analysis and subsequent comparison wasn't economically feasible under his current budget restrictions. Dental records would take a while. But he seemed comfortable with the proffered name as a working hypothesis, especially after he found that the Yarn Woman's description of the man was completely accurate in light of the information in his police record: twenty-eight years old, handsome (good mug shots, at least), extremely well-built, a troublemaker and rogue. Case was, however, unmarried, and no one at the bars, taverns and gyms had seen him with a wife or girlfriend or knew where the man lived if he didn't live on his boat. Avila sounded almost apologetic when he told Ruth that he could find no wife or steady relationship. Her response? "Mr. Avila, I assure you there is a woman involved and she's in great trouble even now. Have you told your brother I wanted to talk with him?"

He said he had.

On reflection, it was clear to me that Ruth's identification of Thomas Royce Case hinged on a single datum: She recognized the yarn – color, breed, brand and twist – used in the sweater. By mild subterfuge, she got Case's name from the dealer, and only time would tell whether her theory of passion, fury and murder might indeed be true. As for the invisible fish and errant strand? Were they supernatural charms? I don't know. For the moment, there was just one fact: she recognized the yarn in a world where there are tens of thousands of grades, breeds, thicknesses, colors and brands of wool. Hundreds of thousands, probably. She knew exactly what went into Case's sweater; but maybe that's not so unusual among the *knitterati*, and only to me does it seem supernatural. In a similar vein, though, I know a sports editor on a small weekly newspaper who can remember the score of every football and basketball game played by the local high school teams back to 1934, plus who scored what in which quarter. And I know a private art conservator who works with museums nationwide whose eye is so discerning he can identify by sight any of the 256 web colors and give you the hexadecimal name — all this while his actual restoration work is far more exacting. So why shouldn't the Yarn Woman know her yarn?

The tale behind the sweater was a little more difficult for me to immediately accept. How, for instance, did she know it was made by a lover and not his loving mother, I asked?

"What did I say about the welt?" she asked, but didn't wait for a reply. "I said the welt was tight to be more flattering, and the chest and shoulders were also engineered for optimum visual impact. The chances of Oedipus rising from the surf are statistically irrelevant," she said. End of conversation.

But wouldn't he have seen the fish, at least? Even I could see the carrying of the yarn on the inside.

"No."

"How could she fall in love with such a macho looser?" I asked, finally.

"Women do it all the time. That's why there's a human race."

"Why'd he wear the sweater if the sleeves didn't work right?"

"He died at sea. He was on a boat. It was cold."

Nevertheless, it appeared to me that the story told by the Yarn Woman, which ended with the imperiled lover — who Ruth was bound and determined to find — was the result of intuitive feeling rather than deductive reasoning. In any case, I accepted the notion that we still had to find that birthmarked woman, whoever she was, and that, if you believe in dreams, we had very little time.

The Akashic Record

It's been said that the immensely long history of the Earth is remembered by the sea. Every single incident over billions of years is logged in its memory, and even the ancient, clocklike movements of stars can be found in the patterns of the waves, or in the rippled, scalloped repeating shapes that they leave in the sand. The Earth, I suppose, is like a giant hologram, with its slightest twinge recorded for eternity. To Friday Avila, who spent most of his time on the beach (except in February and March, when the wind was too bitter and he took shelter at either his mother's or brother's home), the sand was like a hologram and all he needed to interpret its rippled mysteries, read the history of the world and the universe, was what physicists called the "reference beam." Alas, he had no reference beam. All he had was a penlight that he carried in his belt, meaning, apparently, that he could only read bits and pieces, the smallest passages of epic terran poetry.

But still. At least the creatures of mythology – the griffins and dragons of our past – are still reflected in the sea, and their footprints are occasionally visible in the sheets of sandstone that were, at one time, beach sand. Their lives, migrations, even their evolution, are carefully and endlessly noted. And if great Poseidon were to reduce his vast, Akashic memory to flowing, poetic script – something far more legible than the holographic patterns in the sand – surely it would be in the cliff writing at the beaches south of Half Moon Bay frequented by Friday Avila. But do we dare read it? No, because, like Prometheus seizing the flame, it would drive us mad. It would torture us and chain us. We would lose our minds. Unless we were mad to begin with, of course. Then, it might be interesting. And Friday found it interesting.

Friday, who spent his sun-damaged days watching the tides roll in and out, believed he could read the script on the cliff sides, and stumbled only occasionally over unfamiliar grammatical constructions. No one knew about his fluency because he was considered shy. In point of fact, though, it wasn't shyness but shell shock that ailed him, or PTSD, in current acronomy.

The cliff writing is a few hours south of San Francisco. When you're getting near, you start wondering if you missed it because Santa Cruz looks like it's getting awfully close; it's about twenty miles farther south. And you *really* lose track when Mr. Kasparov is driving the Silver Cloud. You can't feel corners in a Rolls. You can't feel acceleration or deceleration. He has a stereo that he installed himself because he can't abide anyone doing work on the automobile. The sound system is like standing in front of a symphony. But he plays stuff like Roger Miller or Allen Sherman if the Yarn Woman doesn't ask for something specific, which she always does out of self-defense.

Deputy Avila said that his brother, Friday, would be at his usual beach or beaches that day, two days after the initial interview at the crab shack. Though she finally rested the day before, Ruth was running on adrenaline and back-to-back Tasmanian Peaberry double cappuccinos. I figured she was in great shape to talk with Friday, whose emotional problems he treated with healthy portions of sea, sand, wind and coffee.

Friday is the man's real name. There's a story behind it, but he wouldn't tell her what it was. We saw him on a stretch south of the area set aside for elephant seal habitat. They don't breed or birth in the summer, though, and the only pinnipeds around were the more common and less dramatic brown sea lions and a few mottled, light gray harbor seals.

"Seals are interesting," Friday said, pronouncing the word 'inner-resting.' He was sitting in the sand, hiding beneath the remains of his greasy Puralator cap. The edge of the bill was beginning to fray. He was nervous, but it wasn't because of the Yarn Woman. His disorder from the war had been aggravated by exposure to weapon chemicals that were burned in the Gulf at the time. Basically, he lived the life of a homeless vet, though he stopped by his mother's house as well as his brother's — and the cafe — regularly but not continually. Some days he would go without food entirely. Other days he would eat five or six meals until he got sick.

Friday collected things he found on the beaches he frequented: agates, driftwood and strange rocks. Sometimes he fished. And he watched the seals.

"There's different kinds, you know," he told us, shielding his eyes by placing a swollen hand beneath the curled cap brim as he squinted from his sitting position. She'd already sat down beside him, and I followed suit. "There's the elephants, and they come over in November and stay until maybe April. I mean the pups stay until then. Six-hundred-pound pups, dude, you know? I mean, you should go to the museum. And there's California sea lions. They come here like crazy. They're all over the island. Once I saw a northern fur seal but no one believes me. One of the rangers called me a liar. I got arrested, dude!"

"Arrested?" she asked.

"He called me a liar, man. I lost it. And then there's the harbor seals. That's the traveler for you. You can find harbor seals that are born right here, but go on north to the Arctic and you'll find them there, and then curve on back down to Norway and even the Hebrides and you'll find the little scutters there. Scotland, too. And the other way around, too. You know? Nobody believes me, but that's par. But that's the only one I know that really travels. The harbor seal, I mean. So if you ever go to Europe, you'd soon learn that British seals are mostly grays, ringed and some harp seals. Bearded, hooded and, guess what, harbor seals, dude! I'm writing a paper on it. I mean, I'm going to.

"But they're philopatric, you know? It means that

they don't travel much more than a few hundred miles from where they're born. They like their homes and keep coming back. That's what they say. They analyze the mitochondria and they can tell that, they say. Well, I've got news for them: There's anomalies out there. Yes, there is. I know for sure there's some here from as far as the Scottish Isles and even Sweden. For sure. No one believes me. My paper'll set them on their butts."

She asked how he knew that. The sun was out beautifully, and the waves were softly lapping on an incoming tide. Friday had a tide chart in his shirt pocket. He'd cut the sleeves of his shirt out so he looked like a shipwreck survivor from the 1950s or 60s.

Friday lowered his head and looked at the sand as if he were a small dog she'd just disciplined. "I mean, you can't tell everything by science," he muttered, "I mean, there's other things older than science, like the old poems you find. Like the old poems on the beach, you know? There could be ancient writing on the beach for all you know. You know, and if there was, you know, you could read it. I'm just saying it's possible."

Ruth was passive, hiding the interest she clearly felt. I could tell because she'd gotten out her knitting and was clicking her needles. It seemed to have a calming effect on Friday. I wondered how long he'd been suffering from post-traumatic stress, how long he'd been back home, if he'd ended up somewhere else for years before returning, like his philopatric seals, to his home.

"Where do you read the old poems?" she asked curiously.

He waited. His right eye was watering, though the sun was to his left. Finally, he said, "On the sides of the cliffs, dude. There's some over there," and he pointed south, waving his hand as if stressing its unimportance. "I'd show you sometime if you wanted. But I'm not in the mood. Not in the mood, dude."

Oddly, though, Friday stood up and began walking

south. We followed, closing up the gap until we caught up with him. Away from the surf, the sand was heavily strewn with stones from sea and cliff, with a lot of chert and even an occasional agate.

After a few hundred yards, the cliff became steeper. It rose about forty feet from the sand. In two places, you could see fossil layers. The cliff was a mix of hard-packed dirt separated by sandstone. The sandstone fossil layer was ash gray and contained white seashells — mostly clams, snails and whelks. In the ancient past, shell upon shell had been deposited, and with time and pressure the silt became stone, or, as I scraped the side and watched it crumble, proto-stone. As the cliff side eroded, the sandstone had been neatly sheared off, showing the cross-sections of the shells. I had to admit, the shells did look like elongated, flowing writing, as if some god with a white pen had written on the gray stone. The lines were fine, brilliantly white, smooth, and beautifully curving. To Friday, they were an ancient text.

"If you look carefully, you'll find the writing. See? ... there's something by Rahman Baba right there. You see it?" He was pointing to a particularly elongated and delicate compound cross-section of thin-shelled clams and sea snails. They flowed in a line because the fossil layer had been so thinly pressed. He read a small portion of one of Baba's poems, and looked up at Ruth as if he'd proved his point.

"Khattak is here, but down farther, dude. And some Rumi. You'd expect more Rumi, but, I don't know. Maybe he wasn't as big a deal back then. No yuppies ... what can I say? They were all Afghans, though. You should know that. Rumi was born there, but he didn't stay. Non-philopatric, huh?

"Then there's the other stuff here," he said, pointing higher on the cliff side, "like the migration patterns of the seals. They're set up like tide charts. The whale stuff, like, it's incomplete. Erosion. I mean, but that's how they read, like, you get so far, and then, like you're missing whole columns. Like from a ledger, you know? Like from Hammurabi's library and all that. Right to left, though. I used to use a mirror. Ask Denny, he'll tell you I used a mirror at first because it was his shaving mirror Dad bought him. Until I got used to it. Read the old stories. Do you like old stories?"

She nodded. "Love them."

"There's selchies here, you know."

"I didn't know." There was no placation in her voice. A selchie, as I understand it, is something like a changeling, a seal who becomes human.

"Yeah, well, there are. Not many. But they like that old lighthouse attendant's building out there on the island." He pointed to a small island about a quarter mile offshore. There was an old stone building on it, barely visible for the low fog and distance. The island's current use was for maritime study by the state university system, specifically UC Santa Cruz. No one is allowed on it anymore. At one time there was a lighthouse and living quarters for two families. There were outbuildings and gardens protected from roving sea lions by fences. But only the shell of the main building remains – one large, empty gothic stone building. Seals populate the island thoroughly, thickly and continually, consisting mostly of California sea lions and a very few common, or harbor, seals.

"They say a harbor seal came across the Arctic from over there, and then swam down. I mean, if you read the script, that's what it says. That's counter to scientific theory, though, which says they're philopatric, like I said. I mean, their range is supposed to be only a few thousand kilometers. So they say. But the script has a different story is all I'm saying."

Ruth finished trying to read the fossils as if they were script. Then she straightened back up and asked Friday if he knew Tom Case.

"No. There's maybe something on him on the cliff. You want me to check?"

"Well, yes," she said, barely hesitating. Why not?

Friday wandered down the beach until he spotted a likely passage in what he described as the "Akashic record of the sea."

He ran his finger right to left along the curlicue shells, over the hard gray matrix, his lips moving as though translating with some difficulty.

"Thomas Mallory Case," he said, squinting. He had the middle name wrong, I noted. He didn't own a pair of sunglasses. "T. Mallory Case, it says, has violated the law, man. It's an old word for law that means, like, the unwritten law, like, you know? The Law of One? What the hell's that?" He pointed out the squiggled side of a long snail shell. "He keeps a soul imprisoned. It says here, let's see, '. . . he keeps a soul imprisoned.' Yep. A journey of many thousands of miles ended with imprisonment. He discovered her secret!" Friday was beginning to shout. His agitation was apparent and, Ruth worried, possibly dangerous. He grew more upset: "He found out her secret, man, and he hid it! Oh, man . . ." Ruth put her hand on his shoulder in an attempt to calm him down, but it was too late for that. His red, sun-battered face grew redder by the moment. His neck reddened. You could see the muscle cords protrude in his neck and the veins above his temples expand. She expected him to go into a seizure and the only thing she could think of was getting him over into the surf to cool down the psychological-physiological fever that gripped him. She pulled on his arm and found him to be compliant. So she pulled until they were both knee deep in the surf, then pushed him over toward the land and he hit the water face-first. I waded in and grabbed him and stood him up; he was tallish but didn't weigh much. He came up choking, but the cold shock seemed to snap him out of whatever his condition was.

"Dude!" was all he could manage to say between

coughing fits. Friday lumbered through the surf, making his way back to shore, and sort of crumpled up against the sand near the cliff. He sat there, trying to breathe regularly and staring off over the sea toward the seal island with its abandoned building as if nothing had happened. Then he curled his head over his knees and wept. After ten or fifteen minutes, he sat up and squinted at the sun. The bad dream had passed and I doubted he could remember any of it. It hadn't happened.

"He's a bad man," he said finally. "He was a bad man. It said his was the body I found. TMC ID'd, dude. Get it? It said there's not much time. There's not much time."

Ruth looked at me. "Deputy Avila and I were both wrong," she said.

I asked what about.

"Tom Case's middle name."

"But that was what they said when you called Wales. The name on the credit card. Thomas Royce Case, right? And it was the name on the police record, right?"

"He must have lied when he took out the card. And I haven't talked with Deputy Avila about the name on the police record. Yet."

I suggested she was taking for a fact what an imbalanced Friday Avila had interpreted from seashells in a sand cliff – Mallory – rather than the legal name on a credit card – Royce. She just shrugged.

Ramsey Snyder

The phone on Avila's desk buzzed. You could hardly see it for the scattered papers and folders. He picked it up.

"Avila. Yeah, put her through.

"Miss M, yes. Fine thanks. Okay, I have it here." He fumbled through some of the papers; he had the Case file to his right.

"Yep. Tom Case. What do you need to know?

"No. That was an alias he used five or six years ago. Royce, yes. Went by Tom Royce.

"His middle name? Mallory. Why?

"No, I haven't mentioned the man's middle name to anyone. My mother? No, Miss M, I have not told my mother Thomas Case's middle name. It hasn't come up. No. I haven't even seen Friday; I was about to head out and see if he was okay. Should I tell him? Is it important? Okay, then. All right. Yes, thanks. Day Eight. Right, plus the day in the water, so that's Day Nine or maybe Ten, I don't know. Oh, no. Nothing yet. We're trying to find a residence, but I'm short on manpower these days and I'm not getting much help from other agencies. Please, help yourself, but stay in touch. I mean that. Okay. Yep. Thanks." He hung up and surveyed the scattered papers, which he tried to put in order. He briefly wondered why he'd given her a green light to continue her own investigation, but he shrugged off her effect on him and went to get another cup of coffee.

* * *

By Day Ten, a summery July Thursday, Avila had located the home of Tom Case and through a mutual aid system had it thoroughly searched, courtesy of the San Francisco Police Department. Avila found nothing to indicate a marriage, and there was nothing in his apartment in San Francisco's Bayview that would indicate a permanent relationship. There was an old Dodge pickup in the alley and plenty of commercial fishing gear, including a few rotting crab traps stacked up behind a nearby garage, and a pile of old buoys amid tangled, aging nylon rope in blue and yellow. Legal papers? Questionable. There was no record of a boat or slip lease. The intent of the search had been to locate Case's next of kin, but there was no kin.

"He must have jobbed himself out to various fishing outfits," Detective J.P. Adams told me. "There's some receipts from Anchorage. Oh, yeah, and the Dodge had the registration in the glove box. Last year's." He showed it to me with a careless attitude. It had his name as Thomas M. Case. There were no bills in the collected mail, just junk that came to the street address. Maybe he had a post office box for the important stuff. Tom Case's living quarters gave every appearance of being only a temporary home while he spent most of the year in high northern waters, and the lack of bills in the mail seemed to back this up.

I left Adams on the battered doorstep of Case's apartment building. He never smiled, but did manage to nod as I turned down the sidewalk. Most of the cops worked with me to some degree because I'd never fried them. Most often, I just covered the city's murders and robberies and if any of the cases were bungled, they were quick to cover it up. Hence, no bad press, which in turn resulted in someone like J.P. Adams letting me in the door of a dead man's residence.

I met Ruth later in the Avaluxe lobby.

"Nope," she said. "If he was the rogue I think he was, he has his own boat. Two things I'm thinking: He couldn't take orders, and whoever might try to give him orders would end up with a fist in his face. Therefore, I suggest he had his own boat. Right? Right."

"How many days has it been?" I asked, changing course.

"Since he was found?"

"Died."

"Probably nine or ten, according to Deputy Avila." She sighed and shook her head. "That's almost two weeks."

"I'll start calling the ports," I ventured. "If he owned a boat, it has to be moored somewhere. I'll talk to the harbormasters."

* * *

The harbormaster at Pier 76 in San Francisco wasn't in when Ruth and I visited his small office at the docks, but rather than wait, she decided to walk around the slips to see if she could find him. She didn't, but she ran into Ramsey Snyder, an old line-baiter who kept a barely functioning flat-decked thing in a slip on the same bobbing wooden dock as Tom Case, about twenty feet farther down the walkway and on the other side. He'd worked mostly in Alaska for some of the larger outfits, but now, in his seventies, just set crab traps from his small green ex-urchin vessel in the winter.

Snyder was tanned from years of exposure and lean from decades of hard work. He was wizened like over-smoked salmon, minus the silver scales. He had a red checked shirt, green jeans and a formerly red billed hat advertising outboard motors.

"Ah. Tom Case," he said. "Don't like the man, myself. He's got a bad disposition, as they say, and not many put up with the likes of him these days. He has a nasty habit of shooting seals, Miss, or at least saying so. Braggadocio! And he's brought no end of trouble to the fishermen on account of it, Miss ..."

"M. Please, call me Ruth. This is Mr. Fisher."

"Him, I read. I tell you, none of us likes seals. They eat up the salmon and every other fish, but it don't do us any good to have everybody — the agencies, the public, even our own families – down our throats about killin' 'em for it. Tourism, you know. Tourists are good for the economy, now that fishing's so poor. Seal-killing? Not good, just not good. It's criminal, anyway. Federal offense."

"What kind of fisherman was he," she asked.

"Was?"

"He's dead," I said. "They've identified the body that was found two weeks ago near Half Moon Bay."

He thought for a moment. "So that body was Thomas Case," he said, shaking his head. He couldn't quite hide the grin on his face, though he tried to cover it by bringing up his pipe. It was a filthy old briarwood thing with a crack in the shaft. He kept the bit in with a twist of wire. "So you want to know something about Tommy Just-In-Case?" he said to Ruth. He squinted, as if evaluating her. He pulled a stainless steel butane lighter out of his pocket and got the pipe going, and since this was the third or fourth relighting, the fumes were particularly acrid. "I do not like to talk ill of the dead, so good day to you," he said, as if the stench of the smoke had made him change his mind.

Ruth wasn't surprised. She just stood and waited, looking over the boats, the yachts. They were just like the cars in the parking lots: a mix of rich men's toys and independent laborers' tools. Several minutes passed as she amused herself with the sights of the harbor.

"Well then, we'll stay to the point," he said, gnawing on the pipe and succumbing to Ruth's catlike ability to hover over a rodent hole until the end of time, waiting. "He was a dragger for years, four, five years after his daddy died. Then, right before the cutbacks, he sold that vessel – it was his father's seventy-footer – and got a good price, turned around and bought him a smaller trolling boat for near-shore work. Rockfish. There's, oh, eight or ten species that's viable. They just call it snapper in the markets. It's not snapper at all! Then the bottom fell out of the fisheries in general, but he's okay because he did this prior, and turns himself to near-shore rock-fishing. Now that's a fine thing ... keeps the fish markets in snapper, you know. And the restaurants. Fish and chips. He was either damn smart or darn lucky, excuse my Portuguese. Some say Tom Case's wife has some witchery in her and it was her idea to sell the one for the other. But I know that to be false, because he had no wife until recent, see, after the boat swap. Common-law, they say. She's a widow now, I guess, poor thing ... maybe not so poor if you ask me. Is there common-law widows? Sorry for her loss."

Ruth smiled to herself. There was indeed a woman after all. "Which boat is his?" she asked.

"Well, then," he said, looking up the walkway. "Still not here. I'd say that boat's been gone for a week, maybe two. Don't keep track of the time, myself. No need do. Boat's called the Doris, standard forty-foot troller, and the trim is green and blue but the white's starting to go."

They walked over to the empty slip, which Ruth studied thoroughly. There were three wood pylons extending from below the water to above the plank decking, and a thick nylon rope was strung from one to the next along the water line and a second strand about two feet above the planking, like a rail. Attached to the lower rope were round orange floats that kept the boat from being hammered up against the dock. There were a couple of extra mooring ropes, also of thick blue nylon, tied to the posts, and these were coiled up none too neatly on the dock. The end of the rope on the easternmost post had fallen into the water.

Ruth inspected each of the ropes — the two mooring coils as well as the end that wrapped around the east pylon and descended into the water. Holding onto the post with one hand, she put her other hand into the water and grabbed the rope. She pulled on it, and it came along for a few feet and then caught on something. She finally had to let it go.

"Do you know where he usually fishes?" she asked, turning around and rubbing her arm dry on her shirt. "I mean, is there an area that he frequents, or where rockfish fishermen find their fish?"

"Sure! He heads north four or five miles and works the Gray Whale Cove area maybe a mile offshore, and sometimes away north of that. But he's after seals as much as anything these days and I'll tell you why. Because he's an SOB, that's why. I'm telling you, no one will talk to him. He's a plague to us. That film crew come up from Los Angeles and give us a hell of a time over the seals." He removed the pipe from his teeth and then started thumbing down the ash in the bowl and fumbled for his lighter again. "Lots might shoot them, I guess, but Tommy Case blasts his mouth off about it. I always said, one of these days Dearest Mr. Thomas Case is going to lose him a slip right here, out of orneriness. All's it takes is for the harbormaster to pencil him out, and that day is surely coming. *Was* surely coming, and now, I guess, it's here after all."

A handful of gulls that had been wandering around on the planks started yelping and then took off, heading south. Snyder watched them fly off. "Tom Case, known by all and many to be a bastard," he said, "was after seals as much as rockfish, I say. Good place for that, up north. Or down south. Doesn't matter. I happen to like seals, myself. Like 'em very much, you know. Then, as the story goes, old Tom met his maker, you say?"

Ruth explained she was looking for Mrs. Case and that the boat seemed to be the only lead.

"But now you're saying the wife is still aboard the Doris," he said, in summary. "Not likely, says I, but as I am curious as hell, and as I have a fondness for the woman, I say let's go on out there and find out. I'd recognize his vessel at quite a distance, I'm sure. She suffered Tom Case mightily, I tell you, and I pray for her welfare. If I prayed, I mean. You can buy me some diesel at the harbor pump and we're as good as gone, hot on his trail." Ruth hadn't exactly asked for a boat trip up the coast in search of Case's Doris, but she wouldn't turn the offer down. But she does think ahead, and she was kind enough to share her Dramamine tabs, which I took without reservation, having been out on a boat or two like Snyder's.

Once we were underway, Ruth asked about Mrs. Case. "What do you think of her?"

"Nice enough, I suppose. Quiet type. I'll tell you, she's got the strangest eyes a man has ever seen. I think it's that woman's eyes that got folks talking. Now Tom, he never did bring her around much, you know. Some didn't know they was married. Thought he was single, and he sure acted like it."

"What do people say about Mrs. Case's eyes?" asked Ruth.

"Those eyes?" he asked, craning his neck and looking up from wheel, "They are so dark brown that you can't see no pupil. And what's more, you can't see no white there. Hardly. Two things, I say: You either think they're the most beautiful eyes you ever saw and they melt your heart away, or they scare the living daylights out of you like she was a sea demon. Me? Maybe a little of both …

"She nervouses people, don't you see," he continued. "One day that Tom Case shows up with her. Now, I don't know if they're married, but it seems like they are. That they were, I mean, if your body there is the remains of dear old Tom Case. If it is, then drive a stake through its heart – if you can find it – to make sure the bastard stays dead. Otherwise, he'll rise up and go out drinking and fighting.

"She's very quiet, Mrs. Case. Never heard her speak much of a word, but one day there on the docks I heard her singing … and never did I hear a sweeter sound. Like the voice of an angel coming from the sea. I don't know how else to describe it.

"I remarked to her that she had a lovely voice on that occasion, you see, and asked her what that was she was singing, for it sounded familiar. Well, she was very kind to me, but never did tell me the name of the song. It's like you've heard it all your life but at the same time like you never heard it before at all, if you take my meaning. That voice was kind of deeper, not a soprano, I'd say. Like an alto, I'd say. She's isn't tall, and she's neither thin nor stout. Last I saw, she had long, straight hair as dark brown as her eyes, but not black. And thick. Very thick, thick as yours there, Miss, but right down onto her forehead. And what's more, she's got stains on her skin. Birthmarks, I suppose you'd say, there on her face and chest, you know. A low-cut blouse she wore once showed some large dark-skin birthmark or other. Other than that, she's awful white-skinned. Pink-white, even."

"When was that?"

"What?"

"When you saw her last."

"Let's see then, that would be a month or six weeks I'd say. But I only seen her three or four times altogether. There at the dock. Maybe she brought old Tom some packed lunch or something, I don't know. I never could see what she saw in him. I mean, other than he was movie-star handsome and big like a weight-lifter. I guess that's enough, but she seemed smarter than that, that's all."

"What do people say about her? What makes them nervous?"

He lowered his voice almost to a whisper, and looked at the ground, avoiding eye contact completely, and said, "They say she's an odd creature born here among the humans when she should not of been. By which I mean they say she's a creature of the sea, and not a land person at all."

His gaze returned to the Yarn Woman. The he cracked a smile, as if he were kidding (he wasn't) and relit the pipe after putting in fresh tobacco on top of the stinking dead ash. "Now, I'm not saying she is and I'm not saying she ain't, but the older people say she's part of a seal, or as they say in the old days, a selchie, and they say it on account of her eyes. They can't look at her eyes without coming up with stories because they have a limited mentality, see. All's I know is that she does have them eyes, and that she's a quiet woman that has little to say, but a lovely soul. Very kind in nature. And yet, there is surely something frightening about her. An electricity in her."

"A selchie," Ruth repeated.

"A selchie. That would be a seal, Miss, a traveling seal akin to the islands, the British Isles, a traveler, that pulls herself to shore of a night, there in the dark, and sheds her seal skin, and there stands a naked woman. Or man. So they say. Old stories my mother told. And they live among us regular people plain in the sight of day, of course with clothes on, with their seal skins hidden away by the sea, for at any time they wish they return to the ocean in their skins, leaving behind children that are half seal and half human. And they say that, or used to. Not much nowadays, you see. The stories are, well, they're old.

"And men would find the skins and ransom them, take the selchies as their wives, and hold them from returning to the sea – for the selchies had no skins no longer, you see, and was hostages."

Snyder grew silent and turned his attention to his boat and the water. For a few gallons of diesel, we enjoyed an afternoon at sea, rocking in the mild swells about half a mile from land. There's only sporadic human development on that stretch of coast, and a lot of sand, and behind the sand, forests of green. The engine in Snyder's urchin boat clacked and at times hacked up black gulps of burned oil, but we were going fast enough in a headwind not to have to breathe it.

"You don't know what she was singing?"

“Nope. Don’t. But they say it was seals that taught men to sing, and that they may sing at night, alone, and that it was seals that learned people melody and harmony. Don’t ask me, though, for I don’t know. I only know what I heard as a boy. And that was a mighty long time ago.”

You Pick Locks?

Sure enough, Tom Case's boat, the Doris, was anchored barely north of Gray Whale Cove and close enough to shore not to draw the attention of do-gooders looking for troubled boaters. "By which I mean," Snyder said, "the Coast Guard and state park cops." It was exactly where it had been for almost two weeks.

The old fisherman cut back the engine and drew it up to the Doris on the starboard, near-shore side. Not waiting for us, Ruth climbed onto the vessel, hauling herself up nimbly over the gunwale. Snyder waited as she looked around. Nothing particular gained Ruth's interest, but she silently examined the deck's perimeter, ignoring the gear but looking under and around it.

The deck was blue-gray and thick with marine paint in which fine gravel had been embedded to reduce slipping. The gunwale was five inches above the deck and was trimmed with forest green enamel. About very five feet was an oblong hole through which the Pacific waves could flow from the deck back into the sea, and Ruth inspected these holes more thoroughly than anything else on the boat. She discovered a single item of interest on the perimeter: a rifle bullet. There were no clips, empty casings or anything else. The bullet had gotten jammed, point first, in a gap between the deck and the gunwale.

Less than three minutes had elapsed since she boarded. Snyder and I climbed aboard. She stood up and went directly to the cabin. The small hatch was, of course, locked from the outside, and the lock was a modern residential solid brass deadbolt with a heavy brass padlock above it. Snyder remarked that most boats had no locks. Sometimes they'd have older locks or just hinged latches.

"Tom Case had secrets," she said. Ruth removed a pair of thin steel rods from her bag and started to pick the lock.

"You pick locks?" he asked. "Shame I'm too old for marrying."

She looked at us quickly, then turned her attention back down to the two little pieces of metal she'd taken from her bag. "Oh, you know," she said slowly as she worked the metal. We couldn't see what she was doing because her shoulder interfered with the view. "I was studying some of the old Victorian fabric bags a few years ago, and got interested in the latches. Latches led to locks, and locks to the doors, doors to shackles, shackles back to deadbolts, those to a short course in locksmithing. You know the story. It's fascinating.

"There," she said and the bolt snapped back. Then she went to work on the padlock, and it, too, yielded to her.

The door swung upward. She looked down the short stepladder into the hold. It smelled unpleasantly, and the thick, damp air was unpleasantly hot. There were jackets hanging close on the right, and behind and below them were long-handled nets. At the moment she started down, she could hear movement in the boat's belly.

Ruth turned around toward us, took a full breath of fresh sea air and ventured down the short, angled ladder into the cabin. The dim interior looked much like that of a large vacation van, with a small bed, a collapsible Formica tabletop and along the walls were cabinets, high and low. But, small as the room was, it was clear it had been ransacked. There was not a drawer that hadn't been emptied, not a cabinet door that hadn't been nearly torn off. The bedclothes had been pulled up and thrown to the foot of the bed near the wall. Even the small rug on the floor had been crumpled up and tossed into a corner. What looked like cut hair was lumped on the floor near the end of the bed. There wasn't much room, and even less when you tried to get through the mess. It was clear there had been a great struggle in the room, surely between Tom Case and his wife.

Ruth looked over the wreckage in the thin light cast by the two veiled ship's windows. Her eyes passed the piled debris and fell upon the form of a woman curled up fetally on a sponge mattress that covered a built-in shelf-bed on the port side. A chair beside a small, fold-down table obscured a full view. Ruth, taking a moment to pull back one of the small window curtains to let in some more light and unlatching the brass-encased window to let some much-needed air into the chamber, beheld Mrs. Case for the first time. Even the small amount of sun the window allowed into the gut of the boat was enough to make Mrs. Case blink and agonizingly move her hand out as a shield.

Ramsey Snyder had not prepared Ruth for what she saw as Mrs. Case. It's one thing to hear an eccentric old fisherman describe the eyes of a "selchie," but it was entirely different to actually see such eyes, selchie or not, staring back at her in the half-light of an otherwise abandoned vessel bobbing on the ocean. It might truly have been a ghost ship. It was no wonder the woman spawned the rumors that followed her.

Mrs. Case raised her head to peer at Ruth. Her clothing was wadded on the floor, her skin glazed with sweat. Ruth wondered if the woman's body heat was responsible for the sweltering room – it had to have been more than ninety degrees, with no air movement or ventilation. The woman's unclothed body was a camouflage of pinkish white skin mottled with grayish brown from head to toe. Just as Friday Avila had described from his dream, her skin looked much like a dog's looks when the dog's fur is shaved off, leaving the multi-colored skin that lies beneath the multi-colored fur.

She lay on her side. She had a lock on her right ankle, the top one.

Ruth edged closer. Among the unfortunate odors of the small room was a thick animal smell, like a dog that had been caged too long. Was it her? Or did the cabin smell from years and years of fishing among sea mammals?

There were no whites to her eyes. And yet, rather than eliciting fear in the beholder, they seemed to be so calm that, in response, the rest of us grew calm. Snyder and I were still near the door, but I could see that Mrs. Case's eyes matched perfectly the color of her hair, which was thicker than any I had ever seen — what was left of it. She'd taken a fish knife and hacked at it. What was before us was an animal, driven mad by its captivity ... the clothes, the hair, the stench. I've seen birds pull out their feathers, or big cats and bears gnaw out large patches of fur in unfriendly zoos. The cage had been too much for Mrs. Case.

Ruth made her way through the wreckage of the room to Mrs. Case, talking quietly and continually to her. Once beside her, she looked at the woman's arms, her face and head and her shoulders as she lay there. She gently straightened a leg. Then she rechecked her, touching her occasionally but carefully, as if she might be a wounded animal. I realized she was checking her medically, looking for bruises, cuts and breaks, or tears. Mrs. Case, obviously in some degree of shock, allowed this without flinching; she watched Ruth as Ruth picked up one arm, talking to her all the while, replaced it on the pad, then picked up the other.

Ruth pulled a cotton pajama top from one of the open drawers and helped Mrs. Case into it. She covered the rest of her with a towel, also from a cabinet, leaving her right ankle exposed. Ruth put her hand on the U-shaped bicycle lock had been clamped on the woman's ankle with a chain extending to a post beneath the small bed. The prisoner had a run of just a few feet, she had water (though none was left) and a covered, galvanized pail, but she couldn't have left the hold even if the door had been unlocked and open. If she could have reached a window to allow her screams out into the wider world, it would have done no good: All of them were sealed shut with marine silicone except the one near the entrance-exit steps that Ruth had opened.

We were beginning to see the real Tom Case, and it was more than unnerving.

"Do you have a ballpoint pen, Mr. Fisher?" asked Ruth. I was struck by her formality.

I descended the short stairway, rummaging through my pockets, and turned up a couple of small pencils, a pen and some lip balm. I handed her the pen.

"I need Mr. Snyder's lighter and his pipe."

She pulled the pen apart and kept the tubular body of it. Then she lit the pipe and held the pen end over the wretched bowl, puffing the damn thing, blowing the smoke out of her mouth, warming the end of the pen over the tobacco coal and then pulling it away several times to keep the softened plastic from dripping. She inserted the end into the small circular keyhole of the bicycle lock and waited, letting it set. After half a minute, she pulled it straight out to see if it had sufficiently taken the key shape. Satisfied, she shoved it back in, pressed and slowly turned. Snick, and it opened.

Mrs. Case watched silently, then, when the iron U-bar had been removed, began rubbing her bruised ankle.

"I see that you found nothing in your search of the cabin, Mrs. Case. I'm sorry," Ruth said to the woman. Mrs. Case nodded blankly. I wasn't sure what Ruth was talking about. "I don't see much reason to look through this a second time; you've gone through it pretty well. Should we try?" The other woman shook her head. "That's what I thought. There's nothing to be gained. We'll have to look elsewhere. You're sure you checked everything? You could reach everything?"

"Not the window."

"Fine."

What had the woman been looking for? Obviously, there had been no scuffle between Tom Case and his victim, as I had surmised. I'd been wrong. Mrs. Case had ransacked the room herself, or as much of it as she could reach. The only unusual or incriminating things in the whole of the room were three rifle clips at the top of the short staircase opposite the hanging jackets and nets. The rifle, which should have lain quietly in an empty rack on that wall, occupying the top pair of hooks, was noticeably absent. There were a few big fishing rods in the lower pairs of hooks, and they'd been knocked part way off, hanging with the reels on the floor.

Mrs. Case, who seemed physically undamaged and reasonably composed under the circumstances, had leaned over to watch the lock-breaking operation. It wasn't until she sat back up that I saw tears streaming steadily from those other-worldly eyes. I remembered, then, what I had read somewhere ... I don't know where ... seals cry real tears. I couldn't get the thought out of my mind and, worse, realized I was buying into the whole selchie thing.

"They do," said Ruth, looking from Mrs. Case to me. Was she reading my mind? At this point, it seemed that anything was possible. "Dogs cry. Wolves weep. Seals, elephants, otters, lab rats. Even humans do, but only occasionally," Ruth said. She shoved the heavy links aside along the floor.

We guided Mrs. Case, half-carrying her, to Snyder's small boat. As soon as she boarded, Mrs. Case walked to the stern, stood silently for a few seconds, her back to us, and then walked off the boat. Once in the water, she shed the pajama top and rubbed herself down, rubbed until she was pink, trying to wash off the effects of two weeks imprisoned. Then she pulled herself back onto to the vessel, whose small loading area was only a foot above the water line.

Ruth had another towel and some clothing she'd taken from one of the drawers. Snyder and I remained at the cabin toward the front. Soon, we were all assembled at the cabin. Ruth pulled a cell phone from her bag, but it wasn't receiving a signal. We waited as Snyder started the engine and ran the boat south. The cylinders clacked and hacked happily. Tom Case's boat melted into the distance as we made our way south along the coastline.

The captive was dehydrated. Snyder had a six-pack of cola and four beers. Mrs. Case chose the beer. She ran her fingers through her chopped hair and rubbed her cheeks.

Back at Pier 76, Snyder pulled gently alongside the dock at the end below the public parking area, killing the engine while we were still twenty yards out and letting her drift gently in. He offered Mrs. Case his hand as she stepped up onto the dock, and she took it. He was very gentle. She recognized him, though Snyder said they'd seen each other only a few times.

"It's good to see you, my friend," she said. Her voice was lyrical; that is, it's very hard to describe, but it had a light roll or lilt to it. "Please tell me what you've heard about my husband."

Snyder looked at the ground, then back up and into her dark eyes. "We're of the mind that your Tom has been killed, and that his was the body that washed up there at Pidgy Point some days ago. Couple of weeks, the story goes. Listen, Dear, I tell you he was wearing a sweater, is what I'm told. I'm sorry, Mrs. Case, I'm sorry for your loss."

She sighed. "Thank you. Mr. Snyder, did Tom have anything with him? Or, was there anything, just anything, on the boat, above decks, when you boarded?"

Snyder looked at Ruth and raised an eyebrow. Ruth shook her head, and said, "Just this," which was the bullet she found, and she held it in her open palm about waist high.

More tears ran down Mrs. Case's face. "I mean," she said, "were there any seals on the vessel, above decks? Carcasses? Or in tow on the cables?"

"There wasn't no seals there," said Snyder. "And what you're looking for, well, only God and Tom knows that, I'm sure. I'm sorry, Mrs. Case. I'm really very sorry."

Seal Skin

Mr. Kasparov made a courtesy call to Deputy Avila to tell him Mrs. Case had been found. Avila was genuinely pleased and frankly surprised. Of course, once the law entered the scenario, things grew more complicated and Mrs. Case was forced to stay the night at San Francisco General Hospital in the city for observation. This was probably for the better because she was extremely weak after her imprisonment, and she was still dehydrated after we got off Snyder's boat. Her food had run out as well. But hospitals being what they are, Mrs. Case was ejected after a twenty-four-hour stay and Ruth decided the woman was still too weak to be alone. Mr. Kasparov was instructed to prepare No. 4 at the Avaluxe for a guest, and he went about his assignment quite joyfully.

Mr. Kasparov then arrived at the hospital at 10 p.m. and Ruth guided a very surprised Mrs. Case to the Rolls. She sunk back into the leather, but her hands remained clenched on her knees for the first few minutes of the drive. Ruth sat in the back beside her. By the time she actually began to relax, they were at the old theater. Its marquee lights were gnawing into the foggy night air, and the perpetual red lettering, crookedly spelling the word "orchid" and nothing else, greeted them. Ruth and Mrs. Case exited the car, and Mr. Kasparov continued silently down the old alley to a small garage that he kept.

I arrived shortly after Mr. Kasparov pulled off, having had to stop by the Bulletin to check for messages. Ruth showed the woman upstairs and brought her fresh pajamas and a soft shawl. They opened the big door to No. 4, almost directly across from Ruth's apartment, and, although I was standing some way off so as not to intrude on their privacy, I felt that Mrs. Case was pleasantly surprised at both the hospitality of a stranger and the interior, visual warmth of the room. Maybe I should say overwhelmed.

She slowly pulled the door behind her, leaving it open five or six inches. In moments, the room was dark and silent.

Ruth, alone, knitted through the rest of the night, lounging comfortably in the night-sparkle-lit No. 8, curled in the red love seat by the circular table in the far corner. I guess the rhythm of knitting helped her think. She suspected that Tom Case owned or rented a house – other than the rundown apartment – somewhere along the coast, perhaps as far north as Oregon. People like Thomas Mallory Case have many secrets to hide, she told me. But we both realized the possibility might not be relevant to Mrs. Case's current situation.

Ruth knitted and she thought. I began scratching out some notes.

Mrs. Case had torn up the boat that imprisoned her, looking for what Ruth had begun to call "it," searching madly.

She knitted and she stopped thinking. Then she stopped knitting and just thought.

Surely the Bay View apartment would also have been ransacked by Mrs. Case at some point – that is, if she knew about it. It was irrelevant because the police had gone through it thoroughly. Nothing unusual had been found, according to my source.

Whatever *it* was, Tom wouldn't leave it within her grasp. She was rarely taken out in the boat, though, or she would not have had to search it. In a way, it would have been a stroke of luck for her, had the object of her obsession been stowed there.

Once again, the needles clicked and clicked. They were sharp pointed. She hated dull-pointed needle brands.

Click, click.

Whatever Tom Case was hiding wouldn't be in the house or the boat. It would have to be accessible, but only to him. If it was so important to her, then it was immensely important to him, and he would need access to it: It wouldn't be all that far away, then. Click. Click.

She dropped a stitch.

It was 4 in the morning when she roused Mr. Kasparov by phone. I had gone back to my apartment after I was assured that all was well at the Avaluxe, which was about 1 a.m. Mrs. Case remained sleeping in No. 4, oblivious to any human activity whatsoever. Ruth placed a note at her door in case she awoke.

Mr. Kasparov called me at 4:10. I was dead asleep. By the time I drove back to the theater, Ruth was fully dressed and very awake. "We need to get down to the harbor," she said. "We'll have to pull the rope up, the one I tried to pull when it got stuck." Mr. Kasparov, the perfect driver, was already dressed.

In another hour, we were standing at Tom Case's slip at Pier 76.

"There's surely nothing to be found at the residence or residences of the Cases, wherever they might be," she told me, testing the blue nylon rope at the end of the dock, "and there's nothing on the boat. We won't have any luck there. I think what we're looking for is at the other end of this rope." She held up the wet blue line. I, for one, had no idea what we were looking for. What did she think was down there? She pulled lightly again at the rope.

"At the end of this line," she whispered, "we'll find a seal skin preserved in a waterproof case of some kind, weighted with, I'm sure, a common lead-ball sinker or iron anchor in the fifty- or hundred-pound range.

"The skin will be from a harbor seal. It'll be lightly colored with darker splotches on it, much like the pattern apparent on Mrs. Case herself. Her entire body is mottled."

Dramatically, she bent down and grasped the rope to heave it up. This section of the dock had a substructure of poles and pylons, and the end of the rope seemed to be caught on the timber crossbars below. She struggled with it for a few seconds, and then I also took hold and planted my feet. But we could gain no more than the same two or three feet.

She looked back at Mr. Kasparov. He moved over silently and took hold of the thick mass nearest the edge of the dock. Ruth and I still had a hold.

"We will pull on this together," he suggested. Ruth pulled up the two feet of slack and again hit that solid stop. Mr. Kasparov planted his polished black shoes on the weathered, cracked surface of the dock, and began to pull and lift. He applied a slowly building pressure to the rope that strained the docking itself. The man was amazingly strong. It made me think of Victor Hugo's Jean Valjean. First the planks on which we stood creaked and groaned. I could hear a series of small snaps and cracks all along our feet and at the edges where the planks were attached to the understructure. Then there was a strange vibration that rattled through the wood beneath my feet, and we wobbled forward and then backward as if the water were moving us.

I was sure the underwater timber framing was giving way. Mr. Kasparov continued to pull. I could feel the decking move. Then there was an enormous crack far beneath the surface of the water, like a boom and a deep-sea echo that you could feel rather than hear, and the impediment gave way, allowing us to pull the rope up hand over hand. We reached the end, pulling in two round, fifty-pound lead weights and metal box the size of a large aluminum camera case.

"Thank you Mr. Kasparov," said Ruth. "We can open it later." She took the case and let the rope slip back over the planks into the water. The weights remained on the dock. Mr. Kasparov wrapped the case in a plastic bag, then a blanket, and placed it in the trunk of the Silver Cloud, where it seemed very small, but, like ounces of gold, hugely consequential.

Mrs. Case

Mrs. Case was awake when we returned. She'd located the small downstairs kitchen and throttled a few eggs into a mash beside two pieces of profusely buttered toast. She was seated in the corner of the lobby near the wide door to the kitchen.

Although she knew nothing about our search for her peculiar Holy Grail, or that such an object would be housed in a modern aluminum suitcase, she immediately knew what the case contained and came to her feet abruptly, almost choking in consequence. In a moment, though, she regained her composure and sat back down; the relief that passed through her permeated the room. She sat at an angle in her chair, facing us. Ruth unceremoniously handed her the box, and we all took a seat near her in that corner.

The latches were locked. Her face grew frustrated and just for a moment I thought she'd panic. But she swallowed it back, looking at each of us as if we had the solution to the twin locks. I have no doubt that Ruth could have sprung them, though they were combination and not key locks, but Mr. Kasparov produced a short mechanic's screwdriver from his jacket pocket and forced the lid in a few quick movements, bending the metal. There was a smacking sound as a waterproof seal along the edge of the lid loosened its grip.

Mrs. Case slowly opened the lid. She pulled at a zipper-type yellow diving bag in the case, and opened that also. Because of the position of the lid, only she could see the contents fully, although I was able to catch a few inches of the interior and could see the diving bag. She spread open the yellow plastic and said nothing. There was no change in her expression.

She gingerly began to remove the contents, but I saw only yellow from my angle. I don't think the others could see as much as me. I looked up at the woman and it was clear to me that she was holding what she had long sought, almost as if she'd found a lost child. The vision was so unnerving that I felt a brief upwelling of nausea and turned away. Mrs. Case then tucked it back into the bag and removed the bag from the case. The bag, the size of which could have held a lap-sized blanket, the kind the elderly might use, remained in her lap, and the case was closed and set at her feet, to the side.

Shortly, Mrs. Case began to talk quietly to Ruth. Mr. Kasparov and I seemed not to exist. For the return of the Grail, it seemed, she offered Ruth her story. Her voice was somewhat rough at times, as if she might have a cough or was getting over one. But beneath that, the tone was, for want of words, musical. Or songlike. It somehow matched the dark, wide oval of her eyes.

"We came out of the sea down there," Mrs. Case began, referring, with a wave of her arm, to the southern beaches. She described the submarine fingers of rock and sand, and how they felt their way below the water's surface in the living dark, and how these formations gave way to the rock spurs and sand of the long beaches, and to the cliffs and finally to the roads and habitations of men. "We could run in the sand in the dark, or some nights under the moon ... under the white light from the moon. And it was so quiet, except for the hiss of the surf. There were a few of us, and we had the wind and the sea with us – the rush and roar of the sea that you can never hear from under the water.

"We often swam north and south for miles, through the rocks underneath and in between the crags when they thrust into the air, and we moved more quickly when we passed the harbors along the way because they were dangerous. A few of us began to watch the inlets where the boats were moored. It was very dangerous to delay our travels by lingering near the harbors ... or to be seen near the boats when they were out fishing. We all knew what it meant to be seen. The guns came out."

She sighed. "We often leave the sea at night. In borrowed clothes, we walk the streets of little towns near the water. We all have, we've always done this. New country, old country, it doesn't matter. We're pulled to it. Once you have had the freedom of running along the sand, of walking amid the lights of the houses, of being with the people in a warm and lighted room, well … How can I tell you about the miracle of having fingers?

"The water there," she said, lifting her arm to point generally south, indicating the coastline, "is at the edge of a cold channel, where the fish go up, especially in the winter, and you can lay suspended in the sea and rise and fall with it like the fishes in the kelp, and your head is just above the water.

"He knew. He saw us once, from his boat, on the beach. I know it was him. Then he saw me from his boat, at sea, at the inlet one night. He was fishing at night. No one else was out. He used to sit there for hours, rising and falling with the waves.

"And then at dusk one day, standing on the shore in the dusty light that the orange sun leaves when it sets, I saw Tom on his boat. It's so sad. That was the end of me. I couldn't keep away. Was it his smile? All of me followed his every move, even though my spirit rebelled.

"I don't know how much he knew about me, about my situation. But he knew I had a secret. He didn't know what. I don't think he ever made the connection. He didn't believe in things, in superstitions. In me or the people of the sea ... or in anything. But he found my skin that day. I can't imagine what he thought … he never said a word about it. I had left it so foolishly folded on one of the rocks. But good lord, we all did that. Forever. That's what we do. He didn't know what it was but he understood it – I mean he knew what it was, of course, but not what it really was, that it was … me. But he knew it was dear to me. I guess that's all he needed to know. His suspicions grew, but he didn't understand.

"He knew enough to hide the skin, and he hid it well. What could I do? I couldn't control my emotions. He owned me, with or without the skin. It's happened to us before. It's happened. I accepted my fate, I suppose. No fate could have been more bitter or more sweet.

"I began working on a sweater for him. I had been knitting one afternoon with some of the fishermen's wives. We usually met at Mrs. Galloway's. She even gave me the first few balls of yarn. I ordered a reverse-twist from the same people, for I knew just what to make him. I started it from some memory or other from long ago. But there wasn't enough, and I eventually had to order more of the same yarn, both types, for the sleeves.

"I had already finished the ribbing and the welt. How well I could remember this pattern! It was as if I had seen it all my life. The people of the sea have memories, you know, and it was mine, or my mother's or my grandmother's memory. They are all the same to us. They're handed down. The wraps of those fishing families were always blue and tight — not as waterproof as a skin, sure — and never did they wear anything different over all the years and the centuries that live in my memory. They were good people … good women, good men. But the men were killers; we had to remember that.

"So I began the sweater with what Mrs. Galloway had so generously given me. I didn't pay her — no money," she said. She shrugged in the silence that had engulfed us, and then continued. "And I wanted Tom to have luck fishing, but he would have none of my thoughts. He was afraid and wore a silver cross on his neck. I told him I would knit something into his sweater for luck, and he hit me. So I hid the fish. I had to save him from the sea, I said, and he hit me twice. He's not like me, and I knew someday the sea would bat him dead with a single wave. How many times have we seen this? I stitched in a piece of yarn I'd borrowed from Mrs. Galloway's knitting basket one afternoon when we were knitting together. I knew it would keep the devil away.

"One day I went with Mrs. Galloway and several others to the beach, north of the big bridge, the big Gate. A sort of picnic. Tom didn't know; he thought I was at home at the apartment. Mrs. Galloway and the others left, something seemed to hold me back, and I got a ride up the coast, in a car. I never went anywhere, usually. I knew where he was ... I could sense where to go. They let me out of the car when I asked, and I walked down to the surf. Walked for three or four hours altogether, first getting away from the road, and then south along the sand. I saw his boat anchored not far out, and I could see Tom as he was working on his gear.

"I was going to wave, but just as I raised my arm he left the deck and went below. I looked around south and to the left of me, and there were some of the seals there in the water, the people. Their heads were visible above the surface. And Tom came out with his rifle. I knew what he meant to do. How could I not know? But how could I not have known this about him? How could I have been so blind? It was late and no one was on the beach except me; I'd walked down from the highway.

"Tom!" I yelled. "Tom!" and he saw me immediately, and ran down below with the rifle and returned to the deck.

"Then everything changed. It was as if I had come back into myself, that I was myself once again, and not the prisoner of this man. I was so incredibly sad and lost, as if the line that held me in the world had snapped. He treated me worse and worse – I'd seen through his masks. He couldn't stand me knowing who he really was; I began to hate him. Time went on. I knew he had begun to hate me.

"Days went by and weeks went by. Without my skin, I could never leave his world, but still he locked me in the apartment anyway. Or he took me along on the boat, never letting me free of him. I was a prisoner.

"I didn't have anything but the knitting. I finished the

shoulder. I picked up the stitches at the first armhole. I knitted the gusset and the arm. I passed the elbow and added just a few stitches to make it wider, just a little. And cast off. Next armhole. Next sleeve, cast off. I left it on the table, of course.

"What could I do? I had learned what he did. I knew which of my people had vanished. I was his prisoner. How could I let him continue?" She paused again as if awaiting our response. There was none. "I knitted the sleeve wide, and the cuff wider. And he took it and wore it. I could nearly see him strutting around the docks and taverns. For barely more than a week, he wore my sweater.

"And one day, he was working on his boat. I was with him, not at the apartment this time. He didn't want me out of his sight. He sent me below and put the chain on my foot again. I realized he was going shooting or he wouldn't have done that. He had the sweater on and there was a cold, wet wind that day. I heard the gun discharge three times, and with each crack I knew a bullet was taking the life of one of us. I mean, I don't know if he hit any of us those three times. I don't know. Mr. Snyder didn't see any of the people hooked to the boat or on deck. That is right? Is that right? I don't know if he was a good shot. I heard him drop some of the bullets; his hands must have been very cold. Then there was a louder crack. Something had dropped on the deck; maybe one of the clips for the old rifle.

"I was below, but it was as if I could see him. He had to reach down nearly to the water because one of the ropes, one of the buoys fell over when he was reaching for the bullets. He had to reach down and down to try to grab the rope.

"One of the people was there in the estuary. I know which one. His head was barely above the surface, enough to watch the boat. I heard the clip, heavy with bullets, hit the deck and I knew Tom crawled down after it and I heard the rope hit the water.

"The ... out in the water, several of the people followed his movements. I know the ones and the one. He snapped his fins and whipped around, leaping out of the water just enough to hit Tom's arm above the surface, and he clamped down hard, trying to get the wrist of him, but managed only to get the sleeve. My sleeve, dangling there under the wrist and hand. And the seal put his weight behind it, knowing this was the only chance, and pulled him in. The others were there in the water and they came quickly, snapping at him, looking for the soft area just like a fish. There were seven seals. He fought. They finally just held him under.

"Then they hauled him out a way and let him drift. The current pulled him south. The rifle had fallen into the water and sank. The bullets sank to the bottom, too, I think. I couldn't see this; I was locked down. But I know what happened.

"He'd left me locked to the table. I was very sad. I knew he wouldn't be back, though, because when he left to go above, he said goodbye. He never said goodbye ... he never said that. There is always something that lets you know. I knew it was good-bye. So I sat, for a day and then more days. I lost track of time. I had killed him. I can't tell you ... It didn't really matter if I had to pay for that. A few more days passed. And then you unlocked the cabin door. I could hear the clicking in the lock."

To the Sea

At Mrs. Case's request, Ruth and Friday had accompanied her south to the seal grounds where the island and its lone, abandoned lighthouse can be seen from shore, where the sonnets of the sea are written in white on the gray cliff side. But, really, they're not recorded for the pleasure of men. "It's more the sea writing for the sea," Friday said. "So it won't forget. … Do seals have broken hearts?"

Mrs. Case nodded, her smile saddened. The yellow bag was in her lap. They sat and watched the tide and listened to the million voices that rolled in on saltwater. They sat in the sun and wind. Mrs. Case leaned into Ruth as they sat, but spoke to Friday.

"Will we see you again?" Friday asked.

"I'll see you," she said.

The day passed as they walked and laughed. And then, when the moon first rose, she walked toward the water. The darkness encroached on all sides, and they could barely see Mrs. Case. As a dull silhouette in the moon glow, not far from the sparkling, obsidian surf, she removed her clothing. Friday turned his head, knowing he shouldn't watch. He'd read that somewhere – not to watch. But Ruth didn't turn her head. There was no need.

And then Mrs. Case was simply gone. The shallow waves pulled her clothes from the sand and they vanished, too.

In the moonlight, they could see her small, human footprints in the sand all the way to the water. They glistened as if they'd been filled with starlight. Friday was very sad. The tide was retreating, so the path was long. It was direct, veering neither left nor right. It went into the sea and it didn't return. Only foam, what old sailors called meerschaum, tumbled in rough balls up from the water's edge and rolled along the sand, losing bits and shreds as it left the sea, until at last they vanished. The froth looked very strange in the moonlight, and slightly green.

THE BOY
IN THE
MIST

At First Sight

She sat in the sand at Ocean Beach on San Francisco's Pacific side, her knitting bag beside her as she stared out into the fog and the bright, refracted sun that tried unsuccessfully to hide behind the mist. In her bag, which had tipped to the side, was a half-finished crimson sock, beaded above the ankle, and Neruda's Odes to Common Things, which was falling out. The book and sock were each marked – the sock with silver ringlets that designated the beginnings of the rows and cables and the end of sanity, in a tightly knitted pattern, and Neruda with a eucalyptus leaf she'd picked up on her way to the beach, marking page 75, regarding an ode to his socks. She'd been there for hours, ignoring the walkers, runners, dog walkers and puddle surfers. She read, knitted, watched the water and the bright gray horizon, and listened to the wind – when the direction's right, you can hear the sea lions barking below the Cliff House to the north, their voices drifting in as if from another world.

Uri Mr. Kasparov, the Ukrainian refugee who caretakes the old theater where she lives and who had taken it upon himself some time ago to drive her around and generally watch after her, had called me: He was convinced she wouldn't mind a cappuccino, and could I possibly deliver it, "you see, to the beach?" My night shift at the Bulletin was over several hours ago, but I was intent on some research and hadn't left work. I was definitely inclined to visit the beach and pick up a coffee on the way, and then take my usual late-morning nap.

By the time Ruth M, the Yarn Woman, looked up from sand and sock, the Pacific mist had crawled steadily closer and wavered at the water's edge, uncertain if it should crawl closer still or retreat. And at the edge of the mist was a boy about the age of five or six, as hesitant and translucent as the vapor but as undeniable in his presence as the unsuccessfully hiding sun. Water dripped from his dark curls. His beach trousers were cut off at the calves and the cloth had been turned up twice, the cuff crudely sutured with millinery cord so coarse and a needle so thick that you might use them to stitch two sides of a cow together if you had the strength.

His ankles were scratched and bruised and very thin. They were clotted with blood up near the cuff, about mid-calf, but the surf had washed away the red near his ankles. Overall, he appeared malnourished. He wore a long-sleeved white shirt that was far too large. It was stained and dirty and the pocket was torn off. His right wrist was oddly bent, and he tucked it up into his sleeve, which was too long for anything except hiding the deformed wrist. When he played on the beach (which was not often), sometimes he shoved it into a back trouser pocket, though the pockets were always wet and never an easy harbor.

His complexion was dark, his hair dark brown tending toward red. His eyes were large and hazel-colored, and, set in a serious, swarthy face, appeared bright and piercing.

Images of sweat-houses and child laborers zipped quickly across Ruth's field of vision, seemingly out of nowhere. Songs of slavery echoed in her ears and were gone, sucked back by the retreating surf. And here, again, was the child with the twisted joint, as if he'd been cursed with an old man's arthritis. She watched him place a rock in that hand, clench it tightly, and then search the sand for similar rocks, which he readily found. They were porous gray sandstone with various embedded shells, mostly clams. These were the fossils of Ocean Beach; modestly interesting and fairly common, though you did have to pay attention if you wanted to find one.

By the time he got near enough, she could hear his high voice. He was singing show tunes – songs from musicals he'd picked up from somewhere. He was very intent on piling sand into mounds and getting as wet as possible as he worked his way farther and farther into the surf, singing "The Song of the Jellicles" from *Cats*. The poppish song seemed drastically inconsistent with the boy's ethereal presence, but, she thought, the show must apparently go on.

I delivered the coffee and sat beside her, sharing an old towel she was sitting on to keep the sand from creeping into her clothes. Eventually, the boy came over and sat on her other side, neither singing nor talking at first, or paying much attention to her at all, just sitting there with himself as his best company and with her, Ruth, as some sort of surrogate for warmth. When he finally spoke, he talked about his desire to have a shirt like one he'd recently seen, solely addressing her but at least not offended by my presence. Yes, he'd be interested in that shirt – an orange, Hawaiian-type shirt that buttoned up the front, whose collar was loose and not buttoned down, whose sleeves were long (uncommon but necessary, under the circumstances) with loose buttoned cuffs and all of which was in rayon patterned with dark brown luggage stickers in various languages … but not English. He was insistent on the rayon and lack of English.

"But don't worry about it," he told her.

Ruth looked at him and rubbed her nose. She didn't dismiss the idea and she wasn't particularly surprised by this odd discussion from a child she'd never seen before and who had never seen her. In a way, he was like so many cats who simply found her company pleasant. So she explained that she would look for that kind of shirt – and she asked if he knew where, approximately, one might be found.

He said he didn't know, but there was something in his voice that said otherwise. There was no doubt that she was earnest in beginning a search for either the shirt or the cloth to make it from; so much so that I expected her to begin later the same day.

"Well," the boy said firmly, "it is not store-bought, if

that's what you mean. It can't have no labels," which itched, "no impressions on the buttons," which would indicate the maker (like Levis or Dockers) and therefore serve as inappropriately free advertising, and it should have "single-stitching along all-a the hems and cuffs" rather than double, which is the commercial standard. Finally, he said, voicing his thoughts to the surf, there should be no polo players or alligators or other emblems on the breast pocket, which should also be single-stitched, and the shirt should be cut straight along the bottom so he could wear it either tucked in or loose, depending on his mood.

She sipped her coffee. I had some chocolate things in my jacket pocket and opened them up on the Bulletin's sports section I'd been carrying around. He took only one; there were at least seven or eight. From what I could tell, he had described an old man's beach shirt, the type that was kind to the pot-bellied figure, except that it had long sleeves.

Where would she find the material? she asked. He shrugged. "I was just thinking, is all," he said. "It would be useful, that's all, and we'd have to hide it, I'm sure. Rayon is a very good fabric, and everyone wants it."

"Hide it from what?" she asked, staring off into the day-fog and setting her cup in the sand.

The boy became nervous, as if he realized he'd just offered too much information. Why had he mentioned hiding it? "I don't really need a shirt," he said softly. "I have one. Really. Do you think it's going to rain? This is October, in the middle. Will it rain on Halloween night, or not?"

After she looked at the horizon all around her, she said it would rain for a week starting in three days but that by Halloween the skies would be dry and clear and the air would be cold. I couldn't tell if she was pulling his leg, if she'd read the long-term forecast in the paper or if she was a weather-witch.

“That’s great,” he said. He had no reason to disbelieve her. He pulled her hand from her lap and put one of his odd little fossil stones in it. He did it quickly, but, using his right hand, she could easily see his damaged wrist. It struck her as especially sad because his hand was so small. She squinted.

He stood up and walked around collecting a few more gray rocks and then wandered off, moving south with the prevailing breeze, and he was gone. The wind buffeted the wide brim of her straw hat. She wondered if the boy was a ghost. Or if he was the personification of the mist itself, or if, outlandishly, he was really anything at all. She looked down the beach but saw only a barren stretch of watery sand and moving fog and sea foam riding the edge of the fog like a finishing stitch.

Then, off with her hat and up with the hair, jamming two No. 7s in the knot from the top and side. Time to leave. She had a conference to prepare for. I gathered up the few remaining chocolates and sat there for a while before going back to my apartment in Oakland. I thought about the boy, but at the time I didn’t think I’d ever see him again and it left me with a strange feeling, like there was a hole in me somewhere.

Fallen Leaves

The leaves of October start out crisp and colored. Ruth always saves a few small red maple leaves and presses them in one of her fat volumes on cotton and wool textiles – or whatever, linen maybe ... her library is immense. The leaves can hide in the pages for months, maybe years, until she has to look something up and they drop out like paper koi escaping from a two-dimensional pond, floating down to the tabletop. After her encounter with the boy in the mist, she pulled out a book on the import and export of Italian rayon. She had some new leaves ready to go inside, and although the volume wasn't illustrated when originally published in 2007, it now had a dozen autumn fish mixed into the text and there were four or five more to go.

The hundred million leaves that don't make it into one of her books turn brown in a couple of weeks and grow soggy with the winter rains that come to San Francisco by November. The narrow sidewalk in front of the Avaluxe Theater, where she lives, becomes a blanket of red and brown mixed with the bright yellow fanlike leaves of a single ginkgo tree that grows at the end of the alley about five buildings south of the theater. They ferment on the sidewalk for weeks or months and when they finally wash away, their souls remain, staining the cement brown, and they really do look like shadows of koi.

Ruth was watching leaves rustle outside the glass doors of the Avaluxe as she sat in the evening working out the pattern in a three-button cardigan when she saw the child a second time. It had been two days since their meeting at Ocean Beach. The weather had begun to change, just as she predicted, and the sky was steadily building up layers of gray as it prepared for an autumn downpour – a rain that would last six or eight hours, back off for a day and then set in for the rest of the week, flooding most of the drains along city streets on both sides of the bay. A growing silence mimicked the spreading of the gray cloud above. You know it'll rain, she says, because if you can't smell it, you can hear it.

"Maybe the rain brought him," she said as she looked over to Mr. Kasparov, who was reading a Canadian paper he'd picked up a few days before. It was the Toronto Globe and Mail, his favorite from north of the border. He liked the Globe so much he might have paid for it, if necessary. He was a strange, large-nosed man who shut himself away for hours to read the world's newspapers. Sometimes he would sit in the ticket-taker's kiosk or out in the theater lobby, carving odd puppet faces in soft basswood with an incredibly sharp penknife. And then he'd read his papers again or comb the Internet on a small netbook that fit precisely on the kiosk's narrow mahogany shelf. On this day, he was seated on the far side of the lobby with a week's worth of newspapers and two days' worth of basswood chips. Most of the papers were in English, two in Russian and one was in French (not the Globe and Mail). The Moskovskaya Pravda, the Moscow daily, was spread open and littered with shavings; Mr. Kasparov was not fond of the Russian mouthpiece and he'd always apologize – to anyone – if he was seen in possession of it.

He looked up from the Globe when she spoke and he saw that she was staring through the cut glass doors as she watched autumn fill the alley with its leaves, with gray, and with silence.

He followed her eyes, and his fell on a boy who was standing outside the doors, moving his head from side to side, and bending his knees over and over, just slightly, as he watched the rainbows created in the cut glass of the doors. The peculiar-looking half-squats allowed the child to catch the bright rainbows cast by the door and by the crystal chandelier that hung over the magnificent north staircase inside. On a bright day, a hundred prismatic splotches might glance off the theater doors and splatter themselves across the walls and woodwork of the lobby. Outside, even the sidewalk and the sides of the neighboring buildings would turn colors. But not today. It had been too gray and was now too dark. The boy was relying on the dim lights inside the lobby for his rainbows and had to continually change his position to catch the colored light.

Mr. Kasparov, whose early life in Ukraine had never been simple, could tell a homeless child at a glance. He could see the child's young life for what it was without having to bother opening his eyes.

"Besprizorniki," he said quietly, using the Russian term for the homeless children who roamed Russia and the Soviet satellites in the 1920s, 30s, and 40s.

She nodded. She knew the old Russian term for street child. And she knew it translated with much more baggage than those two simple English words: street child. There had been hundreds of thousands of besprizorniki after the Bolshevik revolution and though Mr. Kasparov was a generation removed, he was nevertheless intimately familiar with that immense, little-remembered twentieth-century human tragedy because of his mother, who had grown up among the countless roaming, starving children.

The doors were unlocked. Mr. Kasparov rose to invite his guest inside, and though the older man moved slowly, even silkily, the boy flew off like a bird. There was always the probability of flight, Mr. Kasparov thought, but you had to try.

Ruth set the pattern book she'd been deciphering to the side, plopping it on top of the cardigan's cast-on, and rose to go and catch the boy before he vanished. She would invite him in … or something. She didn't exactly know what. But as soon as Mr. Kasparov opened the big glass doors, the boy turned and began walking briskly north up the alley, his boney knees bumping each other as he rushed. It was 7 in the evening and fairly cold, but she grabbed the heavy wool sweater from the back of her chair and slipped on shoes that were too thin for the weather and began following him in the dark. She whistled, trying to get him to turn around. He looked back but continued forward. She threw an acorn at him and hit him in the head, solidly, at twenty yards, but he refused to feel it. He rubbed his head, scratched his curls and wandered on.

They'd gone five or six long blocks west and then south, the boy occasionally breaking into a run to gain some distance between them and then slowing again, and Ruth was closing in when he suddenly stopped at a mound of junk in the street gutter near a drainage grate on Seventh Avenue. In the blue halogen glare of oncoming headlamps of the speeding traffic, the refuse pile looked like a crushed Halloween pumpkin and a sack of clothes and other trash.

As Ruth got closer to the mound, she knew there was something wrong. In fact, she wanted to stop, turn around and go back. Why had she left the lobby? She'd practically figured out the decreases but now she'd have to start over. She slowed to a stop about ten feet from the stuff in the gutter and looked around for the child. He was nowhere in sight. She stepped cautiously forward, as if she knew what she was going to find. She did; she was never wrong about these things. With the help of the car lights and the streetlight on the other side of Seventh, she was able to make out the form of a man lying face-down, shoved up against the curb like a fat sack of rice. She could see the back of his shirt; it was orange, like a pumpkin. She had mistaken his black jeans for a black trash sack. Golden-toe nylon socks covered his feet and his shoes had slipped off. One was about a foot away, and the other lay in the middle of the street, where it had been thrown. She looked at the shoes, the feet, and all she could think about was size eight-and-a-half or nine wide, extra-large shirt, forty-six-inch waist. There was blood pooled beneath the body but she couldn't tell how much.

She carefully touched him, but the flesh was already cool and stiff like clay. He'd been there for a while, though she didn't know how long; calculating the time of death wasn't her department. Her specialty was textiles, not blood. She stood back up and looked around again for the boy. There was still no sign of him.

It took her more than twenty minutes to flag down a car — several hundred passed by, marking the end of the day's commute. People in the Bay Area don't stop their cars for anything, not even murder. They don't slow down. They have to get home or to the bar, and some of not-stopping is because they fear for their own safety; it's not the kindest of urban environments here, after all.

Miraculously, nobody had struck the man in the gutter after he was down. Ruth didn't have a phone with her and was beginning to feel the dampness through her soft lounging shoes, which she'd jammed onto her feet as she darted from the theater. An old Volvo 240 finally slowed down, but the driver was drunk and one look at the body by the side of the road made him swerve back into the traffic and hit the gas. Two other cars squealed their brake as he re-entered, his engine roaring like a lion but unable lurch forward into the flow. Volvos, she thought. She looked down at the body, as if trying to communicate. "Mr. Kasparov is very disparaging about the power of the 240 series, you know," she said to it.

About two minutes later, a Honda pulled over. The driver, who was already on the phone, was in her early twenties and kept brushing her thin, light brown hair out of her eyes as she talked nonstop. She wore a lot of lipstick and her hair was stiff, as if sprayed with copious amounts of uncleanliness. But she did pull halfway out of the traffic lane and stop, which was surprising. She put her caller on hold, looked at Ruth, then at the man in the gutter and made the emergency 9-1-1 call. Holding the phone away from her face, she asked Ruth her name and then gave it to dispatcher. "Where are you?" she asked, and then relayed the location that Ruth gave her. Did she understand that she and Ruth were actually in the same location? Then she perkily said goodnight and clicked back over to her previous call, simultaneously pulling back into the traffic. She managed to keep chewing her gum throughout.

Ruth waited. She thought it would take about ten minutes for an emergency vehicle to arrive. In the meantime, she scanned the ground but didn't see anything peculiar. She looked around on the sidewalk but stayed near the body. There was a construction barricade on the sidewalk about fifteen yards north, so she hauled it over and propped it up near the body to protect it from cars. Ten minutes turned into twenty.

She didn't like the idea of staying so close to the body – Ruth is uncomfortable being around the dead if she doesn't know them – but she remained within about ten feet, studying the roadway, sidewalk and even the grass that grew at its edge. On the sidewalk, there were some leaves, and there were the tannin ghosts of leaves that had blown away. Man should be so lucky to depart the world so cleanly. That's when she saw the bullet casings. There were two brass shells – one on the sidewalk about ten or fifteen feet south of the north-facing body and a second in the roadway about five feet from the curb and north of the body. She pulled her sweater sleeve over her hand and picked up the casings, placing fist-sized bits of cement where they originally lay, and placed them on the curb beside the body. Then she moved the barricade farther into the road beside the chunk of cement. The resulting honking was ear-shattering. People were upset; something had interrupted their commute. Twenty minutes turned into thirty and still no emergency vehicle could be seen.

After a few seconds, she decided to keep the first shell, the one from the sidewalk, and dropped it into her pocket. She didn't know why she did it, but Ruth was way past questioning why she did things that seemed odd.

Then she removed the cement shard that had marked its position. Intuition is a peculiar thing: If you question it, you'll find it's timid and doesn't stand up to interrogation. It'll either turn and run, or rat out whatever's next to it. When intuition leaves, reason prevails once again – and you're left with nothing.

She looked for the boy again but her search was in vain. Finally, she could see the flashing red lights of the first responder about a half-mile north, coming rapidly in her direction. She stood out in the road as far as safety would allow and waved her arms. The vehicle was from the fire department. Behind it was the first of the police cars; eventually, when it became known there'd been a shooting, there would be seven and one from the state highway patrol.

She spoke with the officers, left her name and the number of the Avaluxe Theater (she never answered her own phone), and pointed out the shell casing and the cement chunk that marked where it had originally lain. No, she hadn't touched it with her hand, she said. And she left.

A day in the city. The nagging part, for her, more than the death, was the similarity of the man's shirt to the wish list of the boy on the beach: the orange rayon shirt. Even the pattern with its suitcase drawings matched his words of two days before. Odd. Well, actually not. Not odd. Not a coincidence. Ruth M had never believed in coincidences.

It only took a moment for her to realize the boy in the mist had led her to the body of his friend.

Streetside

Intuition is one thing; luck is another, and the Yarn Woman has her share of each. I've never understood it. But life is half luck, anyway, I suppose.

Three days after her encounter with the boy at Ocean Beach and one day after he knowingly or unknowingly led her to the man's body in the gutter, she saw the child yet again. Ruth was walking north on Seventh Avenue in the Twin Peaks district, having visited a shop on Judah and Tenth, and she was thinking about a cappuccino or maybe a mocha. Her driver, Mr. Kasparov, had remained at the Avaluxe at her request, and she'd taken buses to get herself south and east, wonderfully alone. Mr. Kasparov didn't like the idea, but he never did. He was her driver, after all.

The No. 44 bus was coming from the north and on the other side of the wide, much trafficked avenue. Behind it and mostly out of view was a vintage, half-rusted-out Ford Econoline van of a color formerly known as white. It waited behind the bus as passengers loaded and unloaded, and when the 44 pulled out, the van illegally slid into the red bus zone. If you're caught, the fine is something like $250. The van's side door opened and the boy from the beach stepped out onto the sidewalk, careful not to scrape himself on the rusty edge as the door was pulled closed from the inside. Then the driver cranked the van back into the traffic. He was a big man with big hands, older and African American. Ruth also caught a clear view of the man in the passenger seat: He was white, probably in his early forties, sparse or no facial hair, baseball cap with light-colored hair falling out the sides and back. He had a long nose. In contrast to the driver's broad, almost friendly face, the passenger's was pinched at the nose and mouth, making him look like a rodent. By the way he was seated, he appeared a few inches taller and a few pounds lighter than average. The windows were tinted with do-it-yourself dark plastic sheeting and had hundreds of air bubbles caught between the glass and plastic.

The van rattled away. She couldn't tell if there were other passengers. Her attention returned to the child, who was by now ambling north, the direction Ruth had been heading anyway. He was on the opposite side and about twenty feet in front of her, weaving from one edge of the sidewalk to the other like any child trying to waste time, though he seemed to know exactly where he was going. He stopped at the corner, laid out some junk he'd pulled from a canvas sack he carried over his shoulder, and sat down just off the sidewalk but in the line of sight of anyone walking by. Then he put out a beaten-up paper coffee cup.

The child was a beggar. The realization was troubling, and though she was already aware that he lived on the street or at least spent most of his time there, it was difficult to have her knowledge confirmed. Seeing him beg was like seeing the dead body on Seventh instead of just reading about it in the paper.

She walked over and sat down on the sidewalk beside him. The boy was genuinely happy to see her, though he did look around to see if anyone, God knows who, was watching. His heart was light: She could feel that. And hers became light as well. He had little bent-wire forms in front of him and an irregular ball of stripped residential copper wire and a small pliers. Mostly, he made animals, and they were pretty good for a six-year-old, especially one without full use of his right hand.

"So you have to be pretty careful about being seen by police," she said, sitting, observing the boy's watchfulness as the traffic whizzed by ten or twelve feet away.

"Somewhat. They can't see me from that direction," he said, pointing north. "And they're on the other side of the avenue in that direction. They never look across.

Hardly ever."

"Do you get caught a lot?"

"Not really. I have a card. I give them the card."

"What card?"

He rummaged in his pocket and showed her a 3 by 5 laminated index card with his name, age and the city-approved foster care-giver's phone. "They call and someone comes and gets me. Joey puts on a big show in front of them how I'm supposed to be in school, then he finds a better place for me to, you know, sit. I am a vender and an artist."

"Ah."

"I sell my own work. And I do commissions."

"I see."

The sidewalk was still damp from an early morning rain, but the sky was clear blue and a chilly ocean breeze dodged through the streets from the west. It kept down the smell of car exhaust.

"So, you know, are there a lot of you ferried out in the van to work?" she asked.

"Oh, you know. Four or five. It depends. At a time. Four or five at a time is all."

"And you live there at the foster home with them?"

"Some. Sure."

"Sure."

"There's eight of us right now."

"Wow. That's a lot. Who are the foster parents?"

"Eight all together. Joey Starling and Sabrina Something. Joey Starling, you know? He has Tooley drive the van most of the time, but he goes along. She cooks. Mostly, like, hot dogs. I mean, you know? I prefer all-beef ones. I think they, like, get them from the food bank and, kind of, the color is pink and yellow because they're a little expired, not just pink like the ones from Safeway's."

"Joey Starling drops you all off to, well, beg … or sell wire things?"

"Pretty much. Mm hmm. We have goal-setting, you

know."

"No."

"Oh. Joey Starling, you know, he's management. And, the rest of us, he calls us the 'guild.' He sets goals for daily. He keeps us all in his book. See? The goal is to bring in $30 a day as our minimum. Anything over, we get ten percent. Joey calls it 'tilting' or something. We can stay out for several days in a row, but we can't come back without the cash. He charges us $25 per diem for being absent. But that's how I save money. I mean, one of the ways."

"So if you make thirty a day and it costs you twenty-five a day if you wait and go back after a few days, then you can keep $5 a day?"

He looked up at her and smiled. "Duh."

"So it's really $25 a day."

"Duh. He's generous with the per diem. But Joey calls it thirty. It works like 'incentive.' Stay out and it's miserable out here at night, but you clear $5. Go in and it's warm, you know, comfortable, and you clear zero."

They sat in silence for a few minutes.

"What's your name, anyways?"

"Ruth."

"Oh. I see now. Like the candy bar. Mine's Gabriel."

"Oh, like the angel."

"No. Like the candy bar," he said, and laughed. She smiled.

"So, how long are you going to stay here today?"

"All day, probably. Joey's got bills due. But I might not go back tonight."

"Where do you keep your money?"

He looked up at her, squinting. "Why?"

"Wondering how you keep it safe."

"Not at the house. Not at the house. Other places," he said, his guard now up and visible.

"And then you might not go back tonight? And stay where?"

"I think I might go back. Channel 7 said it would

rain."

"So did I."

"I remember. Are you any good?"

"Pretty good. You are, too: You found where I live. Where do you live?"

Gabriel finished a neck coil on a small dog. Without another word he picked up his wires, shoved them in his sack and walked off. But he waved – that was a good sign, she thought.

Ruth sat for a few more minutes. It was one of those moments that could direct the future. Should she follow him? If she did, he'd probably get even more suspicious and disappear again. She'd lost his trust, anyway, with the where-do-you-live question – as if the where-do-you-stash-the-money weren't enough – and she decided the risk was too high to push it. Let this one go for now. He'd been on the street so long that one more day, or a week, may not matter. But you never knew. Life or death could depend on minutes, hours or a day. She didn't feel good about it, but at the same time she didn't have an overwhelming sense of pending tragedy. She had to trust her intuition. And she decided she had to trust Gabriel almost as much as she had trusted herself at that age.

She grabbed the next bus north and headed back to the Avaluxe. It was mid-afternoon by the time she arrived, and Mr. Kasparov had half a dozen yellow sticky notepapers cataloging the calls he'd taken for her. They were all from the police department. He'd stuck them very neatly in a column on the outside glass of his kiosk. He waved solemnly as she entered, his enormous nose nearly touching the curved glass of the ticket-taker's box.

"Our Detective William Chu," he told her succinctly. "He was very complimentary about your pervasive knowledge of textiles, and Mr. Detective William Chu has telephoned numerous times for you. He would appreciate you looking at a shirt."

"The orange shirt from the dead man the other night,

Mr. Kasparov?"

"Well, I don't know about that. There are a lot of shirts in this old city. Everybody has one these days."

"Here or down at the department?"

"He was very insistent. I relented. You have been invited to the Central Station for 'coffee,' " he said, stressing the quote marks with his fingers and looking at the small, solid gold watch on his thick left wrist, "in about two hours."

"I see."

"I suggest you take calcium."

"What?"

"You might think it's coffee, but it is not. Something for your stomach: calcium." She nodded but otherwise ignored the advice. "Are you inconvenienced, Miss M?" he asked apologetically. "I'm so sorry."

"Oh, no. No, not at all. It'll be fine. I have some questions for Mr. Chu as well. Two hours. That's okay. I'll have time to rip out the cast-on and get the thing back on the needles; there's a mistake in it. The whole thing's a mistake. Sometimes I wonder what the hell I'm doing. Well, then," she sighed, "how do you feel about giving me a lift?"

He didn't quite know how to reply. That's what he did. He was the driver. He always gave her a "lift."

"Of course," he said. "I am your driver."

Joey Starling

Ruth told me about her conversation with Gabriel and we agreed that Joey Starling would be a good subject of inquiry at this point. And so, I investigated. I checked the clip file and police records, and then hit the street in an effort to understand Joseph Lamar Starling, age 39.

I had some sources at the county Health and Human Services office, which oversees the foster care system, if you can call it a system. I'd tried to avoid it over the years because of the sadness. Crime's one thing … it's interesting. Cruel, harsh, even final, but interesting. The foster care system is just sad.

I began by using digital sources; this way I could get as much information together as possible before I moved away from computers and into the realm of flesh and blood. I contacted one of my solid sources at the police department, then moved on to HHS and worked my way through the systems that make our society work, or at least purport to. But really, most of the dope on Joey Starling came from his own neighborhood. People talk. In fact, people like to talk and the people who like to talk the most are either those with grudges or those who genuinely like a person. Joey Starling was proverbially both hot and cold, depending on whom I was talking with. But that's so much better than being lukewarm. I even managed to talk off the record with a few of his wards, and they were anything but lukewarm. For the most part, they liked him.

Joey Starling didn't think of himself as a cruel man. Even his wards didn't hold that opinion of him. But his punishment of choice for the children and youths was a five-foot length of residential electrical wire, the heavy duty kind that runs through house framing with two solid copper strands wrapped in black and finally in white vinyl. He folds it in half with the joint as the handle and the twin whip leads being aimed particularly at the legs and ankles of the youthful offender. To his so-called credit, he rarely resorted to it because he didn't need to.

Joey wasn't cruel. He filled a necessary position in the social matrix of San Francisco, and his counterparts – people he knew, visited and even respected – fulfilled similar functions in nearby Oakland and Berkeley, Daly City and Santa Cruz, and, of course, other parts of San Francisco.

Joey Starling was called a "beggar master." The terminology sounds like it's from an old rhyme – "rich man, poor man, beggar master, thief," but it's not. It might be thought of as something out of medieval Europe, but it wasn't. Or India. Not. It was today, and everything about it reeked of modern justifications, rationalizations, and, in reality, the relative comfort to be had in abject slavery. Joey didn't like the term and didn't use it. Not that it mattered.

Joey's stable included four foster children of various ages, three older dependent adults plus Marnie, or Marina Patricia Leon, who was in her early 20s and didn't look much older than she really was. With one of the few pleasant faces among the ragged homeless who shared the street corners, she was a beggar master's treasure trove. How much easier to give those dollars to a pretty face than that of a toothless, senseless bag of addicted bones.

The children who comprised Joey's foster family lived together in the southern reaches of the city, the bowels, in tenements in the Bay View referred to as affordable housing. With each child came the guaranteed monthly check – not much, true, but Joey was dealing with a factor of four, which, in a sense, is like buying in bulk: A very good value for what is a necessity anyway.

The adults were simply for production purposes.

Joey Starling considered himself an altruist of sorts. What difference did it make that he worked in the gutter, that he provided so little for his workers, that he was no better than the plantation owners of the Colonial period? He provided more than they would have had otherwise. Didn't they have a warm place to sleep? Yes. Didn't they have his protection? Yes. Medical care? In a sense, yes, because he whipped them right into the emergency room of San Francisco General or Laguna Honda when things got severe, and the city ended up paying, not them. Therefore, they had health insurance. And there was cable TV, too. Not bad. All in all: better than working at Wal-Mart, thought Joey Starling.

And the children: Weren't they better off with Joey looking after them? Yes, again. Such is the interesting state of our society.

Joey Starling wasn't born to be a beggar master. He stumbled into the business. He'd been a teacher for eight years, specializing in social studies and geography, grades six to nine. He was one of those public-school teachers who made their students keep a current events notebook filled with newspaper and magazine clippings. At the age of thirty-six, four years ago, Mr. Starling, the teacher, was laid off. The state didn't have enough money, the districts didn't have enough money, the cities didn't have enough money, and a third of the teachers were released at all grade levels.

He applied everywhere, but schools were shedding the trained, certified instructors and backfilling with inexperienced, often uncredentialed workers. His unemployment ran out and his union abandoned him. So the former teacher started a foster home. The begging part happened as naturally as any other system: It evolved so slowly he didn't know what he had until it was fully realized. To his great surprise, other enterprises similar to his little microcosm of functionality existed in other places besides his shabby, three bedroom apartment. In other words, he wasn't the city's first beggar master, he wasn't the only beggar master, and he certainly wasn't the cruelest or meanest in this peculiar socio-economic sector.

Joey Starling. There were no drugs, there was no prostitution in his operation. No pedophilia. No porn sales. He had honor and dignity. That, by itself, classified him as a true humanitarian. But keep in mind that San Francisco is a world where the great are measured not against greatness, but against the utterly corrupt. In the city, a crow is a songbird because it's measured against wingless alley rats, and the lovely morning song of Joey Starling was, therefore, a benefit to mankind.

Off to Work

Joey was boiling water for soup when Gabriel wandered in. The boy had spent some of his day on Seventh Avenue making and selling wire animals and talking with the strange woman who'd asked one too many questions. Yet he liked her a lot but didn't know why, exactly. It was something about the way she listened: She listened really deep, he decided.

Gabriel emptied his trouser pockets onto a low table in the main room by the door, and then carefully stacked and counted the bills. Today's haul was $60, but that's because a nun from one of the hospitals gave him a $10 bill, then came back about a half-hour later and gave him a twenty. He'd also sold two wire animals, a cat and a giraffe, but he didn't tell Joey and stashed the money before walking in the door. Once inside, he poured more than $10 worth of coins into a Kirkland bulk jelly jar from Costco. Gabriel folded the bills in half and balanced the jar on top for Joey and walked into the kitchen. It smelled like hot dogs. Joey and Sabrina made a sort of hot dog soup every week or so, throwing in cabbage and canned white beans and simmering the frankfurters with them for maybe an hour.

Sixty dollars. Joey realized that there had probably been more. He didn't say anything. With Gabriel, he never did. Joey understood that this boy, this one, was a hell of a lot smarter than the rest. IQ? It had to be above 140, no question about it. Maybe 150. He remembered how seldom he'd seen that kind of intelligence among his students. Gabriel was skimming and Joey knew it, but he just considered it incentive. The kid was so smart he was working a system that was working the system, which made Joey laugh when he thought about it. It would be a shame to lose him. Gabriel and Marnie were the best, and

Joey'd done *his* best keeping the boy out of school. Next year he'd have to start first grade for sure.

A child like Gabriel was only good for a few years. Then they grow up and lose that childish magnetism; they lose their cuteness.

Joey never could find where Gabriel stashed the extra money. How much could it be by now? Hundreds, certainly. Maybe close to a thousand over the last year and a half, but there was really no telling. The boy never bought anything, at least anything that Joey had ever seen. Part of his success, in Joey's mind, was because of the boy's curly hair. People really go for that. The broken wrist? ... yes, very big. Then there's the intelligence. Some were intrigued by Gabriel's ability to carry on a conversation with them, to joke, to read the headlines and text of a newspaper story as he stood there, and by God if *that* wasn't worth folding money when a slower child was lucky to get coins. Alas that childhood is so fleeting.

When the boy was away for two or three days, Joey worried. There was no protection out there on the street. But Gabe was smart. He knew what to watch out for. Maybe. Hopefully.

Actually, Joey had every intention of keeping Gabriel happy, within reason. But in truth, it wasn't because of his intelligence, natural charisma or pleasant looks. And though he could make, on average, double anyone but Marnie's take, it wasn't his earning capacity. It wasn't even the monthly foster payment he got for Gabriel and the other three kids. With a sigh, he could accept Gabriel's dishonesty, with a sigh he would let it go because Gabe had a special talent, and that was what Joey simply couldn't let pass into other hands.

Gabriel had a knack for finding things; it was that simple. That's what this evening was all about. Luckily, the boy hadn't stayed out all night in an effort to work into tomorrow. He was here, now, and standing there with a solid sixty bucks in his wretched right hand.

"Get you some twenties?" asked Joey.

"One. Sister Mary Whatever," Gabriel said, but both he and Joey knew the boy knew the nun's real name. "She needs some glasses, she says. But then she stuffed the twenty down in my cup so I couldn't see how much it was. She shoved it down there. Sister Mary's fingers are more bent than mine, even. I think she has arthritis in her hands. And maybe her left hip or her knee. She favors that side and tilts a little when she walks and when she stands. Still. Stands still. I can always tell if it's her coming down the sidewalk because she walks half-over and she prays that way, too."

"Well," said Joey, "bless her anyway, I say. A regular Mother Teresa. Oh, yeah, we've got a little work tonight, so I'm glad you're back." He didn't like the way Gabriel said Sister Mary's fingers were more bent than his. Joey was convinced he could hear accusation in Gabriel's tone.

Gabriel picked up on Joey's vibe and went silent. He knew what tonight's work meant, and he slowly stuck his right hand down in his pocket. It was a reaction without thought. He'd broken his wrist a year ago, fighting the inevitable. Running away, he'd tripped and fallen down the outside stairs, catching his arm in the railing and fracturing the wrist. There was no doctor and no hospital that time, all things considered, so it healed crookedly in place. Joey called it Gabriel's "moneymaker."

"Tooley came back earlier," Joey continued. "He's over at 351D watching that game show with the wheel ... and said there'd been a death over on Noriega about 18th. It's that green-painted four-story apartment building, the second unit from the corner. The building where Mrs. Bolin lived? Remember?"

"I remember Mrs. Bolin. She had very nice rings, Joey," Gabriel said. Something about the memory triggered a sadness that nearly brought tears to his eyes. Old Mrs. Bolin was gentle soul. She died about eight months ago, maybe from a heart attack, but maybe from a broken heart when her Chihuahua, Alexander the Great, died on a Sunday morning. "Al" was all she had — Al and a half-dozen gold rings with full-carat red and clear stones. They'd been hidden all around the apartment. Really hidden, too, not just placed under or behind something.

Joey didn't like Gabriel's tone when he mentioned the rings. What, Joey was supposed to feel guilty? "Tooley was out on his corner there and saw the paramedics arrive earlier today. And then they left with a body. So Tooley asked around a little and found out who it was and what apartment, pretty much like with Mrs. Bolin."

Gabriel wondered how Tooley had met Mrs. Bolin in the first place. He had his suspicions: Tooley cruised for victims, and then he'd just keep track of them and wait, sometimes for years. He'd befriend them, like Mrs. Bolin. His list by now must be hundreds of names long. That's what makes the waiting system work — the long list.

"I prefer not to go this evening," said Gabriel, and, realizing he'd shoved his hand into his pocket, he stuck the other one in the other pocket and rocked back and forth on his heels.

"We've talked about this," said Joey. "Can't do it alone. Take me forever."

Gabriel didn't say anything. He just stood there. Tears welled up behind his eyes. Joey went over to the cabinet under the sink and grabbed the whipping wire. It was time for a reminder. When Joey's back was turned, Gabriel took off at a sprint, making it to the door, out the door and halfway down the second-floor walkway before Joey caught him. Joey was fast, and Gabriel, despite his precociousness and ability to deal with the street, was no match, emotionally, for the commanding demeanor of an adult. Joey was management. He pulled Gabriel gently back into the apartment, joking and smiling — a good show for anyone curious enough to be looking.

The door snicked closed.

A Small-Time Piano Man

Detective William Chu was sitting in his small, impersonal office toward the back of the station, and he came promptly to the front desk when the clerk announced Ruth on the intercom. He looked like a Chinese gangster from a Technicolor film noir, circa 1948. He wore a deep maroon silk shirt with a bronze, patternless tie under a deep-ash suit. He lacked only the snub-nose .44. His hat was hanging from a hat tree in the corner of his office, and his service weapon, a Glock 19, was under it.

"Yarn Woman, Bill," was all that the receptionist said, but she looked up and smiled as she evaluated every possible feminine quality of their visitor.

"So," Ruth said as she approached the other woman's desk, "do I pass or what?"

Chu's clerk turned, pleased to see the detective approaching from the back. She looked back at Ruth and tried the smile again but it was like trying to make frogs jump when they don't want to. The smile ended up somewhere on the floor. Chu looked out the front glass door where parking was limited to police vehicles and just about choked when he saw the big Rolls idling silently in the autumn dusk in a police-only slot.

"He won't be a minute, Detective" said the Yard Woman.

"Oh, fine," said Chu. It always amazed Ruth how the smallest thing – in this case, a "civilian" parking in a police spot for about 15 seconds – could throw a wrench in the well-ordered brain. Chu was absolutely nervous about it.

After regaining his composure, "Bill" greeted her amiably, and buzzed her in. They walked back to his well-ordered room. There were some file cabinets and a cherrywood desk with three drawers on the right and a shallow one in the center that locked. There was a small photograph in a Wal-Mart frame of Chu's mother and, apparently, a brother and sister, a Rubik's Cube, and an inexpensive chrome pen and matching mechanical pencil. On a shelf to the right, beside a window that looked out onto a six-by-six-foot garden with a small maple in the middle, were a number of sports trophies and medals. I was familiar with Chu's office and his background in high school and college sports: All the awards were for track (well, one was for high school football). Chu'd been a sprinter, running anything under 800 meters, with or without a baton. He had made a name for himself early in his law enforcement career by literally running down offenders on his Chinatown beat.

"Everything tells me we should know who this man is," he said of the body she had found in the gutter at Seventh, looking at Ruth as if for the first time. There wasn't much about her that he didn't like, except, truth be known, her intelligence. His mother had warned him years ago to forget about women who were smarter than him, it just spelled trouble, and he had no reason to disbelieve her. Detective William Chu was a good boy and a great cop, but now forty-ish, he was still single.

"But the face isn't easily recognizable," he continued, "due to damage from the impact with the edge of the cement curb. And fingerprints aren't enough when there's no criminal record. He seems like just an ordinary older male. He had on some black jeans; his brown loafers were found at the scene. I don't need to tell you that, of course. Nothing expensive. I think the shoes were nice enough, but let's just say they weren't Bruno Maglis. It's the shirt that seemed odd to me. It didn't have a tag or anything. And, you know, I decided I ought to call and see what you can tell me. I have the shirt here."

He carefully pulled the shirt from a protective plastic bag and placed it on his desk. It was orange with black patterned letters from different languages of the world. It was bloody on the lower front. Chu watched her for a reaction. He placed two latex gloves on his desk for her. "Look," he said, "I feel badly to have you do this. I'm not insensitive to that. I know you called it in, in the first place. I guess you just can't get out of this guy's circle. Anyway, my apologies, but if you could just take a look …"

She stood beside a small, comfortable chair at the side of the desk, snapped on the gloves and held the shirt up to the overhead light but then pivoted over to the window, which provided more raw wattage. She turned it around a few times, and then inspected it minutely from top to bottom, from armhole to cuff and back again. Then she placed it back on the desk, snapped off the gloves and waited for Chu to pick up the conversation.

"Well, I mean, what do you think?" he finally asked.

"Tea? I'd love some, thank you."

"Oh yes, oh yes," said Chu, clicking the intercom and asking the woman in front to bring back two cups of coffee. "I hope coffee's okay?"

"Sure. So this belongs to the man I found and called in the other night."

"Yes."

"You don't have a clue to the identity?"

"It's a big city. If we had the slightest idea of where to start, we'd trim weeks down to days. I don't like cases that linger, especially when we're looking for something as simple as an identity."

"The man's a professional actor and musician, performing in the area," she said. Here or the East Bay. He's small time. I'd start with the local chapter of the acting guild. They'll have a list of several hundred, but he's what, seventy? Seventy-five? Wouldn't you say?"

"Yes, that's about right. But tell me, how do you know he's an actor? And why do you say he's a musician?"

"It's in the shirt. It's rayon from a fabric store in Oakland. I've been calling around, looking for something, well, similar. But you'll notice the design and the stitching. That's the important part.

"Here, I'll point it out as I explain," she said. "See, there's the straight cut of the lower hem. Now, we both know that mature men are fond of that because it takes the emphasis away from their paunch. But notice that the hem is rather wide and not evenly turned under. I mean, it's good but not great. Looks fine from the outside, see. You wouldn't buy this shirt for $180 and wear it to a bar mitzvah, but it's pretty good at $15 to wear to Bill's Diner. That's because it's not a commercially made shirt and it's not the product of a tailor. Then, I mean, look here at the side stitching. You'll notice that there's a single row, that it's not double stitched. Again, it's not commercial. It hasn't been made to last. The person who made this, and I believe that to be the man who was wearing it, was concerned only about the superficial appearance, how it looks when it's worn, and not about durability or quality.

"I happen to know that this is the way stage garments are made for short-run productions of plays or music. On the cheap. You just knock it out, perform in it, toss it. The concern is only for the outward appearance. It's my opinion that your man is an actor, and I say small time because he has to make his own costumes. He made this shirt. Plus, he's a musician, a pianist. Maybe he sings." Her thoughts wandered to Gabrielle, the day on the beach. "Show tunes."

"A musician you say. And what leads you to believe that?"

"When I discovered this person two nights ago, I chanced to look at his right hand because it was flopped up onto the curb while the rest of his body lay in the gutter. It was very sad, Mr. Chu. I do not like this. But it was clear to me, even under the streetlights, that the joints of the distal phalanxes were retroflexed. You know? I mean, how obvious, right?"

"Oh, yes. And?"

"Well, it seems to me that a very high percentage of the piano players I've known or watched have the same condition: the fingertips are slightly bent the wrong way from years, decades, of pressing piano keys. I've seen this occur in no other trade."

"Ah. Very clear. Very sensible," said Chu. "We'll see how close you are, I suppose."

"So tell me, Mr. Chu, about this shooting."

"Well," he said, placing his hands on the desktop, "I just, well you've been a great help, you see, but I'm afraid I'm not at liberty to discuss the investigation. I'm sure you understand."

"That's a load of garbage." She smiled.

Chu kind of shook his head. She just wasn't normal. With anyone else, absolutely anyone, he would have turned as red as his Chinese genes would have allowed, sucked it down, and escorted the perpetrator from his office and from the station. She even called him mister, not detective. But this Yarn Woman, well, he just reacted to her differently.

He was quiet for a little while as thoughts raced through his head and as his blood rushed through the arteries in his neck; he finally got both to slow down and obey. Then he shrugged and said, "Oh, well, it was you yourself who found the bullet casing, anyway. He was shot at fairly close range, probably from a passing vehicle right there where he dropped. We think he was walking on the sidewalk and fell onto the curb, resulting in the facial damage. There was one casing, a .32 ACP from a small semiautomatic pistol, but there were three entry points: one was the lower abdomen with a front entry, a second in the thigh, also from the front, and the other in the chest. There's probably a vehicle out there somewhere with a couple of spent casings on the floor. The shooting wasn't random. I can't see it as random, though I have no idea why the victim was chosen. Or stalked. Is there a nutcase out there who homed in on this man, and decided then and there to shoot him? That would be random. How many shots were taken?" Chu sighed and then smiled. "Now I kind of see why they all say you have your own opinions. I get it now." Then he laughed. "Actually, I look forward to calling on you when I need your expertise, and for now I think I'll concentrate on the actors' guild. I'm sure the department will find a way to thank you, as usual. I look forward to receiving your report."

"I do have one question," she said. He nodded, but his brow was furrowed. "I've heard that there are cases, here in San Francisco, of groups of panhandlers who work for, well, a personnel manager, I suppose. What do you think about that?"

Detective Chu sincerely pondered the concept for a moment and said, "Well, you know, I've heard that, but never seen anything real. My opinion? It's one of those urban myths. I think they talked about it once at Rotary, but it was more like a joke, you know, it got them a laugh."

"Maybe they drop off their panhandlers to work a day at a particular intersection, possibly," she pushed. "And then pick them up at the end of the day. Maybe some of your officers have noticed activities like that? That they move their panhandlers from place to place?"

"Nobody's ever said anything to me about it. Miss M, this isn't the nineteenth century, you know. It's not India, it's not Asia. This is the United States. If I'd ever heard of anything like that, it wouldn't last long, a guarantee you that. Not here. This is America. You'll be telling me they maim their beggars next, so they get more money. This is America."

"I was going to say, the manager wouldn't be crippling a child, for instance, to increase his earnings? I mean, as in Asia?"

"Excuse me. What I said was a joke. There could be

nothing like that here, I assure you," he said. He walked over to his desk and sat down. What was she saying? Did she know something he didn't?

Ruth smiled, shook his hand and turned to leave. The Silver Cloud rolled up to the door and Mr. Kasparov leaned out the window, peered into the door and smiled, his enormous teeth jutting out most of the way to the door. He waved; Chu awkwardly waved back. Mr. Kasparov had been waiting across the street during the twenty minutes it had taken Ruth to steer the detective in the right direction. Then they drove silently off.

Pulling Off a Job

Tooley pulled the '67 Econoline over and set the parking brake. The sound always grated on Joey Starling because it was so unnecessary. The damn thing was too rusted out to roll, anyway. Tooley was frowning and Gabriel was assigned to a chair in the back that had been fastened to the metal wall with steel L-brackets held firmly by a half-dozen sheet metal screws.

"You can wait here, Mike," Joey told Tooley. "Don't get excited or anything. What do we have, like two blocks, right? Give us maybe five minutes to get there, five to pick the door, thirty inside if it's clear, and five back. Don't turn on the van radio or it'll drain the battery and I sure as hell don't want to call Triple-A again, if you know what I mean. So leave the radio off. You brought that one of yours anyway, right?"

"Sure." Tooley pulled out an old Radio Shack transistor set about forty years out of date. It was like listening to tin pans.

"Okay then. But don't listen to music. You remember what happened last time you listened to music. Listen to the Raiders or something. You like the Raiders, right? Put it on the sports station. Just don't fall asleep. Got it? Good. You're sure you got the right room? You saw it when we drove past just now, right?"

"The one that's not with the table lamp on. It's the next one to the right, not the one with the lamp. That one's got this woman and kid. Second floor, west end, second from the end. Mr. Karl Whatever. Randall. Don't knock, Joey, he's dead. He's gone."

"Mike, I know he's dead. That's why we're going up there. Here's how it works: You told me he was dead, then we go up there. We wouldn't go up there if he wasn't. It's very simple. We're going to check for cash, Mike. That's what we do and that's all we do. We're not hurting anyone, we don't have guns, we're just clearing the battlefield like they did after Napoleon's armies swept Europe. It's an industry. We're part of a proud tradition."

Joey was an educated man, thought Tooley. "Yeah. Gabriel's pretty small. Good for crawling," he ventured.

"That's right, Mike. That's why Gabriel is helping. You have your radio?"

"Sure." He turned it on. You could hear something through the static, but you had to have an ear for it. To Tooley, though, that didn't matter. He set it up on the dashboard, pulled out a pack of Maverick cigarettes and settled back into the seat.

"Don't smoke in the car. And don't do it outside, either. Just wait, Mike. You can wait."

Joey closed the door quietly and then opened the side door for Gabriel. They crossed the street and backtracked two blocks to the apartment building. Getting inside was the easy part, and they accomplished it in less than the allotted five minutes. They took off their shoes once they were inside the apartment, and Joey began a systematic examination of the rooms and furnishings, quickly checking the usual stash areas for cash and jewelry. He found a couple of 20s was all. He sat in an overstuffed chair that faced a television that should have been recycled fifty years ago, and motioned Gabriel over. He looked sternly into the boy's eyes. There were no words. None were needed. Joey removed a thick gold ring he wore on the little finger of his left hand. It was a gold band like a damaged wedding band, but it had the word "Loverboy" inscribed in block letters along the outside. That would be the previous owner. He waited for Gabriel to hold out his hand. He placed a straightened coat hanger in it. Gabriel looked down at it silently, exhibiting his last effort of defiance, and then he relented. It just wasn't worth the fight at this point. What could happen? They'd have an argument, someone would hear, they'd call the cops, the cops would arrive and the final outcome would place him in yet another foster home and God only knows what that one might be like.

Joey placed the gold ring in Gabriel's right hand, next to the hanger and he clamped his fingers around both. He stood up and started walking around the room. The first time Joey had seen the boy do this, he thought it was a parlor trick. Gabriel was, at the time, locating dimes and quarters with a pair of L-shaped wire coat hangers. Joey, never a mark for crooks, kept checking his wallet to see if it was still in his pocket. And he kept watching as carefully as he could to detect the sleight of hand, but there was no indication of gaming. There was something weird about it, and he didn't totally believe it until about the fourth or fifth performance, by which time Gabriel had proved he could locate, for example, a diamond ring with a single straightened-out hanger if he held a diamond or the correct precious metal in his divining hand. It was dousing, plain and simple. The hanger was his divining rod.

Joey got his thoughts in order, returning to the present. Gabriel was on the other side of the room, following the hanger, following its lead. It seemed to be dipping up and down like a bobble head. When Joey saw the boy's hand bobbing the first time, he thought he was witnessing a poor job of acting; he thought it was an ill-executed part of a hoax. But he eventually learned that it wasn't. That's just what a divining rod has done for centuries, albeit in the backwoods of Arkansas or Idaho.

Gabriel walked into the hallway, pointing the rod as if it were a flashlight in the dark. Joey followed. Gabriel walked into the kitchen and Joey followed. The boy knelt down, obeying the pull of the hanger as it tapped the bottom of the kitchen wainscot. The flat boards, which ran to about three feet high, were painted in thick white enamel that had been stained by years of splashed food. About a foot above the spot that Gabriel was pointing to was an electric socket. How perfect. Joey pulled a pocketknife from his jacket and opened the flathead screwdriver blade. He removed the plastic outlet cover and shined a small flashlight into the wiring box. He unscrewed the steel box and with some difficulty pulled it free of the wall, careful not to get shocked.

Gabriel watched silently, hoping Joey would close the circuit and fry himself. Too bad it wasn't a 220-volt dryer outlet.

But Joey was too careful. He delicately pushed the wiring behind the box into the space above it and found what he'd been looking for: stiff cord tied to the metal electrical housing. He pulled it up. At the other end was a heavy gold ring with a flat ruby setting. A man's ring, probably size 11. It weighed a ton. Joey held it up to his flashlight. It was a 1954 college graduation ring. But it was something special; it was wider than the usual grad rings, and heavier. The stone was amazing. He shoved it into his pocket.

"That's great, Gabe," he whispered. "Score. Now let's try the bedroom."

They searched the house but found no other gold. Joey had Gabriel return his gold ring and slid it back onto his finger with a smile. God, that thing was heavy. Then he pulled a small handful of change from his pants pocket and flipped through the coins until he found his 1964 Kennedy half-dollar. He handed it to the child, who obediently slid it into his hand and they went through the search routine a second time. They turned up a half-pint Kerr jar of old silver coins in the back corner of a drawer in what appeared to be an unused second bedroom, but no jewelry.

Finally, Joey rolled up a $5 bill, took back his fifty-cent piece and poked the bill into Gabriel's hand. He thought he could understand why the metal searching worked. It seemed sensible, in a way, maybe something to do with ions and electron valences, with the attraction of atoms. If he had the time and interest, maybe he should try gemstones. But that wasn't necessary and Joey had lost his exploratory spirit years ago. But paper money? That just didn't make sense. A twenty or a fifty not only had no ions, the paper itself was an insulator. Shouldn't that have something to do with it? Apparently not.

Joey had heard about dousers from the hills of Virginia. He'd read about it somewhere a long time ago. According to theory, a mountain person, male or female, could cut a sapling "witching stick" from his property and hold it in front of him as he walked across the terrain. If there was water below, and the witch had the talent, the stick would pull down with great force. Water witches, he found, were fairly common in rural areas throughout the states.

Of course, Gabriel's talent was a little different, but not unheard of. Gabriel could hold onto something, gold for instance, and his finger would act as the dousing rod for gold. If he held a piece of quartz, his hand registered movement if another piece of quartz came into range. It was pretty simple. The sympathetic-materials theory had been used for modern dousing rods that were made and sold commercially – mostly through comic books and treasure-hunting websites. They were a poor man's metal detector. Joey had seen the ads in comic books when he was a kid. The rods came with a little chamber where you could stick in a piece of gold or whatever, and search for its comrade. The pictures had Z-shaped bolts of lightning coming from the gold sample and the tip of the rod. Joey always thought it was a scam, like other things you could get from the comics – sea monkeys and dynamic-tension muscle-building flexors and so on. It probably was a racket, unless the user had actual dousing abilities, in which case he didn't need the commercial dousing rod.

That was a long time ago. He looked over at the boy, the $5 bill jammed into his fist. Cash in Gabriel's hand usually spelled payday for Joey, and this day was no exception. One thing he'd learned in the year or so of dousing for valuables is that old folks always kept a stash of cash, and that applied to anyone, rich or poor, black or white, who'd lived through the Depression and its aftermath. And economically, today was really no different, he thought. Not a bit. Old folks always had cash.

Gabriel followed the hanger into a pantry just off the kitchen, waiting for the familiar buzz, which he knew would be followed by a strong pull down on the rod. It was like someone grabbed it and pulled it toward the floor. When this happened the first few times for Gabriel, it scared him and he looked for whoever was doing it. Soon, he decided it was a ghost or devil, which frightened him so thoroughly he had to change clothes. But as time went on, it just didn't seem like a spirit was behind it. It worked more like an invisible magnet.

A small water heater was situated in the pantry and it was one of the older kinds, maybe five feet tall and able to heat only twenty gallons at a shot. This one operated on gas, with the pilot light at the bottom behind a levered metal door about ten inches wide and six inches tall. Joey pushed the child aside and evaluated the situation. The thing wasn't vented properly. He sniffed but there was no gas smell. But there had to be carbon monoxide, the way it had been rigged. Maybe that's what killed the old man. You just can't get good landlords these days, he thought. They don't give a shit for anyone.

Joey got down on his stomach and carefully pressed open the pilot light door and slid a gloved hand in. He expected to touch mouse turds, and he did. They were everywhere and they were old and dry. But that's not why he wore leather gloves. He needed protection from the slamming of mouse traps and, if there were any nests, their nasty little teeth. But rather than brushing against a whole mouse, his hand pressed against a glove-leather wallet. Ah-hah, he wanted to shout, but he didn't. He pulled it out cleanly, closed up the little door, and they left as he pushed the thick wallet down into his front pocket and the gloves into his back.

* * *

When he was younger, Gabriel didn't know there was anything unusual in his ability. In fact, he was just fooling around looking for children's aluminum jacks. He was clutching a little jack that he'd found under a chair when he felt pressure in his forefinger as he stood near a throw rug. There was a jack under its edge. That's how it started. He didn't remember where he was at the time; he had no memory of a home of any kind that long ago.

Where Gabriel's memories began, he had unfortunately made the mistake of helping Joey find a silver tie tack that he needed for a foster-care interview shortly after he'd taken on Gabriel. The boy found it using a silver dime. The discovery was followed by a handful of very friendly tests, by astonishment on Joey's part, by laughing and patting the boy on the back, and by going out for ice cream. What wasn't to like? Eventually, Joey had to admit that Gabriel had an uncommon talent, that it was real.

Once Gabriel knew that Joey meant to exploit his ability, he tried to hide it, but it was too late.

All this crossed Gabriel's mind as he put on his shoes and followed Joey out the apartment door into the dark hallway. They were very quiet. He paused for a moment, wrapped in thought. He realized he could no longer remember where he'd lived, or who he'd lived with, when he played with the jacks in the dreamtime before the Age of Joey Starling. Could this apartment building have been his real home? He couldn't remember any faces or any voices, but it seemed so familiar. He couldn't recall if there were any other children. Homeless. He sighed and followed the shadowed form of Joey Starling down the hall and stairs to the street. It was about 1 in the morning. The floor creaked, but not loud enough to be a problem.

They slid down the sidewalk and crossed over to the van. Tooley was asleep, the radio hissing almost as softly as the buzzing streetlight above.

Joey punched Tooley in the arm and he shot up and hit his head on the van's ceiling. The engine turned over roughly, coughing up burned oil, and Tooley pulled into the street, sulking and rubbing the top of his head.

Henry Berq, Playwright

Once Detective Chu had the information the Yarn Woman had given him on the shirt and character of the deceased, it didn't take long to discover the man's identity. He'd assigned the search to one of his officers, and it was a matter of about two hours of phone calls and databank work the following day. When he had the name, he called Mr. Kasparov to relay the information to Ruth – a true example of official openness.

His name was Henry Berq, age 73. Yes, an actor, though he hadn't been on stage for a number of years – until his current performance. Indeed, a musician. More, a piano man (he couldn't be called a pianist, really, but a piano man, yes). He was currently appearing in a production at the auditorium just west of the Civic Center, one in a conglomeration of buildings that served as venues for most of the symphonies, operas and plays in San Francisco. Berq's was a bit part and it wouldn't be too hard to backfill after his unexpected death.

There's a restaurant maybe two long blocks from the Center where many of the performers and opera-goers hang out, where they can get coffee or soup or a reasonable meal. It's the kind of place where you might find the lead players or major symphony donors, but timing is everything. It's called Mac's Plase, and I'm sure the misspelling was originally an error on the part of the sign-maker forty or fifty years ago. Mac's best soup was split pea and he made a fairly good pastrami or Reuben by California standards. He was past seventy now but still worked at least four days a week, and those were long days.

I was invited for lunch. Mr. Kasparov had called, asking me, on behalf of The Miss, to undertake a moderate research of the Bulletin's library. "Could you seek out," he said in his brusque, formal, accented English, "informations (plural) on our Mr. Berq? B-e-r-q, Henry. Yes, like Henry Miller, but not Miller at all, Berq, b-e-r-q. Entertainment, yes. An actor. You have her fondest regards, Mr. Fisher, I am sure."

I had about two hours until lunch, and that wasn't much time to forage through the files at the Bulletin. They weren't exactly in the best order. The benefit, however, was that the antiquated library system at the paper is by subject – comparable to a keyword search in our current digital world. But you have to know the keywords. If any person has even a modicum of fame, he or she gets his or her own file and his or her own keyword, their name. Otherwise, the categories are broader, sometimes as broad as "opera," by year. In this case, the system was wonderful, and Mr. Berq's portfolio was moderate in size, indicating a long life of newsworthy activities. I leafed through the dated clippings and glossy black-and-whites with their thick black crop marks and white-out globs that typified the technology of the age, trying to get a feel for the man. But two hours isn't much time so I brought the file with me to Mac's.

I was about ten minutes late because of the traffic that afternoon, but she was later. There was a complete turning of the tables before she arrived at 3, and I'd had enough coffee and water to hold me for several days. I think it's her green eyes that compensate for her habitual lateness, but it could be the smile. Or it could be me.

She asked me to tell her about Berq, so I began, handing her the photos so she could shuffle through them as I spoke. She didn't look at them, though, which surprised me at first, but on reflection I decided she may have known him, at least peripherally. The photos I'd gathered were all old; not one was taken in the last ten years because he'd been working largely behind the scenes or in the orchestra pit.

Henry Berq averaged one or two productions a year

for the last thirty years, according to what I could find. Never had he taken a lead role. Most of the productions were musicals. He was noted for playing piano, occasionally singing or playing an organ in the pit, including a performance at the Castro Theater in 2002. On numerous occasions he was given credit for costumes in various productions.

Berq was born in Manhattan but had zipped west about the time he was of legal age. He'd made an early name for himself in the 70s in San Francisco's avant-garde "theater," for which there was little newspaper coverage. After the 80s, like many minor local actors, he faded away. He resurfaced briefly in the 1990s and vanished again, but by the turn of the century had established himself as a grand old master of the musical stage and it was during this period that he achieved both his greatest fame and his best roles. From obscurity, he had become one of the city's lesser living legends.

Only to vanish once again.

I'd been summarizing his life quietly at a window seat at Mac's while I waited for a bowl of pea soup and Ruth awaited a cup of vegetarian minestrone. Mac always gave you all the Saltines you could eat, set up in a nice little basket.

Our waiter was a man in his forties, bald, emaciated and wearing tight black. "I'm trying to find a friend," Ruth said to him as he placed the soup in front of her. "He comes to Mac's often, and I haven't seen him for several weeks … without a word. Henry Berq. Do you know him?"

The waiter paused. "And you are …" he snipped, his voice sharp and sarcastic in tone.

"I'm Miss Ruth," she said simply.

The suspicious waiter rubbed his chin. "Miss Ruth of the flowing blue robes?" he said slowly and hopefully, placing of his fingers on the tabletop.

"That was a few years ago. But, yes." The references

were, I assumed, relating to either costuming or sets she'd created for a production of some sort two years ago, and I had been presented with another obscure piece of the puzzle that I knew as the Yarn Woman.

All of a sudden, the waiter's entire demeanor changed and a light bulb went on in his head — I could practically see it happily glowing through his eyes. "Oh, Miss Ruth, I'm so sorry! I didn't know. Where oh where have you been? Oh, you're so reclusive, but I'm so happy to see you here. But you really must come more often. Please, well, we don't want Mr. Berq's name just bandied about by anyone, do we?"

"Certainly not ..."

"Mr. Landis. Call me Kurt. Please."

"Thank you so much, Kurt," said Ruth, smiling. "But I was wondering if you'd seen him lately. Perhaps the past week or two?"

"Oh. Yes. A week ago. Let me see." He looked at a small book he took out of his vest pocket. It was a miniature calendar about the size of the smallest address book commercially available. "Today is, hmm, Tuesday. Then that would be Saturday a week, I would say. Yes, I very well remember now. He had the special. Afternoon, about 2, don't you think?"

"Can you tell me," she said, "was he alone? I believe he has a great-nephew, a curly-haired boy."

"Oh yes! Oh yes! A darling boy, but, forgive me Miss Ruth, but I thought he was a street boy! I'm so sorry! Mr. Berq met him here frequently and bought him hamburgers nearly as large as the child!" He laughed just a little too loudly and immediately covered his mouth with his hand. "Henry would buy the child an immense hamburger and a mocha — coffee for the child — and they would sit there, and sit there, and Henry would take notes of various things and stories that the child told him. They were so darling, sitting there together, grandfatherly Henry Berq in his scruffy tweed jacket and little gold-rimmed glasses, and the boy, well, in his wondrous curls!"

"You've been so helpful, Kurt, you have no idea. I think I can rest a little easier now."

"He's damaged, you know. The child. His hand is hurt."

"Yes, I know."

"Are you still designing costumes, Miss Ruth? The Acting Conservatory is, as we speak, considering its next production. Oh, it's a year off at least, but."

"I've been occupied," said Ruth, with a smile.

"I'm sure you have been." He looked to the sides and said, as if sharing secrets, "We all see your influence, Miss Ruth, even when you're enjoying semi-retirement! Well, if you'll excuse me, I do have to pretend to have other adoring customers. Anything at all, just look my way."

How amazing. She saw that I was digesting their conversation, and pointed to my soup. Then she put her spoon in it and tested it. Not bad, not bad. Mac came over about five minutes later and they had a similar conversation about Berq and Gabriel. Mac had a long gray ponytail and wore checkered chef's pants and a formerly white kitchen apron, and he stared all the while over a pair of reading glasses that looked obnoxiously like granny glasses from half a century ago. He said he remembered another character sharing Berq's table. Mac described him as a small man in his mid to late thirties, rat-faced and entirely self-assured. An angry man, he said.

"Oh," said Ruth. "And was he ever in the same company as the nephew?"

No, he wasn't; Mac couldn't remember ever seeing the rat and the boy together, even in Berq's company.

"Well, did you ever see him park out front or did he walk?"

"The rat? Parked."

"So, did he drive Mr. Berq to the cafe?"

"Nope; they met here."

"I see."

"Rat-face McDougal drives up in a white van," said Mac, chuckling at his newfound nickname for the man. "Berq and him nearly came to blows over something or other about two weeks ago. Or three. No, two. But, Dear, they were only seen together about twice. Twice at most. It wasn't an enduring friendship," he chuckled. "If dear Berq had a heart of gold, which is the case, Mr. Rat saw only the gold, if you take my drift."

Mac visited every table in the place whenever he was on shift. That's what made the restaurant work. He wasn't a hanger-on or a gossip, just a good businessman. He made you feel welcome, even special. He knew the name of every customer who came in more than once, unless, of course, that person was an asshole, as in the case of Rat-face. I'd been in occasionally in the past, though I certainly wasn't as attached to the place as the acting community; but Mac recognized me, remembered my name and even my vocation.

Ruth had just one more question for our waiter, Kurt, and she managed to slip it in as we left Mac's Plase. I helped her on with her coat and just as she was shrugging it into position on her shoulders, the waiter approached and handed her the reading glasses she'd left on the table. I'm sure her forgetfulness was on purpose. She thanked him, and then said, "Oh, one other thing, Kurt. Do you think Henry was working on something? Maybe some music. I don't know. Has he been writing again?"

I don't know how she deduced the writing thing, but I made a special note to follow up and discover her reasoning. She was still tops with Kurt. "I hear," he said, looking habitually, melodramatically, from side to side, "he's working on a new play. Mum on that, Mum! You didn't hear it here. But, really, Miss Ruth, I think everyone knows. We're excited. He hasn't written since 1986. Depressed, I suppose, like so many great artists."

"Thank you so much. I'll see you again," she said, and we meandered slowly out the door of Mac's, past the red and white enamel sign with pea-green steam rising from a signature red soup bowl, and out into San Francisco – "Miss Ruth" and I.

* * *

I learned from Detective Chu that Henry Berq was returning from a play on the night he was shot dead on Seventh Avenue. He wasn't in it; he was in the audience. Though he did have a small part in another production, he had been concentrating on writing his play. Sitting in the audience as he had the night of his death stimulated his creativity and after a performance he would write and rewrite for hours. Going out was like charging his batteries.

On his return home, he'd taken the No. 5 bus west to Seventh and then boarded the southbound 44. His mind was elsewhere that night, not on the 44 route, and, lost in thought, he missed his stop. In fact, he missed the next two. Finally, when it dawned on him he'd gone too far, he got out and began walking back north on Seventh to his apartment. He'd just wasted about half an hour, though it really didn't matter and it was nothing a cup of coffee wouldn't cure. He'd stay up an extra half hour, the benefits of which were twofold: He'd get another thirty minutes on the play, and those thirty minutes were spent in playwright heaven where the world's common men could never tread.

He was ambling northbound when a rain of bullets ended his life. It was more like a sprinkling than a downpour. Chu said the cause of death was loss of blood from the femoral artery and that the mortal injury had little to do with the gunman's accuracy. It was an infinitely unlucky shot and Henry Berq's most unlucky day. His body lay there for more than an hour, alone and ignored. Pedestrians walked around him, thinking he was just another drunk passed out in the gutter. They ignored him as he died. Could someone have pulled him onto the sidewalk, at least, where he could sleep it off? No. Cities are not made for the soft at heart.

Shortly after his death, Berg's small apartment was burglarized. At first, Chu didn't know for sure whether the break-in was before or after his death. Although he couldn't find anything directly linking his murder to the burglary, the potential relationship gnawed at the detective. There was a reason and there was a relationship, but what? And what confounded him even more was that Berq's third-floor, one-bed flat, maybe 600 square feet, had been forcibly entered not once but twice.

"There's a door in the kitchen, by the stove, that leads down an exposed stairway between two sections of the same rat-infested building. There are trash cans down there," Chu told me. "Trash for the neighborhood rats from the smell of it. And cats. Rats and cats. It didn't take much to push in the door, though. It's an old building and there'd been water damage from a bad roof. The wood was rotting. We had an intruder force the door. The place was gone through pretty thoroughly. Whatever the man had, as far as cash and watches, jewelry – gone. His credit cards were still there, and that says something. I'm not sure what exactly, but in broad terms I'd say it indicates a planned burglary with something specific in mind."

"Two entries?" asked the Yarn Woman. We were talking at the Avaluxe; Chu had stopped by because I think he has a thing for her – a sort of look-but-don't touch fascination. Ruth had asked about next of kin, but Chu had no information about that. It was clear to me, however, that her expressed interest in survivors was minor, and her true interest lay in the case's recent developments – the home burglary topping her list.

Oddly, Ruth had predicted a burglary when we talked the day before, but hadn't had time to find out exactly where Berq lived. She knew there had to have been a break-in even before the police discovered it. It was, she said, the only reasonable expectation. I, of course, remained as blind to her reasoning as I had earlier been blind to her deduction that the man was writing again. Later, I realized she'd picked up the writing theory from one of the clippings that indicated he'd scripted one of the less successful musicals of 1985 (he didn't write after 1986, according to our waiter, Kurt). All I learned from it was that the man wrote; I couldn't make the connection that he was writing again. But the burglary? I didn't get that one at all.

"The other one was less obvious," Chu told us, having accepted the Yarn Woman, with a degree of hesitation, onto the periphery of the investigation. As for me, he knew I'd abide by our general terms of engagement – I wouldn't release anything that could jeopardize the investigation, period, journalistically kissing his butt. "The window in the kitchen ... it's a small window over his microwave, one of the old sliding windows with a counterweight in the wall, big enough for a cat but not much else, anyway, it had been left open and there were scratch marks on the wall like someone came in and then caught the wall with their foot going back out. Right outside the window is a drain pipe. My guess is anyone could have climbed it, slithered in and then left. I mean, not a big man. Not even an average-sized man. Could be a woman, a thin male, emaciated ... you know how these young kids are these days. That doesn't help us much, though. Two burglars, one at the door and one at the window, amount to just one burglary as far as anyone could tell. Were they after the same thing? Very likely."

"Was there, by chance, a half-finished orange shirt in the apartment – of the same type he was wearing when he died?" she asked. There was no reason to ask if Henry Berq had the draft of a play lying around: That's what was stolen. That was the reason his apartment had been burglarized.

The shirt question upset Chu. It actually momentarily

flustered him. How the hell could she have figured that out? At least she hadn't said it was a child's shirt.

"I see," she noted with a smile. "Was it a child's size? About size six?"

He let off a breath that sounded like steam rushing out of a locomotive stack. There was no need to answer. Why should he answer? He just smiled and shook his head. "When you get tired of living in theaters," he said, "there's always a job waiting for you at the department. Tell me, incidentally, is there anything you think I should know? Anything that I don't know but you do know or think you know or might know later?"

"Nope," she said. She smiled slightly, and he didn't know if it was his dismissal or just a lie. That was the thing about the Yarn Woman: You never knew. But the more he thought of it, the more he realized he didn't really want to know.

After Chu left, I returned to the Bulletin offices on Market. She'd managed to gather enough information by now to start working out the relationships, to make certain inferences and leaps of logic to come up with a single, complete criminal scenario. Almost. I couldn't get her to talk about it. She was more interested in where we could find really good dim sum after 5 p.m., and that in itself was particularly troubling because she had to pick up a package at the post office before they closed at the same allotted time. She'd ordered a pattern book and it was in. This was not a clear-cut decision on her part; you couldn't just say that dim sum trumps pattern books, and neither could you say that patterns — even a traditional Fair Isle book now valued at more than $400 (though she found it for less than $60) — could be an outright win over dim sum.

It wasn't easy, but she managed to get the parcel by 4:48 and locate a Chinese restaurant on Washington that served dim sum until 5:30. I somehow got worked into the 6 o'clock spot. She still needed to talk to Gabriel, but she realized it wouldn't be easy to arrange. She had no way of finding him.

Leaving Joey

After they'd finished the job at Noriega and 18th, Joey Starling left Tooley and Gabriel in the van and went inside his Bay View apartment. He was half-pleased with the haul and half-angry with having to put up with Tooley. The older man sat for a minute after Joey slammed the car door, then shrugged, grabbed his radio and followed Joey inside. What did he care? Didn't matter, anyway. He told himself he was too beaten down by life to worry about the color thing with Sir Starling. He looked back briefly at Gabriel and sighed. He knew the boy wouldn't follow them in; he still had a mind of his own, somehow, or at least a piece of it. He was a cute kid, but only one of hundreds. Even if he lived past twenty, his life was over. Tooley knew.

It was six in the morning when Gabriel finally left the van. He thought he actually fell asleep once he'd crawled into an old coat he found in the cargo area in the back.

It was still dark but he knew it was morning. He got up, moving the old coat. Something fell off it and hit the floor of the van with a hollow metallic ring. Then it rolled to the lowest end. Gabriel looked, but didn't see it.

He got up and forced open the door. It creaked even though he pushed it slowly and carefully. He left it open and walked over to the alley and dug a small box out of the wire and trash near the van. He'd temporarily stashed his cigar box behind some iron rebar and chicken wire and garbage that took up the front half of Joey's parking slot because it was the safest place he could think of after he escaped Berq's apartment through the kitchen window. It was probably the one place in the entire city that Joey wouldn't look. More than $1300 in small bills and large change were in the box, the top held closed with a thick rubber band. He shoved it into a small blue nylon pack he carried, and then took the 44 bus across most of the peninsula and caught the N-Judah train at Ninth. The old coat made the morning at the edge of the Pacific tolerable.

He dallied there on the edge of it all, where the sand becomes the city of San Francisco. Things in his head had slowed down and he wasn't sure what he was feeling. He couldn't let himself cry; you break down once and the street takes you over. You lose. And the longer he sat and listened to the surf, the more he realized that he was making a monumental decision: He wasn't going back to Joey Starling's.

Once the words popped into his mind, he nearly vomited. He couldn't remember a time without Joey. It wasn't really that bad, anyway. Thousands of kids had it so much worse, and that was just in San Francisco or Oakland. It didn't count Somalia, wherever that was. And why couldn't he go back? He didn't know, couldn't answer his own question because he knew there was no reason that he couldn't go back. He just wasn't going to, was all. He could go turn himself in to the police. He'd stay with the woman from the beach if he had to. She was nice enough.

He kept his small nylon backpack on his back – didn't let it off his body because it had his life's savings in it. It didn't rattle much because it was mostly bills. Too bad there wasn't a sandwich in there, too.

He wandered over to the cement surf-wall that divided the sand beach from Ocean Highway, the road that runs north-south along the peninsula's west side. Out of view in the shade at the foot, he pulled a few fives from the box and shoved them into his pants pocket. He was hungry and wanted to take care of that with an omelet and toast before he started in with the begging routine. He didn't have his wire and pliers, and he was damned if he was going to dance for money – too much of a chance of getting caught and too many low-lifes that like to hang around, waiting, just waiting. He'd just have to live off his savings like everyone else he'd heard about.

The morning and afternoon passed quickly and the clouds started building up pretty much like Gabriel's feelings. The wind stopped and a dull quiet settled in. It smelled like rain. Crap. He'd steal an umbrella before he'd buy one. Umbrellas were expensive, unless you got one of the Chinese numbers that were good for one rainstorm, and that was only if there wasn't any wind. After a good breezy rain, crippled umbrellas littered the city like a million metal-ribbed bats — enough of them would add to the feeling of Halloween, he thought. Did he care? He didn't know if he cared much about Halloween, anyway.

The sun grew dim, the clouds just grew. Afternoon passed and he left the beach, working his way eastward, walking as if he had a mission. Maybe he did. It was 7 p.m. and dark by the time he looked up the side of the Avaluxe Theater from his spot in the alley. It wasn't that tall of a building, really. It was weird because it was surrounded by alleys instead of streets. But for some reason, the alleys were clean. Even the cracks in the sidewalk were swept except where someone had planted some late-blooming sunflowers. The sunflowers towered over him at about nine feet, and there must have been a dozen placed here and there in the cracks, somehow able to get enough nutrients from below the tarmac.

He peered up at the luminous windows above, not sure what he'd do if someone came and looked down, and not sure what he'd do if they didn't. A smaller window to the north was open and the curtain rustled in the breeze. Should he go around to the front, to the other alley? He was really tired.

He walked around the old theater, inspecting the foundation, the asphalt and concrete, the trimmed tufts of sea grass. He positioned himself across the alley from the entry and marquee, thinking someone should fix the movie lettering. He could read "orchid," and he wondered what movie that was. Actually, he could read anything and he hadn't been in school for much more than two months of his life, altogether. Henry Berq taught him, but it wasn't so much because the old man was a good teacher but that Gabriel was a quick study.

From the shadows, he looked in through the glass doors. He felt like a dog. A stray. A stray that could read. He looked up and down the street. Maybe a long time ago it was a street, but now the theater and the few other strange shops stared out into a narrow tract of traffic-less asphalt edged in rough concrete sidewalks. It was an alley; you expected to see the backs of commercial buildings and dumpsters, oil-leaking automobiles and battered oak pallets, but what you found were beautiful storefronts as they appeared a really long time ago. This peculiarity gave the Avaluxe and the five or six other businesses a strange feeling. One of the shops was a cafe with outdoor seating. The menu, posted in a window, showed salads, one type of soup (depending on the day) and garlic toast.

Mr. Kasparov was the first to see the boy standing outside in the alley in the evening mist. He'd been sitting on the north end with a chunk of basswood and a Japanese carving knife, trying to chisel out a puppet face with a big nose that didn't look too much like himself. Two sheets of newspaper were spread across his lap to catch the shavings. Mr. Kasparov was a cautious man. A Ukrainian refugee from the Soviet Union, he understood the moods and fears of the hunted, especially children, the besprizorniki. And if this child wasn't abandoned and even hunted, then whatever was impinging on his young life was something much akin to both. Mr. Kasparov propped open the door, nodded at the child, and then went back to his chair in the lobby. As he expected, the boy wandered in, inspecting the corners and furnishings like a cat.

"And Ruth is where?" asked the boy when he approached the older man.

Mr. Kasparov turned and smiled, his gapped teeth

shining as if white river stones had been pressed into a misshapen melon. "She's expecting you, my friend," he said.

"Where are you from?"

"The mountains," said Mr. Kasparov. "The mountains."

"You sound like Mrs. Botvinnik," said Gabriel. "Do you like piroshkis? Mrs. Botvinnik makes them and they're to die for. I mean, with the right filling. Like raisins and walnuts and maple syrup."

"Yes. Not bad. But they have to be baked just right, as far as I am concerned. Perhaps I could see her crust recipe sometime? Does Mrs. Botvinnik play chess?"

"I don't know."

"I just wondered. Shall I call Miss M and remind her that she's expecting you?"

"I don't see how she could be expecting me. *I'm* not even expecting me," he said. Then he looked at Mr. Kasparov and waited. But no sooner had the driver decided to phone her than they both heard her coming down the curved staircase from her apartment above.

"You'll never believe what I found," she said, lifting a heavy book up to her chest and holding it with both hands.

"Perhaps a knitting pattern?" Mr. Kasparov ventured.

She sighed. "What's this about piroshkis? Are you making piroshkis, Mr. Kasparov?"

"Well, I suppose I might be. It depends on the wind. We were discussing the finer points of observing the crust recipe of a certain Mrs. Botvinnik, apparently famous for her piroshkis and possibly a player of chess."

"Oh. Mrs. Botvinnik. Does she play chess?"

"I don't know," said Gabriel.

"How are you doing?" she asked. She gave him a large hug. The unexpected action left Gabriel half-frightened: It felt too good, too warm, too surrounding. And too soft. Tears began to well up behind his eyes but he clenched his hand and the pain made them go away.

Once she released him, Gabriel smiled nervously, trying to regain his seriousness. She wasn't supposed to have noticed the hand in the pocket.

"Gabriel ..." she said, as if in passing. He looked up. Something was coming. Joey did that a lot. He was glad he didn't have a middle name, because with the other kids Joey would say both their first and middle names. It usually meant something was going to hit the fan and Joey would get the cord out. He tried to relax. She was just testing him. He had to be careful; she was smarter than the rest of the adults. "I went and had lunch at Mac's yesterday."

"Oh, nice," said Gabriel, only half relieved. "Mac makes the best hamburgers. Did you have a hamburger? He'll put mushrooms on it and you don't even have to ask. I like him, actually."

"I do, too. I had to ask him about Henry Berq. I hope that doesn't upset you. I didn't have any way of contacting you to tell you. I hope you don't mind. I'm sure you miss him."

Gabriel decided it was time to sit down.

"I like Mac. Everyone else treats me like a child. Do you understand? Mac's cool for that. I talked a lot with Henry. We were working on his project. Henry is my good friend. I mean was. I don't know what to do, now."

"Well, I think we can work on that, what to do. We can make some piroshkis, you know, Mr. Kasparov will probably do most of the cooking anyway, and you and I can apply ourselves to getting you out of this situation."

"Yes, I suppose. I could be in a situation, now that you remind me."

"My friend Mr. Fisher will be here pretty soon. He brought a bunch of clippings and photos of Mr. Berq's acting career, earlier."

"Piano."

"Yes, and musician as well. When I was in Mac's, I

heard that Mr. Berq was working on a project with you. Or you were helping him or he was helping you. It was hard to tell. Can you tell me about that?"

"I could," he said. "I'd like some water."

Mr. Kasparov brought a glass of ice water with a squeeze of lemon.

"He was writing a play," said the boy.

"Oh."

"A musical. It was about beggars."

"And you were helping him."

"It was a very good play. Everyone said so. We talked about it at Mac's. Henry took notes. He was making me a shirt. But he never had time to finish it. He was killed in the street. I saw him lying there. Somebody must have hit him. Joey dropped me off about a block away that morning. He told me where to go for the day … which intersection. I worked all day, and then walked right past my friend Henry on the way to the bus. I didn't understand why he was in the street, the gutter. He didn't drink, you know. Henry isn't a drunk and I've only seen drunks in the street like that. I didn't know he would be there. He was very cold to me; I touched his face. He had on his rayon shirt because he likes rayon. It's easy to care for. It drips dry. He said it's easier to sew than silk and isn't as hot. A very wonderful and useful fabric. I don't understand what I'm going to do without him. I don't think I can stand it without him, Ruth. He was my friend."

"I'm so sorry, Gabriel," she said. "And … I think it's a very bad idea for you to go home to where you live. That's what I really wanted to talk to you about. It's not a good idea at all."

"I don't have to. After three days, though, Joey'll come looking for me. That won't be good. Joey has a temper."

Gabriel's Story

It took more than an hour for Mr. Kasparov's first batch of piroshkis. Gabriel, who had been leafing through some books that Ruth brought down from her apartment, put them aside and settled back with three or four piroshkis about the time I arrived. I sensed something in the air the moment I walked in the door ... tension. I could only wait. I looked at Ruth, she looked at me. Her eyes welcomed me, her lips remained silent.

Gabriel fiddled with one of the piroshkis on the plate.

"Henry was my friend," he said simply.

He told us about the old actor and piano man, but it was more of a brief history of his world and its key players – Henry Berq and Joey Starling – and in telling us, he seemed to lapse in and out of consciousness; that is, sometimes he seemed so distant as to be chimerical but only moments later spoke in great animation, even waving his bent wrist, which he was normally very self-conscious of. But he wasn't telling his story to me or Mr. Kasparov – I don't know if he really knew we were there – but to *her*. There is no doubt that Gabriel had never spoken to anyone about his life until he had piroshkis with Ruth.

Gabriel met Henry one night after a performance. Henry was fat, and old, and unreasonably happy, the way old men should always be. His eyes were clear, meaning Gabriel detected neither inebriation nor malice, two crucial ingredients to his safety. The old man had notebooks and papers under one arm and an umbrella in his other hand. Gabriel was bending wire, streetside; it was 6 p.m. on a Thursday. This was up in the Civic Center area, he said. This is the heart of San Francisco, home to its opera and symphony, the concert hall and the Asian Art Museum; however, and sadly, it's no place for a child. It's dangerous and it's filthy. The characters are as frightening as their habits, and it is soaked in predation.

They talked. Henry bought his first animal, a bear. Henry bought the boy, who he understood was probably homeless (if he was not homeless, his parents should rightfully be in prison on child neglect charges), a hamburger at a grill on the same block. It was a cautious evening in San Francisco. After burgers, Henry Berq said good night. He left, walking to the bus stop.

Next night, same thing. Another hamburger. They became cafe friends. At times, they would see each other often, and at other times, only occasionally. Gabriel knew where Henry lived, and found out the same way he learned of the Yarn Woman's home: The stray cat technique.

One day after Joey had beaten Gabriel pretty severely, Henry patched him up. Henry was distraught. Gabriel calmed him down. The battering had been over money because Joey knew Gabriel was skimming but he couldn't find the stash. About a day later, the boy asked Henry to keep his cigar box for him, privately, just to keep it, and Gabriel would check on it now and then. That was fine with Henry. He kept the box. It was a Romeo and Julietta box with a rubber band holding the lid down. Gabriel had hundreds of dollars in it. Hundreds, but Henry never bothered to look.

Henry Berq's apartment wasn't exactly Gabriel's home away from home, but it was a place he had begun to frequent, and within a few months, Henry had become a friend Gabriel could talk with. More than once when he arrived hurt, Henry threatened to call the police, but each time Gabriel managed to talk him out of it. His reasoning? Someone worse than Joey Starling would come along. Though Henry felt he was too old to care for a child, and though Gabriel was averse to becoming a burden to anyone, Henry kept a bed made up so the boy could stay over at any time. It was the best he felt he could do, under the circumstances.

Henry had a little pair of wire glasses he used when he read. He'd actually taken the time to get Gabriel reading, something that hadn't happened because Joey refused to enroll the boy in school. And Joey certainly never had the time or the inclination, though he benefited directly from Gabriel's newly acquired skill: The boy's income increased when he read newspaper paragraphs on the street corners to anyone who would listen. Especially impressive from the child's mouth were the rare five and six-syllable words, pronounced correctly. But, then, Henry hadn't begun with the simple stuff, either. It was *Moby Dick* to start with, and then a translation of Mahfouz's *Harafish*. Halfway through a translation of *Les Miserables*, Gabriel was reading to Henry.

Over time, however, Gabriel wasn't able to keep Henry's place a secret from Joey, who was always out in the van checking on his people. But it was still safe, as far as Gabriel could tell, because to his knowledge, Joey had never seen him go into the apartment, hadn't even seen him near the correct door (Gabriel made of point of that) and Joey remained unaware as well of the relationship that Gabriel had developed with the old man.

Gabriel told Ruth he didn't know many people. He looked up at her, piroshki in hand, and said. "Joey keeps me busy." Isolated is probably a more descriptive word. In any case, a week or so ago – it was his second day in a row away from the house so Joey wasn't commanding him or hovering – he was temporarily free of Joey, and Gabriel simply walked west. He wanted to spend some time on the beach, maybe play in the sand a little. Sometimes you just need some sand time alone, he said.

That was the day he saw Ruth on the beach, just sitting there, staring out into the far-away gray. He sat down with her for a while, and imagined he'd found a kindred spirit. What was she thinking about? The waves rolled in. They retreated. He imagined she was a sea goddess. He knew she wasn't – she had bare feet with toes, not fins.

When she left, he sort of ambled after her, like a dog or like a stray cat, just lagging behind, not really having anywhere to go. He thought it was her smile he liked the best. You don't smile that way unless you, "like, really smile, like you know that person inside," he said, rather quietly. So he followed; besides, he just had places he *didn't* want to go. He watched her enter the old theater. What a strange block he'd wandered into, he thought. There weren't any cars on the street. There were no white lane stripes, no stop lights, no regular street lights, but instead there were a few gas-powered lanterns on elaborate wrought-iron poles. He saw grates in the middle of the narrow alleyway for the water to run off, but he didn't see the usual trash under the grates. They were clean. He walked all the way around the block. The alley ran in front of the shops and the theater, and there was a smaller, more decrepit alley with sunflowers behind the buildings.

He returned to the front alley, looked into the windows of the shops, used some of his coins and bought a mocha latte from a tall, thin Greek waiter who wore a long, curling black mustache. And it was real. He'd never seen a real one. Henry Berq and four or five fake mustaches, including one that looked very much like the mocha man's.

Two days later, Gabriel found Henry Berq dead. He had never seen a dead person, and had never lost anyone he was close to. He told Ruth, his voice at times almost a whisper, that he had walked barely more than two blocks from where he had been conducting his wire-animal business when he saw a man's body by the side of street. He was on Seventh Avenue, walking south. It was dark but not bleak-black. He thought it was probably a drunk — he said "alcoholic" — but as he got closer he recognized the shirt. The man was face down, but there was no doubt. He knew it was Henry. He tried to flag down a car, but no one would stop. He played chicken with the traffic to try to get someone to stop, but he was nearly hit. The only thing he could think of was to go to the sea woman's house on the crazy alley street.

That night when he hovered in front of the Avaluxe, looking in at the lobby, he saw her get up and come to the door. He ran. She followed but she couldn't have seen a sign of him. Not a shadow. Finally, he was a full block north, looking back across the avenue.

He led her back to the body. And still no one would stop! He watched from the shadows across the street, and the cars just kept coming. She played chicken with the cars just like he had, and they almost hit her as well. They just kept driving on and all the while Henry Berq was lying face down in the gutter wearing an orange rayon shirt he'd made himself. What could he do? Gabriel was so mad he wanted to scream. And run. Jump and run, yelling at the fools in the cars and making them all stop for just one minute.

A woman in a small Japanese car stopped. She was talking on the phone and chewing gum like a gum-zealot. The ambulance came. A few cop cars finally arrived. Ruth went home.

He stood there across the street for five or ten minutes, trying to come to terms with the night. He thought of poor Henry, of their afternoons reading together, sometimes after one of Henry's rehearsals, sometimes at Mac's, more often at Henry's studio apartment. The old man always pulled on his reading glasses with one hand, his right one, in a sweeping motion, catching the temple bar on one ear and pulling them across his face and wrapping the other temple bar around the second ear.

Gabriel wanted the glasses. Henry was gone, and Ruth was flagging down cars and all Gabriel could think about was reading Dickens with Henry and whatever happened, he needed to have those glasses to know that

Henry had really been there, that he'd been in his life – that life was more than a Joey Starling version of foster care. And, they were magnifying glasses … they might be useful, anyway.

Gabriel walked on to Henry's apartment. It was only a few blocks north, only ten or fifteen minutes. He went in the front door to the open foyer. He had the key code for that: One-five-three-eight, beep, enter. He climbed the stairway to the second floor but the door to the apartment was locked. So he doubled back and checked the outdoor stairway that led, like a fire escape, to a door that opened into Henry's kitchen. But it was locked, too. There was no reason to knock … poor Henry was dead.

He was stymied twice and it made him angry. He went back down the rickety staircase. He wouldn't recommend it to anyone – it needed some bolts or something to steady it and he figured that one good shake would tear it out by the roots.

When he got back down to the ground, he looked up at the windows to the apartment. There was a drain pipe that ran from the roof edge down past the kitchen window in the front. He started climbing up and it seemed to him the rain gutter was sturdier than the staircase. The window at the top was cracked open for fresh air, and with some effort he forced it open wide enough to crawl through.

The apartment had no lights on except a dull lamp on a small table beside Henry's reading chair. There was a makeup case on the coffee table, and a mustache. And the reading glasses in their bone case. Henry had a pair of opera glasses that he kept by the reading chair, but they were gone. They were probably in his pocket in the gutter. Gabriel felt his hand closing over the glass case almost before he saw it. Then he returned to the kitchen, climbed up to the flour cupboard and took his cigar box.

Gabriel was standing on the counter when he heard the creaking of the fire escape. There wasn't any wind.

Softly, he hopped down from the countertop and onto the green linoleum of the floor. As quietly as he could, he eased himself over to the door and tried to look down through its small window.

There was someone on the staircase, about fourteen feet down. There was nowhere else for them to go but right up to the kitchen door. Gabriel ran to the window and squeezed himself through the gap. He tried to push the window closed but got it to move only part of the way. But he'd made it. Not wanting to make noise going down, he just held on below the window, perched on a small ledge of outthrust, over-fired bricks, his eyes barely above the sill. And he watched.

There was a smack on the door. It made a hollow sound. He could hear the intruder pressing against it, trying to push it in. Every few seconds there was another solid push on the old wood. The jamb finally gave way, and the stair-climber stumbled into the kitchen. Even in the dark, Gabriel could tell it was Joey Starling.

What was Joey doing here? His first thought was that he was trying to find the boy's stash of money. Money was very important to Joey. The most important thing in the world. But he didn't know Gabriel had left it here.

Joey went through the house very particularly, though Gabriel couldn't see much of it from his perch below the window. He could hear the rustling of papers, the opening and closing of drawers and cabinets. Joey entered the kitchen, and Gabriel could hear the folding of money, bills, and the cold clink of coins or rings. He'd be in for a surprise, Gabriel thought, because Henry only had costume jewelry. The glint of gold was something very dear to Joey, but when he would finally see tonight's gold in a brighter light, it would make him furious. Gabriel imagined him taking the Chinese-made Rolex from the living room hutch. He almost laughed, but caught himself.

What kept him from laughing was the sadness. This all seemed so dreamlike. What was real was that Henry was gone. Joey was rifling the place without Gabriel's help. It struck Gabriel as strange, but only for a moment because when he thought about it he realized that Joey had known about Gabriel and Henry's friendship. Of course he wouldn't tell Gabriel he was burglarizing Henry's place.

Gabriel clutched the case that held Henry's glasses and, with the cigar box under his arm, eased himself down from the window. And he waited on the wall in the dark, suspended above the Earth.

Joey left the small flat with nearly $600 in twenties and fifties, a pocketful of carnival fool's gold and half a ream of papers that rattled and ruffled in his hand all the way down the flimsy staircase. That was Henry's play. He was sure it was. What else could it be?

After Gabriel saw the old Econoline pull out and rumble down the avenue, he finally descended, wondering if Tooley was driving or if Joey was alone.

* * *

Gabriel's plate was empty. He smiled at us as if nothing had happened, as if he'd sat there all this time enjoying Mr. Kasparov's piroshkis made with maple syrup from Vermont. I wondered if we should be concerned about his disassociation or grateful that it helped him survive. But he seemed comfortable. Even the maple syrup tin, with its winter scene with horses and sled and a sugar shack with steam rising from the boiler, was comforting. It made him sigh.

In the silence that descended, Mr. Kasparov nudged my shoulder and motioned me with his head. I nodded. It was time for us to go. We said goodbye and walked out the front doors. Mr. Kasparov waited to hear the smacking of the big locks, and satisfied with their safety, suggested a "slight game of chess" at his very small apartment a block east – above a garage where he kept the Rolls.

I knew he'd beat me, and he did, several times.

Stagger Lee

What time was it? Had he talked very long? Did he remember to say that Joey was really an okay guy, like, somewhere deep in his heart? That he wasn't as bad as he sounded, that the foster home was still a home after all? Why had he talked so much? Where had Mr. Kasparov and Mr. Fisher gone? Yet despite the uncharacteristic and even unexpected gush of information, Gabriel's night had barely begun.

"So," Ruth said, "you want to see my apartment?" She closed the narrow door to the kiosk after pulling back to lock lever.

"I guess." He shrugged, but he was interested. How does a sea goddess live, anyway? With seashells on the windowsills?

They took the north staircase, whose grand sweep dwarfed them.

Methuselah was waiting as the oversized oak door to No. 8 swung silently inward. She'd left the bedroom window open to catch the cool pre-rain breeze that came off the Pacific, so the dark room was cool and fresh.

He stood at the door and stared into the half-silhouetted mountains of yarn, softly backlit by city lights reflecting off the low clouds and through the immense windows before him. She flipped the lights on in time to catch Methuselah jumping onto the wide round table in the corner. He could now see the yarn that cascaded like a brilliant rainbow down the left wall and spilled from sacks strewn across the room. He shifted his gaze to the other side: a wall of books — the entire wall, with a rolling ladder to reach the highest shelves.

There was a small red sofa near the round table and it looked comfortable, even inviting.

He walked around the room, sniffing the lavender

bundles that were interspersed with the skeins on the wall, gazing out the ceiling-high windows at rooftops and cloud bellies, and surreptitiously trying to read some of the titles in the bookshelves. Did she really read all that? He tripped over some yarn sacks as he edged along the wall where the entry door was situated. Beside the door were a half-dozen canvas totes holding a variety of knitting projects in various yarns and colors and states of incompletion.

"How much yarn is enough?" he asked, regaining his balance. "I mean ..."

She was sitting with the cat at the table, needles in her hands and lamps on bright. "Never enough," she said, not looking up from her work and smiling.

"Oh. I'm okay with that."

"Ah."

"You have a piano in the middle of the floor."

"Harpsichord."

"Can you play it?"

"Sure."

"I mean, are you any good?"

"Good enough."

"I mean . . ." he paused, trying to figure out the best way to approach the issue. "Can you play *Stagger Lee* on it? I mean, can you play *Stagger Lee*?"

She looked up.

"Bert had an old guitar and a piece of bottle and he'd play *Stagger Lee,* Ruth. He left about, I don't know, a few months ago. From Joey's. I don't know where he went. Outta here's all I know."

"Was he any good?"

"Yeah. He was real good. He was famous once."

"What was Bert's last name?"

"He never said. He didn't have any teeth, either."

"I see." She sat down at the harpsichord. "I mostly work with Domenico Scarlatti. Or Bach. Scarlatti's sonatas, like, if I've had enough coffee. Bach if I'm tired. So ... Gabriel, which version of Stagger Lee did Bert play?"

"Oh, you know ..." He wasn't sure what she meant.

"I mean, in the song, does Stagger Lee pull a .44 on Billy Lyons or a .41? Generally speaking, the arrangements of the two versions are entirely different."

"Forty-four," said Gabriel. He walked over and stood beside her at the harpsichord, carefully lifting a page of sheet music that was on the seat, then replacing it. "There's a lot of notes there, Ruth," he said.

"I like that one better," she said, "the .44. I think the .41 might be older, but the .44's better." She played a few loose chords, then settled into a rocking blues in D:

"I was standing on the corner
when I heard my bulldog bark.
He was barking at two men gambling (pause)
in the park."

A smile crossed Gabriel's face. She could sing, too, he thought. Ruth had seen Gabriel smile a total of one time, when they talked while he made wire creatures by the roadside, when he joked about her name. It was a nice smile, and real. He started tapping his foot, and both hands had worked their way out of his pockets.

"It was Stagger Lee and Billy
Two men who gambled late
Stagger Lee threw a seven;
Billy swore that (pause)
he threw eight."

By the time Ruth was into the fifth verse, Gabriel had started dancing. She tried to concentrate on the keys, the words, the looseness of the evening, the crazy chords emanating from the most unlikely of instruments but which seemed so strongly reminiscent of a Dobro guitar, yet her eyes were drawn magnetically to the scrawny child beside her. To her eye, he had somehow managed to combine the styles of an 80-year-old Arkansas foot stomper with an inner city break dancer. It was the strangest thing she could have imagined. But she knew this: He was really good … more than really good. His rhythm was perfect, his motions catlike and fluid – even the choppy foot tapping and hip swiveling of the octogenarian that seemed to live inside him were perfect.

By the time Stagger Lee had gone home to get his gun and turned it on Billy Lyons, ignoring Billy's pleas for his life, that he had a loving wife and children at home, by the time Billy'd been shot, Ruth and Gabriel were both singing and laughing.

* * *

There was a single knock at the door, and then silence. Both looked up – Gabriel stopped dancing, Ruth's hands fell on the keys one last time. They looked at each other, both breathless.

She shrugged and went to the door. Outside was a small pile of folded clothing. She picked it up and returned to the harpsichord where Gabriel remained standing, waiting and somewhat short of breath because he didn't dance that often. "Clean clothes," she said. "Mr. Kasparov is so predictable. Look, I'll get you a towel and you can go and take a shower. Or a bath. Whatever. There's some stuff here for morning, probably the right size, too, and I'll find something for tonight. We can put some sheets and blankets on the red loveseat if you don't mind sleeping with a cat. He's a nice cat. Really soft."

Gabriel squinted. He looked at the clothes. "You must have a lot of friends."

"On one hand, I can count them."

"Well, he's a friend."

"Yes."

"He's rich, huh?"

"Mr. Kasparov? He doesn't have a pot to pee in."

Gabriel stood, silently shocked at Ruth's candor. Then he sat down on the bench beside Ruth, facing away from the harpsichord, opposite to her. "But he has that car. I've seen the car."

"Oh, that. Mr. Kasparov is, at times, very lucky. He happened to be in the right place at the right time with a $5 bet. It's a long story, but the short version is that he sort of won the car. He's an accomplished mechanic so it runs like a dream. He gets replacement parts from Russia, orders them on the internet."

There was a long moment of silence. It wasn't particularly uncomfortable, but it was definitely quiet. The longer it lasted, the more tired Gabriel became. Methuselah leaped onto the harpsichord. "I hate it when he does that," she said.

"But you've known him a long time. He's not your father."

"Since I was eleven. No, he's not my father. Maybe better, I don't know."

"I don't have a father."

"Me either," she said. She shrugged.

Gabriel twisted around so they faced the same direction. "What?"

"I said I didn't either. I had a mom, though, until I was ten. And a grandfather who died when I was seven."

"They tease you, I mean, call you stuff for not having a father?"

"Sure. I was in a lot of fights."

"I went to kindergarten about a week, and then Joey got me into 'home schooling.' It was better than being roughed up all the time because of it. Not having a father. I'm a bastard."

"That's no big deal in this house."

"So, like, Mr. Kasparov is from Russia I guess."

"The mountain country of Ukraine, the former Soviet satellite. He escaped from the Soviet Union. The first time he escaped, they caught him. He was in a horrible prison for almost five years and then escaped south through what used to be Yugoslavia. He's really smart, Gabriel. And he's good with his hands. He does all the repairs on the Silver Cloud, he plays serious chess, does judo big-time, you know, the sport, and he spends an incredible amount of time making string puppets, marionettes. He learned about string puppets when he was hiding in Belgrade. That's Mr. Kasparov."

Gabriel pondered the information.

"Some of the way you dance reminds me of his puppets," she said. Gabriel, she knew, could make a lot of street money dancing, much more than from selling wire animals or simply asking for donations. She said nothing.

"The money'd just go to Joey," Gabriel said, as if reading her mind. "If Joey ever saw how much people would pay to watch some kid dance on the sidewalk, there'd be no stopping him. He loves money. Very much so. Besides," he said, lowering his eyes, "dancing brings out the freaks." The look on his face when he said "freaks" said more than the word. Ruth understood; old memories surfaced, but the immediacy of the moment blew them away like dust.

She nodded. "You ever think of dancing seriously? Not street dancing, but like in some sort of production, a play or a musical like Henry Berq might create?"

"Sometimes. I wouldn't mind. I would like to be paid."

"How old are you, Gabriel."

Pause. "A little more than six. I don't know for sure. How old are you?"

"Can't tell you. You know that." Tears welled up behind Ruth's eyes, but she fought them back. She wondered if he'd go back to Joey Starling's foster home in a day, or two days, or a week.

"It'd be easy to go back," he said, as if answering her. "I'm afraid. I don't know, I just don't know anything. I know I have a place at Joey's. And it's not so bad. He's okay. Nobody's perfect."

"We can work on you not being there."

"I'm trying. I am. I stay away a lot. Like at night."

"I mean, I have room here. It might not seem like much."

"You have a lot of yarn. Maybe I could visit. Like at Henry's. I'm not in the way." He looked around the room.

"I know." She put her arm around him. "Sure, visit. For now, why don't you go clean up? And wash your hair. I'll make up your bed."

"What?"

"Your hair. It's got, like, junk in it. Methuselah's hair is cleaner, and it has cat spit in it."

He ran his hand through the loose curls. It was his right hand and his fingers got stuck in it. He winced because the fingers caught and bent his wrist wrong. But he smiled.

"I'm kind of hungry," he said softly.

"Oh. Right. Mr. Kasparov left some Chinese takeout with the clothes. You like lemon chicken? Good. This stuff's to die for. After that, I'm going to bed."

* * *

Gabriel curled up in the blankets. His hair was still damp but he wasn't cold. The big old cat was purring behind his shoulder. He found it comforting. Cats were cool.

He slept until 11 the next morning. Ruth was searching the triptych bookshelf for a pattern she knew she had but hadn't seen for four or five years. It was for a sweater that fit tightly at the waist but had belled shoulders and cuffless sleeves. She could see the picture in her mind, but she had about six hundred square feet of books, pamphlets, magazines and folders to rifle through. She'd probably never find it. She'd have to buy more.

Gabriel slipped off to the bathroom and dressed. The

clothes fit. Mr. Kasparov was a good judge of size. But where'd he get the clothes? They didn't look or smell used; in fact, the shirt still had half a price tag on it, though the price itself was missing.

They had scrambled eggs and then went downstairs where Ruth poured him a glass of milk, which she didn't keep upstairs because she didn't use it. She made herself a cup of tea and they sat in the lobby where they could watch the occasional passerby on his way to the Greek cafe down the alley.

Gabriel knew Ruth had something on her mind. And for once in his life, he didn't. He looked over at her, silent. So, he thought absently, what did she have in her hand? It was in her lap, but closed into a fist. There was something in her hand and she started flipping it around. He motioned to her hand with his left-hand fingers.

"I found it in the street," she said in answer to his questioning eyes, "the night we found Mr. Berq's body. I found two, and gave one to the police. To Detective Chu, because he's my friend. I don't know what good it will do." She handed it to Gabriel, who stared at it for a few seconds and then looked up, his eyes wide. Then, as if catching himself, he glanced at the floor. It was a brass, center-fire bullet shell.

"You mean that Henry was shot and died in the street there," he said.

"Yes. Mr. Chu said he was shot. I didn't know how to tell you. I'm not good at this."

Gabriel was near tears. "Don't you have any parenting abilities at all?" he asked angrily.

"None," she said sadly.

He wasn't prepared for the answer. "Oh," he said. What did it matter, anyway, when his friend had been killed, murdered? "But I thought he was hit by a car."

"No, he wasn't."

She had never seen a child *not* cry as hard as Gabriel did that morning. You seem them cry a lot, if you're around children at all, and you see them trying not to cry at times. But Gabriel's lack of sobbing rang in her ears. She seemed almost in tears herself, telling Gabriel how Henry Berq had died. Finally, after five or six minutes, the boy had made his determinations, whatever they were. He hopped out of the chair he'd been sitting on and placed the brass casing in his right hand, clamping over it with his fingers and thumb, his wrist cocked inappropriately downward. Ruth went immediately to the big black phone in the corner of her room. It matched the old model downstairs. She picked it up and telephoned Mr. Kasparov and then me.

Gabriel let his hand drop, forefinger pointing loosely at the ground, and without a word he left her apartment, went directly downstairs to the lobby, walked past the kiosk, then the doors and alley. He spotted a piece of wire a block east, picked it up. It wasn't wire after all, but part of a radio antenna. That was just as good. He followed his own lead eastward at first and then south, way south. Mr. Kasparov pulled up within moments and Ruth jumped into the Rolls as they tried to catch up with Gabriel.

* * *

It took three hours by bus and by foot to arrive at the tenement that Gabriel called home. It was about two in the afternoon. The boy stood a foot from Joey Starling's van. He was absent-mindedly scribbling with his forefinger in the dust that covered the ancient paint job. They were ten or twelve feet behind him. The van was parked in one of several dozen small slots at the side of the building: the junk in front of it, jammed up against the building, was practically a trash dump.

They knew what we'd find inside the van. There was no reason, she said, to enter it. "Mr. Kasparov," she said quietly, "please call Mr. Chu and let him know we've found the weapon that killed Henry Berq, and we've found the man behind the gun and the vehicle from the drive-by. He'll find a missing bullet casing in the van, I'm sure, if not the gun."

Mr. Kasparov pressed the 3 key, Detective Chu's desk number.

* * *

It wasn't easy for William Chu to accept that his city was home to clutches of homeless men, women and children who acted as servants and slaves, willing or unwilling, to a contingent of parasitic beggar masters. It was as if he'd stumbled out of his overly ordered office at San Francisco's Central Station into the rat-gnawed streets of Victorian London or modern Mumbai where a thousand twisted hands shoved their fingers up toward him, asking, pleading, begging.

Chu had a hard time with the cleanup. Joey Starling's arrest and prosecution were the easy parts. His motive was simply to stop publication of a play about him, Joey, the beggar master. Everyone knew Berq was writing it. How could Joey not know? As careful as Gabriel had been, something had slipped through his lips that piqued Joey's interest. It wasn't hard for him to figure out. Joey eventually met Berq once, at Joey's request, at Mac's. Don't go through with it, he demanded, but Berq knew the play, a musical nonetheless, was something special. He didn't listen to Joey. What choice did that leave Joey? Simple: Make sure he got the manuscript and that Henry Berq wasn't around to rewrite it. Joey just wanted to be left alone, free to make a living. Why couldn't Berq have just stopped?

It was the aftermath of the trial and verdict that was more troubling for Detective Chu. There were eight lives that rotated like planets around Joey, their sun. He called in Health and Human Services to help place the older panhandlers. The two named Myra and John were put, machinelike, into temporary housing. But what would happen after their scrip expired in a matter of a few weeks? Would they wander back onto the streets, homeless, in worse shape than they'd been under their master? Marnie was hospitalized briefly with open wounds on her useless legs. Would she go back to the street? How could they be helped? Would they even accept assistance? And Tooley? Would his nights again be cold and wet as winter approached, whereas before he'd been warm and dry? Right is right, thought Chu, but is it better?

The children would be placed in foster homes, yet the arrangements, as always, would be temporary and unsatisfactory. William Chu asked himself, often, if anyone involved had a chance at a better life, but he shied away from the answer, from the possibility that the functionality of a Joey Starling was, in truth, an improvement to the grossly legal social architecture of the city.

Meyer's Boy

It was nearly two weeks after the death of Henry Berq that notification reached Jake Goldstein, his attorney of record.

Goldstein has a perfectly small practice that he conducts from a red brick office building near the waterfront. He inherited both the practice and the renovated historic structure from his father, the renowned (and feared) Romano-family attorney Meyer Goldstein. The Romanos ruled the San Francisco waterfront well into the 1990s, and they remain a prominent family in the city today, with significant development holdings and political pull on the board of supervisors. They were old-school Sicilian, in every sense of the term. Because of the resulting lack of financial stress, Jake could do what he wanted in life, and he was drawn irresistibly to the stage. As a lawyer, though, his clientele consisted mostly of commercial fishermen, the Romanos, a few longshoremen, members of the acting community and enough pro bono work to keep a small army of paralegals employed in the pursuit of common, kaleidoscopic justice. His path had criss-crossed Ruth's for many years, so they weren't strangers. Far from it.

"Meyer's Boy," as Jake is called by his friends, is a short man who bears an uncanny resemblance to Edward G. Robinson – he of silver-screen fame. About six years ago, Jake took a sabbatical from his legal career to act in a traveling stage production of *Little Caesar*, and reviews were rave. His legal business actually quadrupled. Yet, at the peak of his fame, it was with a wide, lipless Rico "Little Caesar" smile that Meyer's Boy retired from his brief foray into acting and returned to Goldstein and Goldstein where he set about paring down the quadrupled workload to something more manageable.

Henry Berq had made out a will a year before his death. It was the first one he'd made and he decided on Meyer's Boy after hearing his name bounced around by other acting guild members. In truth, Berq had little or nothing to bequeath until he began writing his play, but he was so convinced of its genius, or at least its magic, that he wanted any earnings from the production to go toward a good cause if he died.

He had no children, no wife, and no living relatives. The beneficiaries of his creativity were Gabriel and a children's medical center in Oakland, both of which, he decided, would receive all profits from the play while his executor held the publishing rights and negotiating power. That's all well and good, but at the time he died, the play, entitled, "Fifth Street," was barely even a manuscript. The ending was still handwritten on several grocery bags that had been cut to the size of notebook paper. There were some children's drawings on the backs of two of the papers – Gabriel's.

Goldstein drove out to the Central police station to pick up the manuscript, which had been seized when Joey Starling was arrested. Most of the manuscript had been found in his possession, but the penciled ending had been discovered by the police under a chair cushion in Berq's apartment during the investigation. It had been overlooked by Joey Starling.

When Goldstein picked up the papers, Chu suggested that Goldstein speak with the Yarn Woman, should he need any other information regarding his client, Henry Berq, and though there was no need for the meeting, Goldstein decided it was time for a visit anyway. They hadn't spoken for months. So rather than returning to the office, Goldstein drove south to the Avaluxe, telephoning as he drove to announce his arrival.

"The Miss is unavailable until after 10:30, Mey … Mr. Goldstein," said Mr. Kasparov, pressing the heavy black receiver to his ear. "Important?" he continued. "I see. Give me a level of importance between one and ten, Mr. Goldstein, consisting of, in the first place, a figure relating to timeliness one to ten, and a second figure relating to magnitude of the issue in Miss M's life, one to ten. I'll need the average of the two figures."

Mr. Kasparov felt pulled in two directions. He was a friend of Jake Goldstein, and of his father Meyer. They were, in fact, quite close and had been for a number of years. His door was always open to Meyer's Boy. Yet, under the circumstances, he felt impelled to act as Miss M's gatekeeper because he knew she didn't like being disturbed at times. He did the best he could.

"What?" said Meyer's Boy.

Mr. Kasparov repeated the formula as Goldstein continued south.

"Nine, nine and the average, nine," said Goldstein, "for I would use ten only with approval of Her Eminence."

"Excellent," said Mr. Kasparov. "I will inform her immediately. Let me place you on hold for a moment and dial up Miss M. Please hold," and the click was so immediate it almost cut off the word "hold." The "click" on this 1942 rotary telephone is actually a piece of tin that Mr. Kasparov had bent and screwed onto a small wood base that clacked when pressed, like the obnoxious toy of a child. The silence on the line that follows occurs when the mouthpiece is pressed firmly against the thigh. Mr. Kasparov leaned out of his little kiosk and asked Ruth, who was sitting in the lobby, if she was "receiving."

"Who would that be, Mr. Kasparov," she asked, looking up from her knitting. She was working on the cardigan again. "Just a minute. Don't talk to me." She worked furiously for about three minutes and arrived at a good stopping point. "Now, what on Earth does anyone want with me at this hour?" It was already 10:30.

"Meyer's Boy is on his way here."

"Great! That's great, Mr. Kasparov. It'll be like old

times. I mean, is there time to make tea or anything? Scones?"

Mr. Kasparov clicked the phone back on by pulling the handpiece away from his leg and tapping the tin clacker. He spoke very briefly and hung up. Then he was out of the kiosk and into the kitchen without a word.

Meyer's Boy was welcomed with open arms, catered in high style by Mr. Kasparov, who had removed from the freezer a dozen scones that he'd made previously. No friend of the microwave (he didn't own one), he warmed them in the oven until they were crisp on top.

"I hope you did not think I was short with you, Mr. Goldstein," he said to Meyer's Boy. "What can I say? I am a short person by nature."

"I'd like to see your hold mechanism for the phone. It's high-tech?"

"Oh, very," Mr. Kasparov said, blood rushing to his forehead. "I'll make you one."

Sitting with tea in hand, Goldstein explained that he was settling the Berq estate and that he'd learned that Ruth had been involved in the investigation of his murder. "Mr. Berq named me executor, Miss M," he said, "and I'll have to liquidate the apartment. He'd been working on a play, you know."

"Yes. It got him killed, Jake."

"I've taken it upon myself to finish the work, put it in order, find a transcriber for the handwritten parts, see it through the copyright process, and so on and so forth and offer it up for publication and production. I know a few people. He's asked that any proceeds go to the Children's Medical Center and to the boy."

"What else could you do?" she asked sincerely. "I'm glad you stopped by, though, so I don't have to call. I don't like phones that much, you know ..."

"Really?" he said, his voice mocking in tone. But it was all family.

"No, it's true. They're so impersonal. But, here it is:

Can you please guide the county foster home agencies, whoever they are, in picking an appropriate home for the children involved in this case? Gabriel … I don't know his last name yet. He was under the foster care of Joey Starling. His wrist, well, it will require surgery. I'm sure of it. There were also three other children and four adults directly influenced by the man. I suppose the adults may have gone their own way, I don't know. My understanding is that Detective Chu, the police, have made at least temporary arrangements. Maybe it was the social services agency at the request of the police. Or just Chu. He does that. Do you know Detective William Chu?"

"We only just met." He smiled, then the smile seemed to drain away. "Has this been difficult for you, Ruth?" he asked. Clearly, he was bringing up something from her past that I knew nothing about. I didn't dream of asking. Like Methuselah, I would wait. It could be years; it didn't matter.

"In a way," she said, her voice distant.

"What would I do for the children? We need to talk about that. I will see to the wrist myself, immediately."

"I've selected several homes," she said, returning to business. "I have a list. It's taken a few days of inquiry and, well, telephoning. I've been working largely through my knitting underground. It's the old theory that if someone knows someone else, you're only six persons removed from acquaintanceship with the president. Anyway, I have a situation for each, but need your help with the actual arrangements. Specifically, I'd like Gabriel placed with an acquaintance of mine who has a daughter about the same age, very intelligent and somewhat intellectually isolated. She studies music with me two days a week. He could visit as well, you see. Unfortunately, hers is a single-parent household, so, whatever you can do. You know Social Services looks down on single parents. … Here are the names and addresses. Do you need more than that?"

He smiled and said the list was enough. He'd have to call in some markers, but he said nothing. "Sure, sure," he said. "Good as done." He stood and casually wandered around the lobby, looking at the photographs of actors of the gilded screen. When he finally came upon the face of Edward G. Robinson, he smiled. How could he not? It was like an echo of another life to him, maybe a life he'd lived in America's golden age, whenever that was.

"You know," he said, musing, "Berq's play borrows considerably from Brecht's work. The atmosphere. It's the story of a beggar master. Henry worked with Richie B., who did the lyrics more than a year ago, and Henry did the score. It's really very good, very catchy. It could go somewhere. I just kind of have a feeling about it. Richie would get a satisfactory return if it were to go. It's kind of like reading, and hearing, you know, the music, something from a long time ago. Like an old story brought in by the wind, and, honestly, Ruth, as if it had been performed sixty or seventy years ago and we are just seeing and hearing it now. It's so damned odd, when you start reading this thing. Just imagine it being performed."

"Yes. That's just it, I suppose," she said. "There's one other thing. I think there was an unfinished orange shirt at Mr. Berq's apartment. Probably, the police have it. Why don't you bring that by when you find it, and I can take care of that."

"He was making that for the boy."

"Yes."

"I'll find it."

"Thank you," she said.

"You like him."

"Very much."

"He's lucky."

"He is now. And maybe he was lucky before, you never know, really."

"Remind you of anyone?"

She stared, her eyes so green they were gems.

"I met him briefly," Jake said. "He reminds me of you."

Made in the USA
Middletown, DE
03 June 2015